DIAMONDS TO DIE FOR
By: Kathryn Jane

ISBN: 978-1-988790-07-7

www.kathrynjane.com

Cover Design and Interior Format

 © THE KILLION GROUP INC.

KATHRYN JANE

DIAMONDS
TO DIE FOR

What is the
INTREPID WOMEN series?

———

A COLLECTION OF STAND - ALONE novels about women we can all relate to because they weren't born last week, and—scared or not—they do what needs to be done. Modern day damsels who not only ride to their own rescue, but often dig their charming princes out of trouble too.

The series/collection is now nine books deep. Come on aboard, it's bound to be fun, and I promise you nothing but happy endings because in real life, there are too dang many of the other kind!

An old flame, a cold fire, and the will to live.

When the men in her life start dropping like flies, Kate will sacrifice everything to keep an old love safe.

But Jason knows who the killer is...

A horse trainer and a private detective might seem like an unlikely pair, but they have a steamy history neither one would mind revisiting if she wasn't in mortal danger and if he wasn't fighting to keep her alive.

Join Kate while she runs for her life, avoids trouble, and is for the most part successful. As for keeping Jason at arm's length? Well, as a former jockey she knows, you can't win 'em all.

Dedicated to intrepid women everywhere.
Women surviving one day at a time.
Women doing what has to be done.
Women who stand alone.
And women who stand for each other.

Courage is what happens when you look fear in the eye.

PROLOGUE

Fall, 2015

NO, NO, NO, NO, NO. This is NOT happening. But the cop in Kate's living room said it was, and his news filled the air like acrid smoke. Took her back to a different time. A different place.

"Ma'am?"

She'd been blessed. Lucky enough to have three father figures in her life. The one who adopted her as an infant died while Kate was still a teen, and now another was dead, and there wasn't a damn thing she could do about it.

Never again would she hear Tanner's laughter, feel his kind hand on her shoulder, or stand proudly at his side in the winner's circle. There would be no more late-night phone calls because he wanted her opinion on a particular horse.

"Ms. Oliver?"

"I don't know what to do. Say. What—"

"I have some questions," said the officer.

Kate perched on the edge of the nearest armchair, and he chose the one across from her. The one Tanner should be sitting in. *Wrong. This is so wrong.*

"When did you last speak with Wesley Tanner?"

"I dropped him at the airport nearly a week ago." Hugged him for the last time. Teased him about the barn running just fine without him. Said they wouldn't even notice he was gone—which was an obvious lie, but she wanted him to relax and enjoy the vacation they arranged for him to win. Hopefully, with nothing to do but sit in a fancy boat and wait for a fish to bite, he would start to feel like himself again, get some color back in his face, and lose the dark hollows around his eyes.

A sharp knock at the door sent relief shooting through her. She leapt across the room, wrenched on the handle. "Tanner!"

"Katie," said Leo Davis, sorrow etched on his age-weathered face. "I thought I should come."

No. No. Not happening. Not happening. Can't be... "How did you—"

He gestured toward the officer. "He came to the barn first. I gave him your address."

"It's real." She knew it in her head, but her heart was having trouble keeping up. Tanner was supposed to be on his way home tonight. She dropped onto the chair. "What if he didn't drown? What if he's washed up on an island? Lost. Cold." A shiver ran down her spine.

"Ma'am, they were miles offshore. The Canadian Coast Guard worked the area for five days."

The officer had questions, and Leo helped her supply the answers, because they were the only family Tanner had.

She gazed across the room at her favorite photo, a study in contrasts. Kate flanked by Tanner—the funny little red-haired Irishman—and Leo, nearly a foot taller, and with skin as dark as Tanner's was light. The two men couldn't look any less alike, but she could pass as a blend of the two. Tallish, with long, straight brown hair and green eyes.

"What will happen now?"

"We'll go on," Leo said firmly. "You'll notify the owners, and life will go on."

People were not her forte. She preferred to work with the horses and leave the owners to Tanner, since he was so damn good at sharing precisely the right amount of information, playing the social game, and managing the racing stable. On top of that, he was also amazing with his staff. Many had been with him for more than twenty years, and Leo and Kate had worked for him almost that long. Kate worked her way up from hot walker to assistant trainer while Leo's position of night watchman never changed. He called it the perfect retirement job.

"Ma'am?"

The officer was holding out a business card. "The file number is on the back. Call me if you think of anything odd. Or if you have questions."

"Odd?" Her skin prickled and her heart bumped.

"The Canadian authorities were satisfied with their findings…" But judging by the look on his face and the hesitation, he wasn't.

"What aren't you saying?"

"Accidental death is always hard to accept, especially when it happens so far away and leaves behind such limited information."

CHAPTER 1

Spring, 2016
A racehorse training center in Kentucky

EVERYTHING LOOKED THE SAME, BUT nothing was.

Sitting in her car in front of Barn 6, Kate studied the familiar setting.

The red trim, flowers spilling from planters, and red and white silks painted on the traditional cement jockey standing outside the wide entrance were just as they had always been. But the new bronze plaque mounted on the bottom of the statue said it all.

R. TANNER, 1950 – 2016

HORSEMAN, MENTOR, AND FRIEND.

This was no longer Tanner's barn. It was Kate's, and that meant she could no longer lose herself among the familiar scents of horses and hay, leg brace and liniment, camphor and iodine. Or let her mind wander. Dream. Because responsibility meant she always had to be on. Aware. Tapped in to her crew, thirty-plus horses, and all the other details that came with the job of trainer.

At least at this time of day, long after training

hours and afternoon feed time, she didn't have to deal with the owners of the horses, the people who wanted answers, explanations, assurances, and hand-holding. Yes, there were those she liked and respected, but the others? The ones constantly telling her how to do her job because they just read a great new book about training? Or Victor—who was, plain and simple, a nasty human being?

They robbed her of the pleasure she used to get from her work back when Tanner ran interference.

The easy solution was to politely ask them to take their horses elsewhere, but then she would have to lay off staff. Long-term employees with families to feed. Oh, how she longed for the old days. The laughter. The—

"You gonna sit there until the sun goes down?"

She hadn't heard Leo's approach, and while getting lost in her thoughts and memories was perfectly understandable in the weeks following Tanner's death, the time for self-indulgence was past. She needed to damn well handle whatever came her way, just like she always had.

And tonight three new fillies would be arriving. She shook off the crap. Looked Leo in the eye and the lame excuse about being lost in thought evaporated on her tongue. "I could use a coffee."

She filled her go-cup from the pot in the coffee room, then they did a quick tour of the barn before parking on a bench out front to wait for the van.

Caly, Leo's calico cat, paced back and forth between them, purring madly and kneading the wood with her tiny white paws while Leo stroked her idly. When he stopped, Caly gripped the side of his thumb with her teeth, demanding more attention.

Kate chuckled. "What a change from the hissing, spitting kitten you coaxed out from under the hay-shed. You have magic in those hands, my friend." He could gentle the wildest of horses as well.

"It's all about trust," Leo said. He'd spent hours—days—winning the kitten over, and now she was all grown up, she was his shadow. Wherever Leo was, you could find Caly close by. Sort of like Kate used to be with Tanner.

"He'd be proud of you," said Leo.

"How do you always know when I'm thinking about him?"

"Your face gives you away. You'd be a lousy poker player."

A response she'd heard from him on more than one occasion over the years.

Although more than twice her age, he'd some-how become the best friend she ever had. He got her. Always had her back. Kicked her metaphorical ass when she needed it, and sat beside her when life knocked her down.

"I miss him too," he said, reminding her she wasn't the only one still affected by the loss. The two men had been good friends. Comrades who both treated Kate like a daughter.

Kate tipped her head to listen. "Sounds like the truck."

"My ears aren't that good, but she hears it too." Caly was staring past three other barns toward the road that led to the guard shack at the gate.

"Right on time," said Kate. Which was unusual for a shipment of horses coming off an interna-tional flight. Lengthy delays and holdups due to inspection and paperwork were more the norm.

"Time for a little wager?" she asked.

"I think you won last time, so I get first pick."

"Okay, lead off."

Leo looked thoughtful...like he was cooking up something devious.

"Fifty bucks says not one from this load earns out its shipping fees by this time next year."

Doing the math in her head, Kate hesitated. "Victor does his own booking, so I never see the bills. Makes it's hard to know the totals."

"How about a ballpark?"

"About twenty grand for the pallet, and adding in another thousand for ground transport makes it a tidy seven grand per horse."

"What about the cost of paperwork, health certificates, and the equipment he rigs them all in?"

"The grand for ground transport probably covers the paperwork."

"Okay, I'll give you that. What about the fancy equipment, and the guy he pays to fly with them?"

"Brett's on Victor's payroll already, and the equipment is used over and over, so neither count. I'll take the bet at earnings over seven thousand, not a penny more." She held up a hand. "And, I'll bet *you* a hundred one of the three makes it to a race."

"By this time next year?"

"Yep"

"Deal."

Kate grinned because the odds were now in her favor. As famous as Victor was for buying cheap horses with little pedigree and less ability, she was bound to be able to get at least one of the three new ones to a race. She'd lose fifty and win a hundred.

Years ago Kate had a hard time understanding Tanner's attitude toward Victor's inept choices. In the beginning, she thought Tanner should disabuse the man of his ridiculous notions about finding a bargain basement special that could run a hole in the wind, and instead help him buy good horses. Or at least just stick with the nice ones his family raised. But when she voiced her opinion, Tanner ignored her. Back then he ignored a lot of what she said.

Once she achieved the position of assistant trainer, she learned her place with the owners and realized people like Victor were only harmful to themselves.

Tanner's agreement was to take only six imported horses a year from Victor. But since the trainer's passing, Victor had slipped his leash, and tonight's arrivals were numbers seven, eight, and nine—in less than six months.

Should she talk to Victor about slowing down? Tough call, since she didn't like being in his presence, let alone trying to reason with him. Which meant his usual practice of sending her a text message about his purchases with a time and date for their arrival worked well for her.

Since his family was in the business of cargo transport, he handled the travel arrangements himself, claiming he had ways of circumventing some of the import paperwork. Details of which Kate certainly didn't want to know.

All she had to do was order new halters and name plates, prep stalls, and be at the barn to receive the newcomers.

The stalls were deeply banked, and hay nets plump with a nice timothy-alfalfa mix for the weary travelers. New halters hung by each door, and no matter how she tried to fight it, Kate hated those halters. Every other horse in her barn wore brown leather with a brass name plate.

Victor insisted his horses have black with silver—his way to easily identify a horse as his when he walked through the barn—and it messed with Kate's sense of order.

Worse still, the man was obnoxious. Treated her staff—the people looking after *his* horses—like they were invisible.

The only good part about having Victor as an owner was the packet of cash he handed her on the second day of every month, without fail. She depended on it to cover payroll.

As a Canadian trainer working in the US, Kate was only allowed to train for Canadians, and although they were all "good," it took ten days for their checks clear, which made Victor's cash a godsend.

But once Tanner's affairs were finalized, and his attorney signed off on everything, Kate would have to make changes, drastic changes.

"I'm thinking about firing myself," she told Leo.

"You'd have to lay everyone off."

Or hand the whole business over to her assistant. She only owned a couple of horses herself. Maybe she would take them to Florida or California. Or home to Canada.

"Did we shake on our bet?" asked Leo, bringing her back to reality.

Kate held out her hand, and they shared an exaggerated hand-pump followed by much grinning. Even though they were total sceptics where Victor was concerned, there wasn't a horseman alive who didn't hope the *next* horse would be a great one.

When the van pulled to a stop, the driver gave them a wave, then hopped out and got busy setting up the ramp. Kate studied the man climbing down from the passenger seat of the van. Brett, who always traveled with Victor's horses, was an odd sod. Didn't talk much—which wasn't a bad thing—but he had a watchfulness about him that put Kate on edge whenever she was in his company.

"How was the trip?" she asked.

"Good. Ate and drank well. No spikes in temperature." Short, sweet, and facts only. He didn't mention they looked weary and their eyes were dull, but Kate could see the three days of travel had exhausted them.

Leo led a chestnut filly down the ramp. Bedecked in a fluffy sheepskin-covered halter and head bumper, an oversized canvas blanket, full leg wraps, knee boots, hock boots, and bell boots, she was the equine equivalent of bubble-wrapped.

Kate coaxed a dark brown filly off next, and the van driver followed with the last one, a tiny gray.

Leo held each horse while Kate crouched underneath to remove the bandages and boots and drop them into a large laundry sack. Leo's gentle hands slipped under the padded halters to soothe the tired fillies while she worked, and once the blankets were off, he removed the headgear and passed it to Brett, who stowed it in a separate tote.

Once the horses were settled and the paperwork

complete, Brett and the driver loaded the equipment into the van and were on their way.

The whole process had taken less than thirty minutes, and now, as the sun dipped below the horizon, quiet descended over the barn once again—except for the occasional curious nicker among the horses.

Leo and Kate went from stall to stall, looking over the doors at the new acquisitions.

"Not bad-looking, and reasonably correct conformation," said Kate. "And since they're so small, there's a good shot at resale for polo ponies at least."

"My wager's looking good."

"Should I pay up now or later?" Kate asked with a grimace.

Leo laughed. "Where's your sense of adventure? You haven't even put tack on them yet. And odds are, one day he *will* come up with a runner."

"Somehow, my friend, I don't think it'll be one of these." She was frowning, staring at the tired horse who'd been dragged halfway around the world for a future that was going to be okay at best. "His family has a good breeding program here in the States, and they raise decent racehorses, yet Victor insists on importing the likes of this adorable but undersized creature. I just don't get it."

Leo let his fingertips brush across the diamond in his pocket, the one he'd managed to work out from under the padding of a halter. Wondered what Kate would do if she knew.

He shook off dark thoughts and summoned a smile. "Victor's not the brightest bulb, and it's his brother who runs the breeding farm. Maybe he's hoping to one day show him up by finding a champion overseas."

"Huh. He's always calling them his diamonds in the rough. But, hell, they turn out to be more like cheap imitations. Glass."

Startled, Leo studied her face. Saw nothing. "Pretty expensive glass."

There was a muted thud when one of the fillies lay down, and the other two looked like they'd be doing the same shortly.

"They're tired."

"I'll keep an eye on them. You might as well head home and get some sleep too."

———

Summer passed.

Horses came and went, races were won and lost, and Kate's days stayed blessedly predictable.

Each began with her and Leo enjoying coffee at four-thirty in the morning before everyone else arrived, and after that there were dozens of chores, her favorite being to climb aboard Anchor and escort the first set of gallopers to the track at six. They were the go-getters, the ones most eager to train. Horses who absolutely loved to stretch their legs and fill their lungs with cool morning air.

She missed having Tanner at her side, quizzing her about what she saw in each horse, asking her how she would prep a particular horse. They would discuss different training styles and argue good-naturedly.

But now she sat alone, watching, making mental notes, and occasionally fighting the loneliness.

By nine, training was finished, horses were

tucked into fresh, clean stalls, and grooms were busy brushing sleek hides, rubbing legs with a brace Kate made herself. Bandages were put on, feet were packed, and all other needs were tended. At eleven, grooms scooped steaming oats into sparkling clean feed tubs and, while the horses dug into their lunch with vigor, hot walkers raked the shedrow one last time.

At eleven-thirty, feed tubs were pulled out of the stalls, and dinners were mixed and left waiting to be put in at four.

At noon Kate sat with Mark, her assistant trainer, to discuss their morning and make plans for the next day—yet another reminder that Tanner was gone, and all the responsibility rested on her.

Kate usually went home for a quick nap in the afternoon, then drove back at three-thirty to hang out in her office while legs were unwrapped, temperatures taken, and the horses fed.

She used to head home at five, but these days she hung out in her office until six, when Leo would bring her a coffee and together they would stroll the shedrow looking in on each horse, making sure they were settled for the night.

It was one of her favorite times of the day. The horses were content, and everything was neat, tidy, in its place. The quiet was almost hospital-like.

Tanner would have been proud of how she maintained his level of perfection. Every stall looked the same, with white door screens, red rubber chains, and glowing white stall plaques. Bandage holders shone from daily polishing, as did the footlockers, and each groom's equipment was stored as precisely as the wash buckets stacked in sets of three.

Tanner had long ago drilled it into her head that looks mattered. Owners were drawn to a tidy operation just as certainly as they were put off by messy disorder. Even the tack room was immaculate. Bridles, saddles, and other gear hung at precise angles, and stacks of white saddle towels looked like they'd been folded and stacked using a mathematical formula.

Her life was just as orderly. And predictable. And she wondered if she dared to break the pattern... wish for more.

CHAPTER 2

Summer 2016

SEVERAL MONTHS HAD PASSED SINCE Victor's last load of South African horses arrived, and it looked like Leo would win the bet. Two of them were sold as polo ponies after showing absolutely no racing interest or ability, and the third, the pretty gray, was currently turned out at the farm due to a minor ankle injury.

As Kate arrived at the barn in the pitch black of four-thirty one morning, she was thinking about the gray mare, and a few others who were also turned out for rest and recuperation. It was time for them to return to training and she needed to arrange for transport.

What the...?

Not a single light on, and the side door was half open.

Something was wrong.

The moment Kate stepped inside, the sound of hungry thoroughbreds—who should have been fed already—bombarded her with their impatient nickering, whinnying, and stomping of feet.

She flicked the main switch, and light flooded

the long shedrow. She hit the switch again and the courtyard was bathed in a soft light that created eerie shadows, but lit her way to the door of Leo's room.

When knocking brought no response, she pounded, then tried the handle, but it wouldn't turn. She pounded again. Then tried his cell. No answer, and it didn't go to voice mail.

More important, she didn't hear the cell ringing in his room, which should mean he wasn't lying in there sick or injured.

But the man *never* deviated from routine. At three-thirty every morning he fed breakfast oats, then set a bag of fresh shavings across from every stall, dropped a bale of hay in each groom's section, filled the oat cookers and got them started, then made sure the coffee was fresh and hot for when Kate arrived at four-thirty. That's when they would sit together and relax until the rest of the crew arrived—nine grooms, eight hot walkers, four exercise riders, a barn foreman, and assistant trainer—by five-fifteen.

Kate called security, and then quickly went about getting Leo's morning chores done. When each arriving staff member asked, "Where is Leo?" All she could say was, "I don't know."

Bob, the head of security, showed up with a master key for Leo's room, and assured Kate that Leo had not been seen leaving the grounds, nor had anything unusual happened in the barn area the night before, no loose horses, no rowdy gatherings, nothing remotely worrying.

Leo's room was neat as a pin except for an indentation on the side of the bed where someone had been sitting. His barn shoes were by the door, and his jacket hung on a hook just above them.

Kate heard a faint sound and looked down just as Caly—wide-eyed and looking frightened—crept out from under the bed. Kate picked her up and backed out of the room.

There was a sickly feeling in her gut and she didn't know why, but she pulled out her phone. "I'm calling the police."

Bob shrugged. "I have to get back to the gate. I'll let in whoever shows up."

Luckily, in this corner of Kentucky there wasn't a whole lot of crime, so the police department wasn't run off its feet, and even though the dispatcher sounded less than concerned, they were sending an officer out to speak with her.

By the time the cruiser parked beside her car, she'd brought Mark up to speed and left him in charge of the barn.

"Ms. Oliver?"

"Kate. Thanks for coming."

"Officer Rylie. Tell me exactly what happened."

"I don't know what happened. Leo's just not here, and he's always here." She pointed out Leo's shoes and jacket. "He always wears slippers when he's in here, and I've never seen him step outside with them on. But his slippers aren't here now. Just his shoes."

The officer made careful and detailed notes.

"And his cat came out from under the bed just now looking frightened. Leo never left her in the room unless he was leaving the racetrack grounds to go shopping—but he never went on foot, always used my car."

"You probably don't want to hear this, but people disappear on purpose all the time."

She shook her head. "Not Leo. He wouldn't do that to me."

He stared at her for a moment before saying, "I'll put him in the system."

"Thanks."

He opened his mouth to say something and changed his mind. "Feel free to call if anything else comes up." He climbed back into his car, and while Kate watched him drive away, an awful ache grew around her heart.

Leo was gone. And now she was completely alone.

———

Two weeks later she was still sleeping fitfully—pretty much the norm now—so when her phone rang at two o'clock in the morning, she grabbed it quickly.

"Hello?"

There was a weird, hissy noise, like old-fashioned static. "Kate."

The voice was unsteady and whispery, but she knew it was him. "Leo!"

Hiss, spit, crackle, then, with the voice seeming even farther away, she could only catch a few words before the line went dead, or at least went quiet enough that she couldn't hear anything over the pounding of her heart.

She stared at the phone. Clicked it off. Waited. Prayed it would ring again. When it didn't, she hit redial, and a long string of numbers, mostly zeroes, filled the screen, but nothing happened. With a sinking heart, she grabbed a pen and jotted down the words she'd recognized. *Run. Hide/high? River. Jason. Trouble. Sorry.*

She sat on the edge of the bed waiting for God knows how long before she lost hope. Well, almost lost hope. She still kept the phone within arm's reach while she washed and dressed for the day. Tried to force down her usual breakfast of a banana and yogurt, but her stomach rebelled.

"Got to get a grip."

She glanced at herself in the mirror. "Did I dream it? Was the call a prank? Or was Leo calling for help?"

What did the words mean? *Was* he calling for help? Telling her to run? Hide? Go to High River in Alberta? Call Jason for help?

She dug out Officer Rylie's card. Left him a voice mail. Then sat for a minute, staring at the picture of her with Tanner and Leo. Flicked a glance to a higher shelf, to a photo of her at eighteen and madly in love with the tall, scrawny kid at her side.

The last time she bumped into Jason—more than fifteen years ago—he gave her a card with just a company name and a phone number and told her if she ever needed anything, *anything*, this outfit would either help her or find him for her.

She raced up the stairs and dug the card out the bottom of the wooden box where she kept her few pieces of jewelry.

Meyers Security 24/7. A way to contact Jason. But should she reach out to him? Would she be able to deal? To not lean on him, get caught up in the whole relationship thing again?

Good grief, even the thought of that was laughable. They both had lives and careers now, and had even less in common than before.

Before, when she learned that loving someone didn't mean they could have a life together. When she walked away because, in spite of the love and lust, they didn't want the same things in life. He lived for law enforcement, she wanted—no, needed—a career in horse racing. Both driven, both determined, they had no future together, so she walked away, because love just wasn't enough.

But she could still call on him as a professional, couldn't she? Without getting involved? Of course, because she loved her simple life. Was brilliant at avoiding complications…

Maybe she should think about this one a bit longer.

But the phone call, the faraway voice between bits of static, played over and over in her head while she drove to the track. She'd be early, but could help the new night watchman with chores. Anything to take her mind off all the crazy ideas rocketing around in her head and the niggling worry about what exactly Leo had been trying to tell her.

Officer Rylie responded to her voice mail by showing up at six am, and Kate took him to her office to explain about the early phone call and how sure she was that it was Leo.

He listened carefully but, unlike before, he took no notes, didn't even open his little book, and in the end shook his head and told her there was nothing he could do with so little information.

Kate saw red. "What if he was kidnaped? Why

won't you investigate?"

"I'm truly sorry, ma'am. But policy dictates how I can proceed, and without some kind of evidence, I'm afraid my hands are tied. Mr. Davis is an adult, you aren't family, there is nothing to suggest foul play, and, to put it simply, he is allowed to disappear if he wants."

Kate was dumbfounded. What if Leo was being held somewhere and eventually died because she couldn't find him? Officer Rylie didn't look her in the eye even once, and before he got into his car and drove away, he seemed to make a concerted effort to not even glance her direction.

Odd. Really odd. The gallon of coffee she'd already consumed soured in her gut. Something was off. Way off.

She tried to shake free of the uncomfortable thoughts and feelings and concentrate on her job. Gallopers, workers, walkers, the horses all kept her busy, and later, when the vet came for his rounds, Mark, her assistant, suddenly interrupted and asked to speak with her in her office.

Once the door was closed he asked simply, "What the hell's going on?"

"What do you mean?"

"You just told the vet to give a restricted medication to an in-tomorrow horse."

"Oh, no."

"Don't worry, she was as confused as I was and did nothing."

"Thank God." Otherwise she'd have had to scratch the horse and explain why to her owners.

"You've been off all morning, Kate. Even before that cop came. What's going on?"

She shook her head. "I'm not sure." She shoved her hands in her pockets and the tip of one finger bumped into the card she put there hours ago.

"Kate?"

It was time. "I need you to cover for me. Take over in the barn for the rest of the morning. I have to make a phone call," she said.

"Got it. But you'll tell me if there's anything else I can do?"

"Promise. Thanks."

As soon as he was gone she dialed, and held her breath.

"Meyers."

"Hello, my name is Kate Oliver. I'm an old friend of Jason Grant's. He gave me your card years ago and said you could help me find him if I ever needed his help."

"Please tell me your *exact* location before we continue, just in case we get disconnected." The woman sounded rather like a 9-1-1 operator.

"Wells-Radley Training Center near Lexington, Kentucky. Barn 6, in the office." Kate could hear the clicking of computer keys.

"Okay, Kate. My name is Eve Meyers, and I need you to tell me exactly what's happened."

"Well, nothing at the moment."

"What made you call?"

"A friend who is like family—and works for me—disappeared several weeks ago, and I think he tried to contact me this morning, but the police won't do anything about it." When prodded, she told the total stranger on the end of the phone, every detail, starting with Tanner's disappearance months earlier. It felt right. For the first time in ages she felt like she was doing the right thing.

After she'd been drained of every bit of information, including the fact that she was a Canadian citizen, the woman said, "Calling us was an excellent decision, because this is a very unusual situation." Her pause was only for a millisecond, but it was there. "I'm going to ask you to do something rather extreme now."

Instantly wary, Kate asked, "Such as?"

"You need to leave the training center immediately."

"Okay." Not such a big deal. She'd head home.

"I have an agent ready to meet with you to discuss Leo's disappearance and help you find him, but there's a bit of a drive involved."

"No worries. I'll go wherever I have to."

"I'm glad you said that. The agent will meet you in Niagara Falls. The Canadian side."

She held the phone out to stare at it for a minute while she wrapped her head around the request. An eight-hour drive? There was no one closer she could meet with for help? She heard her own voice in her head, saying she would do whatever was needed to find Leo. Of course she would. "I have to be back here to run a horse tomorrow afternoon."

"I don't foresee any problem with that, but I suggest you still make alternate arrangements just in case. Never hurts to prepare for the unexpected."

Kate's gut said *go*, and she always trusted her gut. Mark could hold down the fort. "I just have to swing by the house for my passport."

"Make it quick. Just in and out, then onto the highway. The agent will be waiting for you at the north end of the strip mall beside the Westbaker Hotel. Park near the restaurant next to the hotel, then walk north."

CHAPTER 3

WATCHING KATE'S APPROACH FROM THE far end of the mall, Jason's heart took a hit, and his smile exploded into a grin. She was everything she'd always been, and more.

Her long legs, purposeful stride, and the defiant angle of her chin screamed, "Back off, I'm in control." And her none-too-subtle sweep of the area reminded him of the first time he ever laid eyes on her. She'd been a girl on a mission that day, and now she was all woman and owned the mission.

When they'd met she was only eighteen, but there was a worldliness about her, a certainty he envied and admired. *He* had wanted to look that brave, feel that sure of himself, and he wanted her.

She wanted him too, and life was sweet—damn sweet…until it wasn't. And then she was just as happy to part ways as he was. Law enforcement was calling him the same way riding called her.

And now look at the two of them. Still connected to their old goals, but in much different ways, and for the first time ever, she needed him.

When he stepped into her path, she stopped and stared for a couple of beats before recognition lit her beautiful green eyes and the mouth he'd never forgotten widened into a grin. Two quick strides and she launched herself into his open arms. He held on tight, spun her off the ground while her laughter rang out.

She still felt the same, smelled the same, and all the warning bells in his head went off, but he didn't let go until she did.

Kate smoothed back her hair and stared at him. "You've changed so much I almost didn't recognize you," she said.

"You haven't."

"Ha ha. Thanks, but not true. The old me would have been fixing my own problem, not looking to you for a quick fix."

And there was one more reason she was who she was. Most women would have made a comment about looking older, or heavier, or something else about their appearance, but not Katie. She was all about who she was, not what she looked like.

"Congratulations, you're human."

"Ouch." She shook her head. "Not like I didn't deserve that. But I want you to know how much—"

"Not a good place to talk." He slung an arm around her shoulders and leaned in close. "There's a possibility we're being watched, so we need this to look like it's a reunion and all about sex, okay?"

Not many women would take that in stride, but he was fairly certain Kate would, and she never so much as flinched away from him. "Sure. Whatever."

"Come on, then."

She strolled alongside him until they neared the hotel, then he could feel her hesitancy when he veered off to the parking lot. "Where exactly are we going?"

"To my car for a minute, to help with the visual."

He grabbed a small suitcase from his SUV, then took her hand, and keeping his voice low said, "We need some time without distractions."

She moved away from him the second the door on Room 403 closed behind them, and Jason pulled the curtains and turned on a couple of lights while she checked out the minibar.

"Do you want something?" she asked.

Besides you? Whoa. Needed to shut down those thoughts here and now. He cleared his throat. "Any beer in there?"

Kate handed him one and opened a club soda for herself before taking a seat at the table in the corner.

He sat across from her. Got down to business. "Meyers briefed me, but I want to hear it in your words, right from the beginning."

Kate told the story, finishing with, "I think the police are either in on whatever happened, or they've been paid to look the other way."

Shit. "Never say that out loud, again, ever. Anywhere, anytime."

She pinned him with a searching look. "You agree it's possible?"

"Let's just say I think you have good instincts." Which might or might not be a blessing in the long run.

"After the officer left, bits and pieces of the day Leo disappeared started to come back to me. Things any good television cop would have checked on. And there were questions he should have asked."

Kate's heart skipped a beat when Jason's expression suddenly went blank and he focused on something behind her. She glanced over her shoulder. Nothing there but the curtain.

Up until that moment she was confident about her decision to call him for help. Felt safe in his company, although somewhat distracted by his appearance because he had aged so well.

Better than. Maturity looked damned good on him, as did the new body.

All arms and legs back in the day, but now? She wouldn't easily forget the hard body and strong arms she encountered about an hour ago.

And when those soul-searching black eyes met hers? She was toast. Certain he could see all the way into her soul.

She took a long swallow of her soda, wishing it was something with a lot more kick, and left her chair to stroll across to the window on the far side of the room. The instant she put her hand on the curtain to move it aside, Jason's voice cut through the air.

"Don't."

Startled by the sharp tone, she swung around. "I'm sorry."

He was at her side in an instant, raising his hand in a familiar move to touch her face but as the last second stuffed it in his pocket. "I'm the one to be sorry." He shook his head. "You have no idea what kind of a mess you're involved in, and frankly, that scares the shit out of me."

"The mess or my stupidity?"

"Your life could be in danger simply because you're smart enough to recognize when things don't add up."

She didn't want him to confirm her suspicions, dammit. "In my gut I knew this was something ugly, and I just didn't know who I could trust."

Using just one finger to lift her chin, forcing her to meet his inquiring gaze, he said, "So you were after my investigative skills, and not looking to rekindle the flame." It was a statement, not a question, and now was a fine time to notice his voice had grown deeper with age, sexier—God help her.

He *was* joking, right?

"Ha ha." She shook her head, which broke the contact between them, but she took a step back for good measure because she wasn't sure she could trust herself not to fall into his arms if invited. And this wasn't about *them*. It was about finding her friend. "I don't think Leo left voluntarily, and now he's depending on me to find him."

"What makes you believe that?"

She shrugged. "Did a whole lot of thinking on the drive up. Only two reasons for him to make that call. Either he needs my help, or he was trying to tell me to run because I'm in danger too."

"Plausible theories."

Well, hell. "Not the answer I was hoping for."

"What exactly do you want from me, Katie?"

The fifty-thousand dollar question. On the way here, she had convinced herself she was meeting an agent who would help her find Leo. But now, with Jason right here in front of her? She wanted a friend. A person of her own. Someone she could lean on.

Not that she dared lean, because depending on others left you weak once they were gone, and broken when they died.

But wouldn't it be nice to have Jason to keep her warm for a while? It had been ages since she spent time with someone purely for pleasure. She wasn't into dating. Never had the time, energy, or inclination to bother with romantic relationships. And really? Thinking romance right now was highly inappropriate.

"Last time I saw you, you said you were planning to leave the police force and become a private detective. If you did, I want to hire you to help me find Leo."

Silence hung in the air like dust on a hot summer day. Did he not want to help her? "I can pay whatever your rate is. Give you a retainer, if that's how it works."

"How about I order us up a meal? What would you like?"

Talk about a question coming out of left field. "I'm not hungry."

Something unpleasant flickered across his face before he picked up the phone and ordered a couple of steak dinners complete with dessert, coffee, and liqueurs.

Unpleasant memories tickled at the edge of her mind, but she shoved them away and reached for a safe topic of conversation. "Assuming you did go private, what's it like? More exciting? Less?"

"Less paperwork, less bureaucracy, and less exciting. Long hours doing surveillance on cheating husbands and wives mostly, except for when I'm working contracts for Meyers. Some of them get the adrenaline pumping. What about you? Any great horses, Derby prospects in your barn?"

She smiled. The Derby had been her obsession

back in the day. Determined to one day have a mount in the most prestigious race of all, and ride under the twin spires on the first Saturday in May. But now, while she *would* be thrilled to saddle one amid the pomp and circumstance of Derby Day, it wasn't a goal.

"No outstanding youngsters, but I have a handful of really special mares." He prompted her to talk about the horses, and before long she was relaxed again, at least until there was a sharp knock on the door.

"That was quick," Jason said. "Go into the bathroom. I don't want anyone to see you."

She didn't like taking orders, but did as she was told, and when he tapped on the door a few minutes later, she emerged to find the table nicely set, and the bed stripped down to tangled sheets.

"Nice touch." She couldn't help but smirk, and loved the way his responding smile made his eyes light up.

"Old trick. Show them what they expect to see, and you can keep flying under the radar."

The seriousness of what he said brought her back to reality with a jerk and she nodded. Sat. Ate while he asked her a million questions about the details of her business, with an unmistakable focus on the people she trained for. Wanted to know how wealthy they were, did they all have obvious sources of income, did she think anyone was shady in the slightest way, were they easy to train for or demanding, were they only in it for the money or were they concerned about the animals themselves?

His questions went on and on, and dinner had

long been finished when Kate began to yawn. She looked at her watch and was amazed to see it was nearly midnight.

"I'd better be heading back."

"Not a chance. I won't have you out on the highway in the middle of the night."

"Excuse me?"

"It isn't safe."

Hmmm. "I'm not sure how to tell you this, but not only do I make my own decisions, but I'm not one of those helpless females you see on television."

He half laughed, but didn't sound amused. "You're one of the smartest and strongest women—no, people—I've ever known, and Lord knows you managed to get us both in and out of trouble a time or two, but this is different."

He shoved his fingers through the hair he wore much shorter than in the old days. Back then it was a wave of silky blackness he kept tied back except when they were at home. "I agree with your assessment of Leo's disappearance, and if a man like him could get nabbed, you're easy pickings."

His direct gaze pinned her now. "If you want my help to find him, you will have to put up with me protecting you. Package deal. Non-negotiable." He waited a beat. "Deal?"

She was too tired to argue, and instead glanced at the king-size bed. "I suppose it would be silly for one of us to sleep on the floor." And at the moment she was too tired to care about details. She'd been up for almost twenty-four hours, and there was no fight left in her. All she wanted was a flat surface and a pillow.

She stretched out on the far side and pulled the blankets up over her.

"Oh, for heaven's sake, Katie. You can't sleep in your clothes. You'll look ridiculous leaving here in the morning all wrinkled up." He dug around in his small case and produced a white T-shirt, which he tossed her way.

She'd slept in jeans and a sweater before, and looking wrinkled up hadn't been an issue, but the T-shirt would be a whole lot more comfy. She picked it up. "Thanks."

When he turned his back and peeled off his shirt, she couldn't help but stare. She had always loved the perfectly even golden brown of his skin, but now it was stretched over a wealth of muscle and it was even more enticing. When he stood to remove his jeans, she quickly turned away and made a quick trip to the bathroom.

When she emerged in T-shirt and panties, Jason was stretched out on the huge bed with the white sheet pulled up to his bare chest, and there was way too much skin visible.

She fought the urge to stare and, with what she hoped looked like quiet dignity, climbed under the covers and turned her back to him.

His soft laugh tickled the back of her neck, the light flicked off, and she closed her eyes, praying sleep would be quick enough to rescue her from self-destruction.

The sound of his voice, and the constant twinkle in his eye—even when he was being dead serious—were lethal weapons.

———

Jason studied the rhythm of her breathing and smiled to himself when the long day took its toll and sleep claimed her.

He, on the other hand, was destined to lie awake for hours, listening to her breathe and revisiting their past.

He was the most experienced hot walker in Tanner's barn when Kate was hired, and he was assigned to train her.

The attraction was instant, and within a couple of weeks they moved into an apartment together, and life was perfect until she locked onto her goal. Decided she wanted to become a jockey.

She told Tanner what she wanted, and he took her seriously, started her on a program to learn the ropes from the bottom up. For a couple of months she walked hots, then she shadowed a groom for a week before being given the task of caring for the stable's lead ponies.

Before the race meet was over in December she was a full-fledged groom, and when spring training started, she worked the track in the mornings and spent the afternoons at the farm, learning how to be an exercise rider—she'd ridden lots as a kid, but getting on racehorses was about as similar to that as paddle-boarding was to surfing.

While Kate honed her skills on horseback, Jason added more night classes to his load at the community college, and slowly worked his way to a criminology degree. He wanted to be a homicide

detective like the one he got to know after dis-
covering a dead man in a horse's stall a few years
earlier. The bizarre nature of the case had always
stuck with him, and Ted Gallagher, the calm, cool,
and sharp detective on the case, eventually became
Jason's mentor.

Gallagher's sudden transfer to the West Coast had
been a blow, but they stayed in touch, and with
Ted's help, Jason was able to realize his own dream.

One that didn't mesh well with Kate's.

In the beginning, it was simple logistics.

He was either walking hots, in class, or home
studying, and when she wasn't working at the track
or the farm, she was sleeping like the dead.

Their third spring together brought even more
changes, because Kate was ready to ride in races,
but needed to shave off ten more pounds, which
meant starving herself and working harder than
ever.

Jason hated that even though she was bone-thin,
she still ate hardly anything, and she was getting
weaker and bitchier by the day. Eventually there
was nothing good left between them, and she
exploded at him one night, packed a bag, and left,
never to return. She moved into a tack room at the
track, and he washed his hands of worrying about
her.

When he was accepted into the police academy
a few weeks later, he was more than ready to start
a new life. But now, with Kate sound asleep beside
him, he had to admit that even with his ex-wife
he hadn't experienced this feeling of belonging, of
rightness.

For a while he lay on his side, staring, unmoving,

until he finally gave in and slid close enough to drape his arm over her waist. She groaned softly and snuggled back against him, and he held his breath for a moment, then let it out slowly when she didn't move again. He stayed very still, taking in the faint coconut scent of her hair, and refusing to think about whether what he was doing was right or wrong.

———

Waking up to the sound of the water running, Kate glanced at the clock.

Holy Hanna! She scrambled out of bed, dragging on her jeans. Mark would already have the first set on the track by now, and he'd be wondering what the heck had happened to her. Didn't help that Jason had insisted she shut off her cell phone last night.

Suddenly realizing the shower had stopped, she grabbed her sweater and was ready for her turn in the bathroom but when Jason emerged—wearing only his jeans—her breath caught in her throat and her feet didn't move.

He laughed. "What? You forgot you had a room-mate last night?"

Ha ha. Kate swallowed and hoped her face wasn't as red as it felt. "Something like that." Then swept past him.

Trying to ignore the steamy swirl of Jason-scented air, Kate concentrated on winding her hair into a knot on the top of her head. Washing and drying it would take far too long and she was in a hurry to get on the road.

She showered at warp speed, and was surprised when, the moment she stepped onto the bath-mat, there was a loud knock on the door, quickly followed by, "Hurry up in there, your breakfast is getting cold."

This bossy side of him was unfamiliar. Must have come from his law enforcement training, and she wasn't impressed. She hated taking orders almost as much as she hated having food forced on her, so he was batting a thousand. But by the time she emerged, her annoyance was carefully hidden behind a pleasant smile. No point giving him the pleasure of knowing he was pushing her buttons with deadly accuracy.

"Perfect," Kate said, looking at covered dishes. "I'm starving."

The glint in Jason's eye said he wasn't fooled by her carefully crafted demeanor, but they sat eating together like polite strangers until the effort became too much for Kate.

"What happens next?" she asked.

He smiled. "A few details to get out of the way before you get on the road." He handed her a cell phone. "This is the only phone you use to call me. Unless it's life or death, of course, at which time do whatever's necessary."

Kate was startled by his tone and the look on his face. "Life or death? You're serious."

"As a heart attack."

"You really think someone wants to hurt me?"

"You'll only be in danger if you antagonize or get in the way of the wrong people. With that in mind, you need to make a concerted effort to get along with everyone. That's contractors, staff, and owners. Even if someone wants you to run a horse completely out of line, or use a jockey you think doesn't suit the horse, or whatever, give in gracefully."

"Tell me you're joking." But his face said it all. "How out of line? Like a claimer in a stakes race? Not a chance."

Jason took her hand and held it very tightly, "Katie, my gut tells me Leo was removed because he was in the way, so you can't present a roadblock of any kind."

"I don't understand."

He opened and closed his mouth a couple of times, but no words came out.

"Say whatever it is, for heaven's sake!"

He took a deep breath and let it out slowly. "Before we met—my first season at Tanner's barn—the night watchman was murdered. I was the one who found him in an empty stall when I arrived one morning. At first glance it looked like he'd taken a hoof to the side his head, and everyone assumed he'd gone in to help a cast horse and got himself kicked."

Jason was watching her closely. "The horse who belonged in the stall where he was found was eventually found in a remote corner of the barn area, also dead. Oddly enough, after the initial on-scene investigation, both deaths were ruled accidental."

"Night watchman," she murmured. Like Leo.

"I got tight with the original investigating officer—who eventually became my long-distance mentor."

"The man who used to call you from Vancouver? Ted?"

He nodded. "Ted suspected a cover-up, and when he started investigating on his own time he was suddenly pressured into taking a job on the West Coast."

"Are you saying the problem was within law enforcement?"

"Some of it. He's got proof, but the connections go way high, and he's never confronted anyone, or made more waves. But he's continued to collect data for years while working contracts for Meyers."

"Another connection," she murmured and then a metaphorical lightbulb blinked on in her head. "Tanner was murdered, wasn't he?"

Jason nodded. "Meyers has amassed a ton of circumstantial evidence, but nothing to nail a suspect. All we know for sure is the auction was rigged and the boat fire was staged."

"Fire? What boat fire? The police told me he fell overboard and drowned."

"Tanner was in the water without a life vest because the boat was on fire. The captain and crew 'apparently' went off the opposite side and couldn't get to him, but miraculously they survived." His expression was grim. "The whole situation was far too neat and tidy right from the get-go—him winning the trip."

"That part was us. It was the only way we could get Tanner to take a vacation." Kate went cold clear down to her bones. "And now Leo's missing..." Her voice faded.

"We have a fair idea who might be involved, but unless you're willing to go into hiding here and now, I can't tell you."

Seriously? She leaned back in her chair and

worked at maintaining a cool demeanor. "Instead, I'm supposed to go back and continue with things as usual, even though I know there's a ticking bomb somewhere very close by."

"You can do it," he said with a smile, and her heart did an annoying backflip. Seriously? In the midst of all this turmoil, wishing she could crawl into that smile, those strong arms, was wrong in too many ways to count, and just as ridiculous as her sudden attachment to the word seriously. Both had to stop.

If Jason suspected she—or her operation, more likely—was being used for something illegal, something worth killing for, money laundering would be at the top of the list. Gambling was an easy way to turn old money into new.

But then there was also Victor, throwing away bundles on the horses he imported, but how did he get the clean money back? He had some success with one or two locally raised horses, but there wasn't nearly enough profit involved...was there?

He passed her an envelope full of cash once a month. What if… Her eyes widened.

"Could I be implicated? Be guilty of a crime and not even know it?"

"Possibly." But his face said not probable. What did that mean?

"Leave it alone, Kate. The less you know, the better."

She swallowed hard. Chewed toast about as appealing as pressed paper. "If I go missing, or end up dead—"

"I will never forgive you." He shoved his chair back. "Or myself," he muttered on his way to the window, where he used one finger to part the drapes and look out. "Would you consider going to a safe location?"

She frowned. "Now? As in pick up and leave my career—hell, my entire life—behind and go into hiding?"

"Yes."

She wanted to deliver a heartfelt "Hell, no!" But hesitated. She was smart. She knew something was very wrong. Was her career worth going back for? Of course it was. She'd worked hard for her position, and still worked hard every day to stay successful.

She glanced at the serious face of the man studying her. A man she could have had a life with if not for a career she was doggedly determined to have. One she'd been forced to give up anyway.

He'd begged her once to give up her dream of becoming a jockey, and now he was asking her to walk away from training. But the two requests were worlds apart. They could have had a life together if she'd been willing to quit race-riding.

Now, if she gave up training? She would have nothing. No purpose. No reason to even get out of bed in the morning.

"It's more than a job. It's what I live for." A faint shudder ran through her when she realized it was exactly the same thing she said to him the first time.

"Time to go, then." He grabbed the T-shirt she'd left on the end of the bed and stuffed it into his case. Set it by the door.

His face was expressionless. Likely a trick he developed in the police academy.

Kate was sorry she'd upset him, and once they were in the elevator, she slipped her arm behind him to hook her thumb in a belt loop. His arm circled her shoulders, and he drew her closer, not relinquishing his hold until they arrived at his car.

"We're going for a drive before you leave," he said, opening the passenger door for her. She shrugged, already resigned to Mark taking care of business until she got home.

Once out in traffic, the realities of traffic and all the other bits and pieces of the world around her made the night before seem somewhat surreal, and the old connection between them little more than ancient history. They didn't speak until they had circled the town and were parked beside her car.

"Meyers Security is a family-owned-and-run business with headquarters on a ranch in Texas. James and his wife, Julia, are at the helm, and many of their grown children work within the company. Going forward, any time you can't reach me, call them, and they'll either find me, or get help to you ASAP. They're good people. A really solid family."

He got a faraway look in his eyes, and she was reminded that, like her, he was an orphan, and finding a family, that sense of belonging, had been part of his drive toward law enforcement. He'd wanted to be part of that brotherhood.

Yet, he had left the force and struck out on his own. Maybe because of this Texas family.

"They'll send help from Texas?"

"There's a huge network of contracted agencies for them to tap into, no matter where you are."

Good to know.

"Anyone making contact who's been sent by me

or Meyers will identify themselves with the name of a horse from the years we worked together at the track."

"Like a code," she said, half to herself.

"The phone I gave you is secure, but any time you use it, also open a line on your own phone. Your line will show up to anyone monitoring you, and they'll waste time trying to hack your signal from the nearest microwave tower."

"If they're successful, won't they be able to hear me talking to you?"

"We'll never be on the line long enough."

He walked her through a few useful tricks for communicating with him when they might be overheard and, most importantly, he went into great detail about ways to cover her own tracks if she thought she was in danger.

Kate listened carefully until he said, "I want you to hire a new night watchman right away, and clear out Leo's room."

"No. I can't, *won't* give up hope."

"That's not what I'm asking you to do. We have to make it *look* like you're moving on. And I need access to Leo's belongings to search for clues."

Well okay. That made sense.

"Box up everything and ship it over to your storage locker. I'll send someone to pick them up so I can sift through for evidence."

He handed her a small black notebook. "I'll need the address, unit number, and pass code."

While she wrote it all down, he went on with his instructions.

"From now on, when we meet, and while we're together, it will appear that we have reunited and

taken up where we left off. We only talk business if
I deem it safe."

"No girlfriends you're going to piss off?"

"No."

"What about your ex-wife?"

"Nonissue," he said. "More importantly, you need
to be careful. Avoid acting out of character, but at
the same time give in eventually to whatever your
owners want. Then let me know what's going on."

Kate nodded. "In the meantime, you'll try to find
Leo, right?"

"I will." He shut off the car and unclipped his
seatbelt. "There will be times when, in order to
look natural, and especially if I know we're being
watched, I will need to kiss you without warning.
Will that be an issue?"

"No, I trust you." And that was the utter truth.
Besides that, she liked— Nope, not going there.

He hit the release on her seatbelt and with gentle
hands cupped her face. "I'll be in touch," he said,
and his mouth lowered to hers.

It was a pretty simple brushing of his lips, but
her heart climbed the back of her throat and she
was suddenly leaning closer. Embers she'd thought
long cold were ignited, and when he pulled away
to look in her eyes, his voice was deep and just a
bit scratchy. "I should have known."

She blinked. "Known what?"

"You still pack one helluva punch."

And so, dammit, did he.

———

Jason wasn't sure what he'd expected after the

kiss, but what he got was nothing. Without a word she climbed out of his car, into her own, and without a backward glance left the parking lot and headed for the highway.

He shook his head. Wrapping a bow on Victor and handing him over to the authorities was going to be interesting…and frustrating as hell.

When the Kate he used to know got an idea in her head, there was no damn stopping her. In spite of the years gone by, he suspected convincing her to do what he needed when he needed it was still going to be a challenge and a half.

CHAPTER 4

———

AFTER A FEW SHORT HOURS in Jason's company, Kate's foolish heart was playing games with her mind. Did they still have a chance? Could they overcome what she had always believed were their insurmountable differences?

Jason's drive to solve crimes was still there, front and center, but Kate's dream of becoming a famous jockey had gone up in smoke—and she was glad he hadn't witnessed her epic crash and burn.

He had been there for the endless hours, days, weeks, and months of sweat and sore muscles while Tanner put her through the toughest kind of training there was. Never giving her an easy day. No pity when she was sore and exhausted. But when she was almost there, standing on the verge of becoming an apprentice jockey, Jason was gone. No longer a part of her life.

Kate had neither the time nor energy to miss his companionship—not to mention the great sex— until the day she won her first race and suddenly longed to share it with him.

She could imagine his pride in her accomplishment, and it would have been so perfect to jump off the horse in the winner's circle and right into his arms. He would have picked her up and swung her around in celebration while they laughed joyously.

Instead, she skipped back to the jocks' room, where the valets and other riders blocked the doorway, buckets in hand to deliver the traditional ice-water dousing. Once she'd been well soaked, the crowd parted and, as she made her way inside, she survived dozens of cheery slaps to her ass while she was showered with words of praise and congratulations.

"Well done!"

"You're a natural, kid."

"Way to go!"

"Man, you can horseback!" She savored that one, because it was the highest possible praise. Anyone could "ride," but if you could read horses, understand them, connect at such a profound level they would willingly give you their all? That meant you could "horseback."

But still, amid the shouts of ego-boosting words, she heard what the journeymen—the senior, well-established, jockeys—weren't saying.

Guts, ability, and dedication would never be enough, because she couldn't do the weight. Her height set her up to fail. At five foot nine, she had to starve herself to stay under a hundred and five pounds, and that left her trying to do a physically demanding job on no fuel, with almost no muscles.

She lived on coffee and cigarettes. Her biggest meal in a day consisted of a bowl of green peas topped with one tablespoon of diet mayonnaise because, try as she might, she couldn't master the art of flipping—puking. She didn't dare put food in her mouth that she couldn't afford to keep. A couple of the taller jockeys tried to teach her how to flip, claiming it was the best way to satisfy hunger, get a tiny bit of nutrition, and still keep their weight to a minimum, but she simply couldn't master the art, which meant she had to avoid food altogether.

For almost a year she managed to control her weight by using every means possible, including long runs and water pills—diuretics. And then one day everything came apart.

It was a sunny Saturday in August, and she had five mounts on the afternoon card.

The horse she rode in the first race was a front-runner, broke from the gate like a rocket, and was in front by three almost instantly. In riding terms, Kate was sitting chilly, which meant she was poised above the saddle with her entire body weight resting on thin aluminum stirrups while she kept a steady grip on the reins and did nothing to interfere with the filly's running style. Until they turned for home. That's when the riding started.

Kate shoved her hands up the filly's neck and made chirping noises, urging her mount to edge even farther away from the rest of the field, and she did it so easily Kate knew there would be no catching her now!

Adrenaline pumping, an indescribable thrill coursed through her, and a grin burst free when they hit the wire.

Yes! This was what she'd been born to do. Heart soaring, she stood straight up in her irons and punched the air, reveling in the roar from the grandstand.

The filly cruised on, flying into the clubhouse turn with apparently no desire to slow down, but lucky for Kate—whose arms were now like limp noodles—one of the outriders was there to help her pull up. He galloped alongside, grabbed one of Kate's reins and brought her mount under control.

They slowed, then stopped. "Thanks, Carl," she managed with a gasp.

By the time they loped back to the winner's circle and he handed the filly off to her groom, Kate had recovered enough to hop off and into Tanner's arms for a celebratory hug. With her heart still thumping madly and her knees weak from excitement, she kept an arm around Tanner for a bit of extra support after the photo was taken and they made their way back toward the paddock and jocks' room. Kate kissed him on the cheek, scooted away for a quick change, and was soon back out in the parade ring wearing blue and black silks with the number three on her sleeve.

The ride on the next horse would be completely different, because he always broke slowly and needed the entire mile to pick off the competition. Kate needed to concentrate on traffic and pace. She would probably have to steady him several times to keep a safe distance from another's heels until there was a clear path to go around.

When the assistant starter led him toward the gate she drew a long, deep breath and then let it out slowly. Rolled her shoulders and grabbed a handful of mane. When the last tailgate closed and the horses all had their heads pressed forward into the vee-shaped front of their stall, she sucked in

another breath just before the brrrring of the bell
and the loud clang of ten steel doors flying open.

Her mount jumped out with the rest, but as they
accelerated ahead of him, he was at the mercy of
nine horses kicking back clods of dirt. Kate tucked
her face in as close to his neck as she could without
impeding her vision and patiently waited for the
field to space itself out.

After a quarter of a mile, she spotted an opening,
pointed her horse toward it, and he lumbered on
through. In heavy traffic now, she maneuvered him
into yet another opening, only to get boxed in—
two horses to the outside, one on the inside, and
three across the track in front of her. She steadied
her mount, but he resisted, tugging at the reins as
though he could see a clear path, but she pulled
with all her might and forced the bit back hard in
his mouth, demanding he listen to her and wait.

Her entire body began to scream with the pain
of controlling a thousand pounds of thoroughbred
with just her hands wrapped around thin strips of
leather. A burning sensation began at the ends of
her fingers, shot up her arms, across her shoulders,
down her back, through her hips, and right to the
very tips of her toes, as if being poured full of liquid fire.

Blinking back tears, and her vision further
impeded by dirt on her goggles, she barely saw an
opening to the right when another horse began to
tire. Kate loosened her left line a fraction, and that
was all the invitation her mount needed. He dove
for the opening, dropping his head and picking
up speed, nearly tearing the lines out of her hands
while passing horses and ranging up alongside the

leader.

For nearly a quarter of a mile they went head-to-head, horse against horse and rider against rider.

Kate was bellied down, urging him on with every fiber of her being. One stride before the wire she delivered a slap of her whip on his right flank, and he leapt forward, giving her just that little bit more and sticking his nose out far enough to win the photo finish.

Again, Kate needed the pickup rider to help her get back to the winner's circle. But she was on top of the world. Tanner told her she had "plumb out-rode" one of the best riders in the country, and there was no better praise. She smiled so hard her cheeks hurt, and adrenaline or endorphins or what-ever had her floating about a foot off the ground on her way back to the jocks' room.

She had the next race off but, too pumped to rest, she pedaled a few miles on a stationary bike while watching the action on a video monitor.

First out of the room when the riders were called to the paddock for the next race, she shook hands with the trainer. It was her first ever mount for him, and she listened carefully to his instructions.

"This filly is fast enough to run on the engine, but if you let her set too fast a pace, she'll come up empty before the wire."

He legged her up, then patted her boot when she slipped her foot into the stirrup. "Remember. Take ahold early so you have enough horse to fin-ish." His voice suddenly seemed very far away, and during post parade Kate felt sort of odd, but shook it off.

Two jumps out of the gate, the filly started pulling, resisting the bit, swinging her head from side to side and putting up one hell of a fight, but Kate stayed strong. Was finally able to convince her to relax and go easy until a competitor loomed up alongside, and matched her stride for stride. Tension built between them, and their ingrained desire to race had them digging in, picking up speed.

Kate leaned back, got her feet out in front of her so she could use her legs and hips for leverage to help her maintain some control, and again her body began to burn.

For nearly three-quarters of a mile, Kate was immersed in battle while her mind ticked off the furlongs until they finally turned for home. That's when she was able to tuck her heels back under her butt and chirp. The jock beside her did the same thing, and the race was on.

Kate was crouched low, with withers against her middle and mane tickling her face, when tingling began in her fingertips and tiny flashes of light made her blink her eyes rapidly to clear her vision. But darkness slipped in between the flashes.

She dropped a set of goggles, but it didn't help. Kept blinking and blinking, and then they were past the wire and she was bracing against the filly's neck for support. Balance.

The pickup rider wasn't there this time, but luckily the horse was tired and slowed on her own.

Kate was still blinking and shaking her head when another rider came up alongside her. He asked if she was okay, and she said sure, then prompted her horse to lope back alongside his until they reached the unsaddling area. But when she slid to the ground, she crumpled, her legs refusing to support her. Someone helped her to her feet and to the fence, where she leaned heavily.

There were voices, but they had a funny echo, and she couldn't make out the words exactly. Her body was heavy like lead…yet oddly feather-light.

She woke up in the first aid room, pulling at the oxygen mask on her face. When she opened her eyes, the bright light from the ceiling sent a butcher knife stab of pain through her head, and she quickly closed them again, swinging her legs over the side of the bed.

Sat up.

And held on, waiting for the spinning to stop before she opened her eyes again. Just little knives now.

The doctor spent a couple of minutes checking her out, and then insisted she drink at least eight ounces of water before she got on her next mount or he would give it to her intravenously.

She refused. Told him she couldn't afford the weight, and he informed her that without fluids he wouldn't allow her back in the tack today.

An hour—and eight ounces of water—later, her vitals were back within normal range, so he gave her clearance, and the ride was uneventful.

The horse was a long shot with little ability, and there was nothing for Kate to do but sit still and guide him around the oval while being thankful her strength had returned.

When she stepped on the scale before her final race of the day, Kate was thrilled the clerk of the scales seemed not to notice she was half a pound overweight. She had heard that he sometimes turned a blind eye, but had never been on the receiving end of such a gift until today.

Things were looking up for sure, and she not only felt better than she had all day, but she was on the favorite. A horse who had never been outrun going five furlongs on the turf. All she had to do was ensure he had a safe trip.

But when she was being loaded into the starting gate, things took a downward turn. Her heart began thumping hard in her chest, and she didn't need the sudden sparkling around the edges of her vision to know she was in trouble She leaned forward and took a couple of deep breaths to fight off the tingling in her fingers. Squeezed the reins. Released. Did it again.

Fifty-seven seconds was all she needed. She could hang on that long. Needed this one for the hat trick.

The air began to sparkle, and her peripheral vision went black. All she could see were lighted circles of what was directly in front of her. She stared out the front of the gate, blinking. Dammit, she could do this. Would—

When the doors sprang open she wasn't ready.

The horse lunged forward.

Her hands jerked on the lines.

He faltered, stumbled, and righted himself, but not without losing ground to the rest of the field.

He ran full-out at the wall of horses in front of them, and Kate somehow managed to stay on, scrambling to steer while he closed ground, catching horses one at a time and blowing past them.

He was out of control, and she was little more than a passenger.

When her foot brushed against another rider's

boot he yelled at her to "Take ahold!"

But she couldn't do much more than try to stay aboard, and even that was becoming a chore. She grabbed for a handful of mane and held on for dear life while the world spun past her at breakneck speed and she fought for air.

They flew past the grandstand and suddenly the outrider was there beside her, a galloping blur, an arm reaching for her reins…

And the world slid away.

Kate came to with her chest aching and her throat burning. There was a steady beeping close by. She opened her eyes just a crack and faces swam into view.

A man in scrubs asked her questions and explained in great detail what had happened to her, but nothing more than the basics sank in. She was in hospital, had collapsed, was being hydrated.

Tanner leaned over, and when her eyes met his, he said, "Starvation and dehydration are killing you. If you don't die from falling off during a race, your organs are going to shut down, and they're not talking years from now."

When she was released from hospital ten days later, she was five pounds heavier than the day she went in, and the doctor told her she needed another ten pounds before she could be called anything close to healthy.

She was horrified. Needed rid of the extra weight, and in a hurry, if she didn't want her career evaporating before her eyes.

She would run, and swim, and then hit the hot-box. She'd start with the treadmill as soon as Tanner dropped her off.

But when he let her out in front of the tack room where she'd been living since she left Jason, fatigue won. Just a quick nap, she thought, crawling between the covers on her cot.

For two days the only time she moved was to stumble over to the washroom or fill her water bottle from the tap outside.

When anyone came by to check on her, she told them to go away.

On the third day, Leo pounded on the door and refused to leave. She let him in, then propped herself up on the cot, wrapped in a blanket.

Leo sat in the only chair and stared down at his hands for quite some time before he spoke with that gentle, no-nonsense tone.

"Stall rest is over. It's time you got some exercise and fresh air. If you were a sick horse, I'd take you out for a walk in the sunshine and let you eat some nice green grass."

"Please don't make me eat grass, Leo."

He smiled. "How about a walk in the sunshine, kid?"

"I don't want to see anyone."

"I'll come and get you after training hours, when things are quiet."

"Okay."

Leo got up to leave and reached into the pocket of his coat to pull out a banana and a chocolate bar. "I thought you might like these."

Tears welled in her eyes, and she nodded. Without another word, Leo set the treats on her tiny table and slipped out the door.

Kate ate the banana right away and savored every mouthful, but put the chocolate bar up on a shelf. She couldn't remember the last time she had eaten chocolate.

When he came for her around one o'clock that afternoon, she was dressed and ready. He handed her a small white bucketful of ice.

"What—"

"For later." She set it inside, then locked her door and strolled through the barn area with Leo.

They saw almost no one because this was the usual naptime for most horsemen. Leo should be sleeping too, because he worked nights, watching over the horses in Tanner's barn.

"Why are you bothering with me?" Dammit, she sounded pathetic, but there was no fight left in her.

"You needed someone to prod you."

"Why you?"

"Nobody else seemed to have time."

"Thanks." Tears threatened, and that was just stupid.

"No problem."

When they reached the barn where Tanner's horses were stabled, Leo took her to the lunch room. "Sit," he said, and brought over a box from the fridge.

"Got us a snack from the cookshack."

He put two fat roast beef sandwiches and two cartons of chocolate milk on the table between them.

Kate carefully avoided looking at the sandwich and took a sip of the milk. Closed her eyes and savored it, swallowing barely a drop at a time.

Kate watched Leo eat his sandwich and drink every last drop of his milk. But she couldn't bring herself to even taste her food.

"How long have I known you, Kate?" he asked, with a deadly serious expression.

"Two years?"

"That seems about right." Sorrow clouded his eyes. "My wife has been gone nearly four years. That's how long I've been with Tanner."

Kate was shocked. She had no idea Leo had lost a wife. "I am sorry. I didn't know."

"Nobody does, aside from Tanner. I came here for a fresh start. Didn't want to bring any of the past with me."

"Did it work?"

He smiled with his mouth and his eyes. "Nope. Got the new life, but the past is still with me. Guess it taught me a thing or two."

"You can run but you can't hide?"

He laughed. "Yeah. That. But never mind me. You're the one in trouble at the moment."

"Don't worry I'm gonna be fine. I just have to get back in training, get strong again."

"It's more than that, and you know it."

"No, really, he said—"

Leo stopped her with a hard look. "Time to grow up and face reality, Kate. I know how much you love riding, but it is killing you. You have to either ride at a higher weight or hang up your tack."

Quit?

"You could probably stay healthy if you were tacking fifteen."

The sound that came from her was a grim laugh of sorts. "Who the hell will ride me at one fifteen when they can get one of the journeymen at a twelve? If I can't tack ten or less..." She couldn't say the words.

"You'll be dead in a year."

"That's crap. I just have to make healthier choices. Work harder. Riding is my passion, my dream. It's what I live for. I can't quit. I can't!" Kate began to cough and struggle for breath.

Leo stood, put his hands on the table, and got in her face. "Listen to yourself. You can't even yell at me and catch a breath at the same time. For God's sake, girl, pay attention to what's going on here. You. Are. Going. To. Die."

"Quit saying that!" She coughed. "I'm not going to die, Leo."

"You bet your ass you aren't. I won't allow it, and neither will Tanner."

"I'll be fine, I just need some rest." She held up the plastic-wrapped food. "Maybe a sandwich."

"If you were a horse, or even a damn barn cat they'd be shoving a tube down your throat and pumping food into your belly." He locked eyes and wills with her, and Kate began to crumple under his stare.

"But my dream," she mumbled weakly. "I can't just give it up, it's my ticket to..." She began to cry silently.

"Dreams change, Kate, and shit happens. Do you have any idea how many people never even get close to their goals, let alone get to live them for even a few minutes? You did it. You became a jockey, and a damn good one. But it's over, girl."

She sniffed, swiped tears off her cheeks.

"Dreams are like rainbows, Kate. They don't last

forever. But when they're gone, the sky is wide open and ripe for another. There will be more goals to reach for. Many, many, more."

She looked at him through her tears and shook her head. "Riding races is all I ever wanted."

"Kate, I watched my wife starve to death because a cancer was consuming her body bit by bit, and she couldn't keep food down. She didn't have any second chances, but you do. You, are only being eaten up by your own stubbornness."

He took a deep breath and continued, "Time to grow up and face the fact you can't have everything you want." Then he straightened up and said, "I have to get some sleep." And left her there, staring at his departing back.

Sandwich in hand, Kate walked slowly back to her tack room. Left the door open to the afternoon sun while she sat on the edge of the bed and picked the meat out from between the bread and ate it. Then she savored every bit of the ice cream sandwich she found wrapped in plastic in the bottom of the bucket of ice.

A week later she sat across the desk from Tanner and asked him if he'd consider teaching her to be a trainer.

When he said yes, she was once again on the road to a new career, and from that day forward she worked hard at getting her health back, blossoming into a muscular one hundred and twenty-five pounds. She was happy and healthy for the first time in a few years, and only then realized how miserable she'd been while she struggled with her weight.

When Tanner moved his training operation from

Toronto to Kentucky, Kate and the rest of the crew went with him. She eventually became his assistant trainer, and over the following years learned how to read horses, anticipate problems, and mold equine athletes. Being a successful trainer required a perfect mix of intuition, horse sense, and eyes that missed nothing.

And now here she was, thinking seriously about giving it all up. But this time it was more like shifting gears than starting over. She didn't want or need to give up training completely, just needed to adjust a few things.

Kate glanced at the highway sign. Lexington, 47. She would be home in less than an hour. Home to where danger lurked, where someone was using her or her business for illegal gain.

Tanner had been murdered.

Leo was gone.

And she didn't want to be next.

CHAPTER 5

——

CLEARING OUT LEO'S ROOM WAS a task that needed to be completed now. Period. And Kate dove in without allowing herself to think about what filling those boxes meant. She just couldn't go there. Couldn't consider—

A scraping noise on the outside of the door had her freezing in place instead of adding the sixth and last filled box to the stack.

Was someone trying to get in? Jason's warnings about safety echoed in her head, and she shot a glance at the handle to reassure herself she had twisted the button to a locked position. Like that would stop someone determined to get in.

She grabbed for her phone, only to remember both hers and Jason's were in her jacket pocket. In her office. On the other side of the courtyard.

More scraping.

The knob rattled slightly.

A soft thud.

"Meow!"

Kate's breath whooshed out, and she yanked the door open. "Caly, you scared half the lives out of me," she said, picking up the cat and holding her close until the rumble of her purring soothed Kate's bumping heart.

"You miss him too, don't you?" She lay her face against the cat's warm fur and an idea gelled.

"What if I redo this space as my hideaway, and instead of going home for my afternoon snoozes I hang here with you instead?" Fewer hours alone for both of them.

Caly didn't answer, but Kate's decision was made. She loaded the boxes, chair, table, and folding cot into the pickup she borrowed from one of her grooms, and headed for the storage center.

Next stop was a discount furniture store, where she bought what she needed to repurpose the room, and as soon as it was loaded she hit the road, anxious to get back and get set up. She was looking forward to a fresh space to hang out in, and wondered if maybe it was time to do some redecorating of Tanner's townhouse—where she now lived—to really make it her own too.

Could she give up the constant reminder of someone she would never see again? Erase his presence as she had Leo's? But that was only done so Jason could examine Leo's things for evidence. And if—no, *when*—he came back, she would totally set him back up in his room. Or maybe he would finally accept the apartment she had offered him in a nice complex not far from the training center.

Sure, he said he preferred the simplicity of living in a tack room, but—

Flashing blue lights suddenly filled her review mirrors and she steered onto the shoulder, expecting the car to fly on by. But it pulled in and stopped behind her.

Her heart thumped hard against her ribs while waiting for the officer to get out of his car. But what if it wasn't a cop? What if this was some ruse connected to Leo's disappearance or Tanner's death...murder?

She cracked her window open and carefully placed both hands on the wheel so they were completely visible. Dammit. She should have opened a line on the cell phone. Too late now.

"Ma'am?"

The voice was familiar. She looked up, and Officer Rylie smiled.

"Ms. Oliver. Could you open the window, ma'am?"

"Oh, sure. Sorry. I was a bit startled by the lights and all. I'm not used to getting pulled over."

"Didn't mean to frighten you. But I recognized you when you went by, and I wanted to ask how things are going."

"Going?" she asked.

"Have you heard anything from your missing man?"

"Oh. Ugh, no. But I have heard talk around that he had some personal problems and he just up and left."

"But you said that would be out of character."

"I guess I didn't know him as well as I thought."

"I see. I guess you've had to hire someone to replace him."

"Well, for now I'm using the on-site security company to patrol my barn at night, and I've put in a few more cameras."

"Good for you. Well, I guess I won't keep you then... Ah..."

"Yes?"

"Nothing, have a good day." He walked away, leaving her wondering what it was he didn't say.

Kate waited until the cruiser pulled back onto the highway before she continued on her way, and was about a mile down the road when Jason's cell phone vibrated in her left front pocket—never again would she be caught with it out of reach. She dug it out along with her own, pressed speed dial on hers to her home phone number, dropped it on the seat, and answered Jason's.

"What was that about?"

"Hello to you, too."

"What did the cop want? He never wrote a ticket or even went back to his car to check your ID."

"Where are you?"

"None of your business." His voice was edgy. "What did he want?"

"He's the one who came out when I reported Leo missing, and he wanted to know if I'd heard from him again."

"And?"

"And I told him I realized I didn't really know the guy, and now assume he moved on. When he asked if I had a new night watchman, I said I was using track security, and installed more cameras."

"Shit."

Okay, now he was scaring her.

"I want to put a man in your barn, and that would be the perfect scenario."

"But I gutted his room and bought new stuff for it, for myself."

"Which explains the furniture shopping."

She swiveled in her seat, looking in every direction. "Where the hell are you?"

"Closer than you think." The line went dead, and she was left with her heart doing a ridiculous pitter-patter. Most annoying, and *his* damn fault.

Kate, who really didn't care for being unsettled, shook off the frustration and continued her journey, forcing a smile for the guard on duty at the main gates, and another for a fellow trainer she passed on the main road.

She parked the truck in the courtyard, went into the barn, and toured the shedrow, looking into each stall, making eye contact with every horse. Afternoon feed time wasn't for another hour, so most of them were only vaguely interested in her presence. For the most part they simply watched her go by.

Except for The Princess, of course. The Princess knew everything, acted as though the barn belonged to her, and *nothing* went on without her knowledge. Kate rubbed the mare's face and thought about Leo. He'd also had a soft spot for The Princess, and Kate was certain both the mare and Caly knew exactly what had happened to their missing friend.

Kate wrapped her arms around the big mare's neck, and she lowered her elegant head until her jaw pressed between Kate's shoulder blades, holding her in place.

They stayed that way for a long time, no movement, no sound, pure comfort shared between them, and when Kate's emotional turmoil eased, they parted slowly.

"Thanks, old girl," Kate gently kissed the soft, velvety nose before moving away.

As feed time drew closer, the barn filled with the voices of grooms changing water, picking stalls, and hanging feed tubs filled with grain. Laundry was brought in from the lines, bandages were rolled, and tack was set for the morning. Only then was the barn tucked in for the night.

"You want to keep the truck until the morning?" asked Zeke, the groom she had borrowed it from.

"Nope, thanks, I'm done with it. Or will be as soon as I get it unloaded. Wouldn't mind a hand with that."

"Oh, that's stuff's staying here, not going to your place?"

"Yep. Fixing up Leo's room for myself."

His eyebrows shot up. "You're going to live in a tack room?"

She laughed. "Been there, done that, and no. But Caly needs some company, and it will work well for me to hang out here with her in the afternoons."

Once the truck was unloaded and gone, Kate fastened a new padlock on the outside hasp and headed home, grabbing a burger on the way and wishing she had the jam to call Jason, because her unsettled feelings had come back, and she longed for reassurance.

———

Jason flicked off the feed from the security cameras in Kate's barn.

Hacking into her system had been simple—too simple, because it was lacking any kind of protection, including a passcode. Along with that weakness, the cameras only monitored the shedrow, with feeds showing the front of each stall and the insides of a couple.

He shook his head. Perimeter and egress views might not be *her* priority, but they were definitely his.

Even getting inside the training center's own security feeds didn't give him a view of the side of the barn, or the courtyard area, and he needed to fix that, get cameras set up ASAP. The problem was keeping the installation discreet, and he'd need to hook them into her barn computer but keep the program hidden. Such a pain in the ass, not being able to tell her more, but his hands were tied.

He flicked a glance at his watch. The boxes had been moved from the storage locker by now. He slid the car back onto the road, drove past the training center at a normal pace, and made his way to the motel, where someone contracted by Meyers Security would be waiting to hand over everything Kate packed up from Leo's room.

Meyers was stretched thin these days, working several other missing persons cases in various parts of the country, which meant when Jason needed an extra hand he was sent one of their highly skilled contacts instead of a family member. But Eve Meyers *was* monitoring Jason's case and always available for consult.

If he was lucky, he would find a clue somewhere within Leo's possessions. But something in Jason's gut told him the search would be fruitless. He needed to shove all the negative thoughts to the back of his mind and focus on finding an answer. Then he could concentrate on the most important task of all—keeping Kate out of trouble.

Meanwhile, Max had been brought on board to watch over her. Would she be pissed about that? If she found out, maybe, but he didn't care. He wouldn't risk losing her. Especially now she finally needed him.

———

Arriving at the barn on Saturday morning, Kate grimaced at the thought of extra people in the shedrow. Several of her owners liked to come to the track on weekends to visit their horses and watch them go through their morning workouts on the track. It was something Kate struggled with because it interfered with her routine, her concentration, and her staff, on a morning when everyone needed to get their work done with quick efficiency. There were horses to get ready for racing later in the day.

At six am Kate climbed aboard Anchor, an ex-racehorse who spent his retirement days escorting thoroughbreds on and off the track. His calm presence was a good influence on young or nervous horses, and he really enjoyed his job. Stood waiting calmly at the place where the gallopers would pull up and stop, then walked them home. He was a pleasure to ride, allowed her to be out on the track among her horses, and the youngsters loved him.

Riding back and forth to the track also kept Kate out of the way of her very well-organized staff. From five-thirty until nine, grooms and hot walkers never stopped, and the barn hummed with energy. Stalls were cleaned, horses were tacked, bath and drinking water set out, dry blankets hung over rails, ice wraps prepped, mats swept, and everything else brushed, cleaned, raked, or removed. The work would appear chaotic and endless to an outsider, but it wasn't. The ebb and flow as sets of gallopers left and returned created a comfortable rhythm Kate loved, and which eventually wound down.

But on this Saturday things nearly ground to a halt when an owner showed up at seven and wanted to watch his horse go out for her morning exercise. He actually owned only an eighth of the filly, but he was still an "owner" and merited Kate's attention.

Instead of riding to the track with the third set, she stepped off Anchor and handed his reins to Mark, her assistant trainer. She would have to follow on foot with the owner while Mark rode with the horses, and her morning would now be consumed with explanations.

"You said the riders would be setting them down for a quarter mile, and I don't know what that means."

"Asking them to go as fast as they can for the last half of their work."

"So it is just a work? A breeze?"

"Not exactly. A work or breeze means covering ground at a race-like speed as opposed to a simple gallop. While that means they're going much faster than usual, it's still a controlled pace."

"Why is today different? And how do you tell *them*, the horses? Will they be whipped?"

"No whipping." She hesitated to tell him more, because it would only beg more questions, but...

"The riders all carry whips just in case of trouble. They're used mostly to tap a horse on the shoulder to get its attention if it's going off course. This keeps them traveling straight and not interfering with others."

"So how to you make them go faster?"

"We match them up with others of like ability and send them out together. Being thoroughbreds, they're naturally competitive, so it normally takes very little urging to get them to try to outrun each other. On a normal day they are being restrained at all times, but today they'll be allowed to do exactly as they want."

"Why today?"

"Today is like writing a pre-test for finals. All three of these girls have reached the point where they're almost ready to run—to be entered in a race. By setting them down—encouraging them to go their fastest..." Kate hated trying to put things in layman's terms "...we'll get a true showing of their abilities. Then, after opening up and using all their resources, we'll carefully monitor their recovery, which will give us another way to gauge of how ready they are to be entered."

Kate watched the fillies galloping toward the half-mile pole, and as they picked up speed, she became deaf to questions, immersed in studying the action of her charges.

Before the morning was over a total of seven owners had showed up to demand her time. Among them they owned sixteen horses, either individually or in partnership or syndicate, and there had been endless questions. Kate understood their desire to know the ins and outs of how their stock was being cared for and managed, but Kate only had so much time, and inevitably someone would be slighted. Today it was Victor's turn.

He was pissed when Kate finally caught up with him when he was about to leave. "How about I meet you for coffee between races?" she suggested. "I'll have some free time between the fourth and fifth." She had horses in the third and sixth, so there was a decent gap of time she could devote to him then.

He grunted an affirmative, and she was relieved. Doubly so when he left.

Mark joined her in the office. "Victor was pissed," he said with a grin.

"I'll smooth his feathers later." Because Jason had emphasized how important it was not to rile anyone.

"I'd tell him to take his horses and go away. It's not like he has much for stock, and he's just not worth the aggravation of having to deal with his snarly attitude."

"I'm working on it, but just go along for a while longer, okay?"

"He's rude and disrespectful."

"You'll get no argument from me. What do you think of the new guy?"

He shrugged. "Seems to want to learn, but there's something off about him. Can't put my finger on it yet. Syndication guys can be a pain, at least the ones who own about a sixteenth of a horse but act like they're breeder and owner of a world-beater."

Kate laughed. "We want them to be excited. Otherwise, what's the point?"

"True. I guess."

She tipped her head. "You interested in going solo anytime soon, having a barn like this of your own?"

He sat back and grinned. "Give up this cushy position? Have to deal with the business end, set up from scratch?"

"That's a no?"

"For now. It'll take me a couple more years to save up for equipment."

Something Kate hadn't had to do. She'd taken over a fully operating barn. Hadn't needed to buy so much as a hoof pick.

———

Jason rode a free shuttle from Sea-Tac to an airport hotel, then grabbed a cab into downtown Seattle, where he picked up a rental car. The process was convoluted but necessary, because this morning Eve Meyers had identified the organization Victor was working with, one that it turned out had tentacles everywhere.

Jason was surprised, because Eve was the doctor in the family and didn't usually work on cases which didn't require a medical perspective. But she was incredibly sharp, and had spotted something that led to the discovery that Victor was working with a criminal group well-known for its unscrupulous use of minors for transporting drugs.

On the up side, the sheer enormity of the organization reassured Jason that Kate wouldn't even be a blip on their radar, and it was up to him to keep it that way.

Before pulling away from the rental agency, he

activated the high-tech communications device he recently obtained from Meyers. The new earbud, combined with what looked like a button on his shirt, acted as both an audio and video recorder, and a completely secure, voice-activated cell phone.

"HQ," he commanded.

"Connecting." The Texas drawl of the canned voice made him chuckle.

"Good morning," said Eve.

"It is so far. How are things elsewhere?" At the rate new tech was being developed, even though they were secure, it was always best to say as little as possible.

"The target was a morning visitor." Eve would have monitored the video feed from the Kate's barn.

"And?"

"Hung around for thirty-two minutes, then had a short exchange with her. Appeared to be angry. Left immediately after."

"Shit."

"She had at least six extra people there this morning, spoke with one exclusively for almost two hours. The target's exchange was after that one left."

Relief eased the tension between his shoulder blades. "Ah, that makes sense, then. He wouldn't like that someone else had her attention. Is she still there?"

"Negative. Cleared the east gate eighteen minutes ago."

"Perfect. Thanks," said Jason.

"Catcha later."

As though swimming upstream, he maneuvered

through rush hour traffic to get onto the I-5 and out of the city. Then he gave the command, "Kate."

"Connecting."

"Jason?"

"Are you somewhere you can talk?"

"In my car, in my own driveway, so I'd say yes."

"What are you doing there? I thought you were running horses today."

"Just home for a quick shower and change, then off to the track."

"Ah."

"I'm glad you called, because I have a question."

"Fire away."

"Is Victor Bellamy the person you suspect, or think is connected with…" she trailed off as though uncertain what exactly was going on, which was good. "I annoyed him this morning, and now have to meet with him later to smooth his ruffled feathers."

Shit. "Where?"

"At the Turf Club. He has a table there."

Public. Crowded. She would be safe there. "Good choice."

"Victor's a jerk," she said. "I don't remember you liking him much back in the day."

"True."

"You never answered my question."

"I didn't." And wasn't about to. It was bad enough that she was suspicious.

"Then let me put it this way. You said I had to be nice to everyone. Does that include Victor?"

"Yes."

"Well, that sucks. I was fantasizing about telling him to stuff his horses where the sun don't shine."

Shit. Fuck. Damn. "Don't."

"You know that's not my style, just a fantasy. He's the one, isn't he?"

"I can't go there."

She sighed. "Fine."

Jason felt bad, but before he could say anything, she said, "I hate groveling." The sudden steel in her voice shouldn't have surprised him, because he *knew* she was capable of switching from one emotion to another in a heartbeat. Kept him on his toes when they'd lived together. Made her one helluva lover.

"Try the other approach. Put on a pretty dress and schmooze the man." She had legs Jason could stare at all day.

He could almost hear her hackles go up. "I don't wear dresses, and I don't schmooze."

"Okay, not a good choice of words. Remember it's all about business. Distraction is a useful tool, and being nice to someone you don't like is just part of the deal. I know you can pull it off."

There was a long beat of silence. "I'd forgotten how much you love pissing me off," she said.

"I'm going into a tunnel and going to lose you for a minute, hold on," he said, lying outright and cupping his hand over the mic button. He glanced at the odometer, and after half a mile said, "Okay, I'm back."

Silence.

"Kate?"

"I'm here. Still not pleased, but here anyway."

"That's one of the things I love about you, Katie. You're a stayer."

More silence, but he could have sworn he heard

her heart beat. "Awful quiet on your end. Where are you?"

"I'm here, but I have to get going."

"Call me later and let me know how it went with Victor."

"Okay."

"I'll be thinking of you..."

"Stop messing with my head." The line went dead.

Hell, he was the one with the messed-up head. Thinking about her far too much. Worrying. He'd worked hard to shut it down when she was riding races, but apparently the switch had been flipped and he was in full-blown protection mode again. And wasn't that a pain in the ass?

He shot across three lanes of traffic and made it to the exit he needed in spite of the device signaling an incoming from Meyers. He tapped the mic.

"Clear."

"We have a problem."

CHAPTER 6

KATE'S HORSE IN THE THIRD race finished a respectable third, and she took a minute to talk to the jockey before going upstairs to the clubhouse. She ordered herself a beer at the stand-up bar and talked to a couple of trainer friends, Bud and Lynn, while she worked herself up to meeting with Victor.

"Owner approaching," said Lynn quietly.

She refused to wince when Victor gripped her shoulder none too gently.

"I thought you were coming to my table." His tone was sharp, as always.

Kate pasted a smile on her face and turned. "I'm a little early and didn't want to interrupt if you had other guests."

"I was waiting for you."

Kate smiled at her friends, said she'd see them later, and headed for the table Victor had reserved for the entire race meet.

He barely waited for Kate to be seated before beginning his attack. "I don't know why you give so much time to people who have no future in this business. That guy you couldn't drag yourself away from this morning will crash and burn within a year and leave you with a useless horse to get rid of."

As useless as one of your imports? Kate put a Herculean effort into smiling sweetly. "I know it's annoying for you on the weekends, Victor, with so many others vying for my time, but I'm glad we're able to meet now instead, where there are no distractions."

"I had important business to discuss and couldn't even get a word with you."

"Like I said, Victor, I apologize, and you have my full attention now." She swallowed hard. "What do you want to talk about this morning?"

He continued frowning, as though he wasn't finished scolding her, and she bit the inside of her cheek to remind herself to get along with him at all costs.

The waiter came to take his order, and the interruption was enough to distract him from this morning's irritation. When they were finally alone again he said, "There is a race for the mare. In Toronto."

"Rainbow?"

"Of course Rainbow. There's a mile and an eighth for mares on the turf, in a month."

"The Mandolina Stake?"

"It's a grade two. Would boost her value as a broodmare."

Two facts of which she was aware. Of course, she would have to run first or second for it to affect her worth. And the Mandolina was a prestigious test for turf specialists, one Kate had ridden in when she was an apprentice. "A four hundred thousand-dollar purse," she said, and quickly pulled it up on her phone. "Nomination fee of four grand is due before midnight tonight."

"I paid it yesterday, and I booked her a flight for next week."

What the—? With Jason's warning ringing in her head, Kate clamped her jaw shut on the words threatening to burst free. Sucked in a calming breath. "Did you name a rider while you were at it?"

"Well, no. Should I?" he asked, completely missing her sarcasm, which was a good thing.

"Actually, Victor, I can take care of it today when I complete the required paperwork. Do you have a rider in mind?" Kate would put in a call and see if she could get the mare's usual rider to travel to Toronto for the race.

"I think we should use a jock from there, one with experience over the course. Wait and see who contacts us when the nomination list comes out. Let them fight over her and do a little groveling. Put the arrogant little pinheads in their place."

"Okaaay," Kate said slowly, then added. "Would you excuse me for just a minute, Victor? I must run to the washroom." She fled, barely in control of her temper.

Once in the washroom and certain she had the place to herself, Kate made several loud frustrated sounds and stomped her feet a couple of times. "Damn him!"

Not only was the unqualified buffoon telling her what to do with a horse she was managing, but he held the purse strings, and therefore a big chunk of the control.

Contacting the Canadian track's racing office to make the nomination himself was pretty much going over Kate's head. Making arrangements for Rainbow without consulting Kate or even considering the horse's work schedule added insult to injury. But deciding to not secure a commitment from the best possible rider for the mare was stupid, arrogant, and irresponsible.

Rainbow took a little getting used to, and had never run well for a jockey the first time out. It was always the second and third times they were on her that she ran well, because it took that long for the average rider to figure out her temperament and running style. It wasn't something they could be told, simply because Rainbow had to develop a rapport with a rider before she would put out. She was quirky, and Kate worked hard to keep her happy.

Traveling and new surroundings would probably make her nervous, and then she wouldn't eat properly. She hated change and, most frustrating of all, here at home there was a great race for her on the same day as the one in Toronto for a purse that was only a few thousand dollars less. Kate could see no point shipping to Canada. It was an unnecessary risk, taking Rainbow out of her comfort zone.

Booking the mare on a flight next week was the final straw. Kate would have to split herself between two tracks and put needless pressure on her crew. The mare would be much better off shipping just a couple of days prior to the race. By going next week, she'd likely lose a hundred pounds before race day.

But Jason didn't want her making waves, which

sounded good in principle, but in reality? This was going to be tough.

Kate shot a look upward. "Help me with this one, Tanner. How do I go back out there and not kill him?"

Lynn walked into the ladies' room and noticed Kate. "You okay? Your face is beet red."

Kate's laugh came out a little squeaky, "Aggravated, but okay."

"Take a deep breath, then let it out, and keep exhaling as long as you can to get rid of all the angry and frustrated air and thoughts."

Kate followed her friend's suggestion, and after every last bit of air finally left her lungs, she looked at Lynn with eyebrows raised.

"Inhale."

Lynn went into a stall, and her voice came over the wall, "Feel any better, hon?"

"Yes, actually. Thanks. I have to get back. Talk to you later."

Returning to the table, she sat across from Victor, who was halfway through a steak the size of a dinner plate and a pile of fries swimming in gravy. Kate decided to be grateful she hadn't had to watch from the beginning, because for a man belonging to the wealthy upper class, he had appalling table manners. Seemed to always have grease or sauce on his mouth and/or chin, never used his napkin until he finished the meal, chewed with his mouth open, and talked with his mouth full.

She was amazed his expensive suits never showed evidence of what a slob he was.

Kate fixed her gaze on the track, where horses were warming up for the next race. When the server came to take Victor's plate, Kate said, "Is there anything else we need to go over, Victor? I've got about ten more minutes, then I'm off to saddle for the next race."

"Just the travel plans for Rainbow. Her flight leaves at six in the morning, so you'll have to put her on the van at four. My man is booked to ride with her, so you don't have to send any of your staff. Just the stable pony for company."

What? Anchor, too? "Great," said Kate. "Have you also booked a barn for them to ship into?"

"Oh." Victor's face went blank. "Well, that would be your job, wouldn't it?"

All of it's my job, you fucking jerk. "Fine," she said between clenched teeth. "I'll make the arrangements." She tried to smile, but imagined it was more of a grimace. "I really must go now. If there's anything else, Victor, please don't hesitate to call me." She swallowed hard. "And I do apologize again for this morning."

"Oh, not to worry, my dear. I'm sure it won't happen again." Victor's glance flicked over her for just a second before he began stabbing at his cell phone with greasy fingers, effectively dismissing her.

Still fuming, she marched across the paddock to where Mark was waiting…and staring at her oddly. Why? She was wearing her usual outfit for running horses, white shirt, black pants, black boots, red leather jacket, and her hair was in a tidy French braid.

"What?" she asked when she reached him.

"You look ready to take a bite out of somebody."

"Ugh. Last thing I'd want is a taste of that bastard."

His eyebrows shot up.

"Victor." She filled him in with the details.

"Why don't you just tell the guy to take a flying leap? You don't need this shit."

He was right. But Jason said to make nice for as long as it took, and she needed Jason to find Leo.

"Soon, trust me. I've just got a couple of ends to tie up first."

"Want me to saddle this one?" he asked, tipping his head toward the filly.

"Nope, I've got it." Kate shook her hands to get rid of the bad energy. Looked the horse in the eye, and her soul settled. Saddling went smoothly, and Kate gave the rider the simplest of instructions. "She's got one helluva kick for a quarter mile, but then she's empty, so use it wisely."

And he did. Turning for home, he pointed her at an opening between horses, and she ran through like she had wings on her feet, galloping home a winner by two lengths.

Kate's usual level of excitement was missing, but she faked it in the winner's circle with Mark and the nice young couple who owned the filly. There were high fives all around, and Kate got a great big kiss from the jockey that left her wiping racetrack dirt off her face and gave everyone a good laugh.

———

Kate joined the owners for a celebration drink before heading for the barn to make sure both the day's runners would be in good form to ship home to the training center in a few hours. Checking was, of course, unnecessary, because her grooms were top-notch and had everything well in hand.

With nothing else to do, Kate headed home, and by the time she got there around eight-thirty she'd almost forgotten how furious she was earlier in the day.

Quickly stripping down and donning her favorite oversized T-shirt, she poured a big glass of chocolate milk, grabbed a handful of oatmeal cookies, and settled into the cozy leather armchair overlooking the garden. Then called Jason.

It only rang once before he answered with, "Nice win."

"Why thank you," she said.

"But I thought you were going to wear a dress."

"No, I told you I wouldn't."

"You looked good anyway."

Did he drop his voice on purpose just to get to her? And how did he know what she was wearing? "You were there?"

"Nope."

"Then how?"

"Got the live feed on my phone. Do you always kiss your jockey, or just that one in particular?"

Was he jealous? "None of your business."

"Okay," he said easily, dashing any thought that he might care.

"How was your meeting with Victor?"

"Awful." She took a big swallow from her frosted mug.

"What are you drinking?"

"Water." Why had she lied? Just to be contrary?

"Hmmm." Jason sounded like he didn't believe her, which made her curious.

"Are you going to tell me about the meeting?" he asked.

She did then, gave him all the details, barely able to repeat them calmly.

"So the horses ship at four am on Thursday."

"Not if I can help it," she said.

"Don't mess with his plans. Just go along, remember?"

"But—"

"Katie, this is important. I know the welfare of your horses comes before everything else for you, but I need you to do as I ask. Do it for Leo."

Sucker punch well delivered. She rested her head against the back of her chair. "I'll do whatever you say. But for the record, I'm going to hate putting Rainbow through unnecessary stress."

"Why don't you send her groom on ahead? A familiar person when she steps off the truck."

"I can do that?"

"I'm sure it won't mess with Victor's plans."

Jason had a way of sounding like he was certain about everything. "I'll book him a ticket as soon as we hang up."

"Good. And as for the mare's travel plans, I'll need all the details, including flight numbers. Did he book a return?"

"He didn't say."

"Interesting."

"Jason, is there anything about this you can tell me?"

"Not yet. Just be patient, be alert, and don't forget to be charming."

"Oh, you would have been proud of me today when I didn't rip Victor's face off. The charm was sickening. At least for me."

Jason laughed. "I wish I'd been a fly on the wall for that. I know kissing butt isn't your style."

"Thanks."

"Kate, I'm sending someone to your barn for a job. He has no horse experience, but has a farming background. Could you take him on for chores? You know, laundry, raking, filling hay nets, cleaning tubs, that sort of thing?"

"I suppose that would work. Is he a spy?"

"Somewhat. But he won't talk to you about anything, so don't even think about asking him. He'll be there as eyes and ears only, and hopefully he'll fit in well enough to find out a few things."

"What's his name?"

"You won't know until you meet him. And try to point out the horses going to Toronto. He'll need to keep an eye on them."

Jason was silent for so long she finally asked, "What are you doing?"

After a moment's hesitation he answered, "Listening to you breathe, Katie."

Her heart jumped at the tone of his voice, and at a loss for words, she downed the rest of her drink.

Electricity flickered in the silence between them until Kate spoke, her voice thick with the emotions he'd stirred up, "Jase...."

"Chocolate milk. I knew it wasn't water..."

"What?"

"Sweet dreams, Katie," and the line went dead.

Her gaze flickered around the room. Was there a camera in here somewhere? Was anything out of place? She looked out the window at the apartment buildings about a mile away. Could he be there with some fancy, high-tech telescope? She got up and closed the curtains, then walked around the room, still searching, but found nothing. Gave up and went to bed.

She tried to go to sleep, but her mind wound around the events of the day, trying to figure out what Jason thought Victor was up to. Stood to reason if shipping horses was a key factor, smuggling would be the game, but smuggling what? Drugs? Money? Weapons? People? With only two horses on the pallet, there was certainly space to work with.

The cell phone beside her suddenly sang its tune, and she grabbed it quickly.

"Jason?"

"Katie, quit fretting about everything and go to sleep. I need you to have your wits about you tomorrow."

"Do you have a camera in here?"

"I don't need one to know what's going on with you."

"Why?"

"Because," his voice had gone from businesslike to dead sexy. "I told you before, Katie. I'm in your mind." Click.

If she didn't know his sense of humor so well she'd be creeped out, but she did know him. Well enough to wonder if he was simply trying to keep her off-balance.

Shortly before six the next morning, a young man named Erik Jansen stopped at her barn looking for a job. He had no experience with racehorses but said he'd grown up on a farm and was used to hard work. She hired him on as a spare hand and left him with the barn foreman to get set up, then treated herself to a ride on The Princess.

The big mare was a handful to gallop, but Kate made a point of getting on her at least once a week anyway. It was good for staying on top of how her favorite horse was feeling, and, better still, after a couple of laps on The Princess, everything in Kate's world seemed brighter.

Kate's full attention would be required due to the mare's penchant for picking up speed without warning or spooking and jumping away from imaginary predators. And when she was in a really good mood, she would buck and jump all the way back to the barn after her gallop, totally joyful and happy to be alive.

Tanner had bought her as a weanling to keep another, freshly-weaned filly company at his farm. They became devoted playmates and were frequently seen racing each other around the field. When they were nearly two, Kate was the one to begin their schooling, and was the first rider on their backs, working slowly to gain their confidence and teach them to gallop like ladies. The Princess had been somewhat hotheaded, but Kate remained patient, refusing to give up, until eventually the filly grew to trust her completely. But for the next year The Princess would not allow anyone else to get on her back.

Tanner gave her the filly for Christmas that year. Said they obviously belonged together. Said the youngster would probably teach her more about training horses than he ever could.

Kate swore they would make him proud, and in time they did. The Princess only raced once as a two-year-old, and finished fourth. But she'd been excited and run green—more concerned with the other horses and riders and dirt tossed in her face than watching where she was going.

Kate spent the next few months teaching her patience and tolerance, how to listen to the jockey's hands while they steered her through a crowd of horses, how to pass on the inside or outside, and when to just keep on running.

The Princess soaked up knowledge like a sponge, though she still had her moments of silliness when Kate would have to laugh at her.

Tanner often shook his head at the two of them, and eventually warned her that getting too emotionally attached could cloud her judgement. He didn't want her to train with her heart but with her head. Heart wasn't a bad thing, but sometimes it got in the way.

He taught Kate more than she ever realized until after he was gone. Most important, he taught her to listen to her gut. And that's what she was doing today. Getting on The Princess because she needed that connection. Somehow she knew it would help her sort out all the craziness in her life. Maybe help her get through what was to come with Victor.

When she arrived back from her ride, the new guy went past her with a laundry basket full of bandages.

"How are you making out, Erik?"

"Fine, thank you, ma'am. The horses sure are beautiful, aren't they?"

Kate smiled. "Yes, and this one is particularly special. We call her The Princess."

"I would have called her Precious One."

His expression hadn't changed even a whisker. "Funny, I knew a horse by that name once…a very long time ago." That was the code. Jason said not to trust anyone unless they mentioned the name of one of the horses in Tanner's barn back when the two of them had started working for him.

"Yes, ma'am. I'd better get these bandages rolled. Zeke's waiting for them."

She handed The Princess off to her groom. "I need to talk to him myself. I'll go that way with you."

Zeke's charges were stabled at the far end of Kate's barn, since he liked having the end of the shedrow to himself.

When she told him Rainbow would be leaving on Thursday for Toronto, he was crushed until she explained he'd be flying out the night before so he could have her stall set up and ready for her. Kate knew it would mean being away from his girlfriend for a month, but he said it wouldn't be a problem.

While they discussed plans for a hotel room and a car for Zeke, Erik sat quietly on a footlocker, rolling up the fresh, white bandages, seemingly oblivious to the conversation. But Kate was certain he hadn't missed a word.

Back in her office, she called an old friend in Toronto and arranged for Rainbow and Anchor to be stabled in his barn.

On the way home Kate swung into the grocery store to stock up on snack food for the barn crew in the morning, then gave in to the smell of barbecued chicken on the rotisserie. Added it to her cart. It would be good for lunch and dinner, plus leftovers for tomorrow.

Back at home, she perched on a tall stool at the kitchen counter and picked her way through nearly half of the chicken while looking at the Jason cell phone and weighing the pros and cons of calling him.

Startled when it rang, she grabbed with greasy fingers and it slipped through her fingers, flying out of her hand and onto the granite floor, where it hit with a rather ugly sound of surrender. She dove and snatched it up, and like something out of a comedy sketch, it once again shot free like a bar of wet soap. This time when it landed, pieces flew off.

"Oh, dear." She scurried to the sink to wash her hands, then used a paper towel to pick up the disastrous-looking cell phone remains. The poor thing was covered with barbecue sauce and looked like the victim of an assault.

"Shit, shit, shit." Now she couldn't phone him. She laughed. "Well, at least I don't have to talk myself out of it now."

Kate's laughter quickly evaporated. "But he called me. And now I can't call him back."

Looking at the phone, she said, "I was starting to like having you there at the touch of my fingertips,

Jason. Kind of like a tub of chocolate ice cream in the freezer. For those desperate moments."

Kate's own cell phone rang. "Hello?"

"Are you okay?" Jason's voice sounded strained.

"Yes, I'm sorry. I dropped the cell phone."

"Into the garbage disposal? My ear might never recover."

"Hmm. Well… It kind of shot out of my greasy fingers and across the kitchen a couple of times."

"I don't want to know why. I'll get you another one right away."

Grateful he hadn't asked for a detailed explanation, she said, "Thanks." And he hung up without saying another word, leaving her wishing the phone was still intact so she could heave it at a wall.

CHAPTER 7

———

AN HOUR LATER KATE WAS on the couch
trying to read a book but mostly dozing off
when the doorbell rang.

What the heck? She crept to the door and looked
out the peephole at a strange man with a huge vase
of flowers.

She left the chain hooked and opened the door
a crack.

"Can I help you?" she asked.

"A delivery for Trucker, ma'am."

"From who?"

"It says Cricket, ma'am."

Trucker and Cricket were the barn names of
horses both she and Jason cared for years ago.

Kate opened the door to accept the flowers,
and the moment they were in her hands the man
turned and jogged away.

Once the door was again locked properly, she set
the flowers on the coffee table and stared at them.
About two dozen of what used to be her favorites.
Orange roses.

Kate rubbed her finger over the softness of one
half-open bud, then leaned over one to inhale

the wonderful aroma, but jumped back in shock when the frigging thing rang like an old-fashioned phone. She reached into the middle of the stems and pulled out a cell. Pushed the green flashing dot and slid it off the screen.

"That's twice," she said into the phone.

"Meaning?"

"Twice today you've nearly startled the life out of me."

Jason laughed. "Nothing wrong with a good cardio workout."

"Have I mentioned lately that you're a very annoying man?"

"I guess that means you're in better shape than the phone you beat up earlier?"

"I didn't exactly beat it up."

"But it's dead."

"Pretty much."

"Moving on. Does Erik fit in okay?"

"Yup, no problem."

"And speaking of problems, have you heard anything more from Victor?"

"No, but I made the travel arrangements for my groom. I couldn't get him a seat until Friday afternoon."

"What about you? When do you go?"

"Not until the day before the race. My friend Jim will oversee the mare's training in the meantime."

"No good, Kate."

"What do you mean?"

"I need you out of the barn."

"Why?"

"Is this the same woman who pledged to do whatever it took, and promised to trust me no matter what?"

She frowned. Didn't like where this was going. "I don't remember any pledges. What do you want from me?"

"Oh, Lord help me," he muttered.

"What?"

"Nothing, Kate. What I need you to do is book to go to Toronto."

"When?"

"Friday's fine." For him maybe.

"How long do I have to stay? I have a business to run, you know." But luckily no horses entered to run this weekend.

"Relax. You can buy an open return and proba-bly go back in a couple of days. We'll have to play it by ear."

Kate hated being pushed around and Jason knew it, but she had to remember this was all about Leo. "Okay, Toronto on Friday. Do I get to pick the airline and the hotel?"

"Book to go with your groom, but you're gonna get held up at the barn and miss the flight."

"Then what?"

"Then you'll get on a charter and fly into Ham-ilton instead."

"Really?"

"Really. I'll meet you there."

"What about hotel reservations?"

"Book into the same one as your groom and guarantee for three nights. Pay in advance."

"Something tells me I won't be staying there."

"I can't tell you anything more than that."

"Okay."

"That's it? Okay? No argument?"

"You've taken the wind out of my sails. I prefer to make my own decisions, and I hate being away from my horses, so I'm seriously considering a good, long sulk."

"The horses will live without you. You have a great assistant, don't you?"

"Yes, but with one major drawback."

"What's that?"

"He can't stand Victor and hates that I put up with his nonsense. Keeps telling me I should get rid of the arrogant son of a bitch. If Mark had his way, he would send Victor packing."

"I think I like your man Mark. But you have to make sure he keeps his cool. Promise him you'll tell Victor to shove off at the end of the meet. Bribe him to be nice if you have to."

"Victor *is* the bad guy, isn't he?"

"I don't know that. But even if he isn't, you *should* get rid of him. He's not worth the aggravation and abuse."

Kate didn't say anything, and Jason's voice came back quietly, "Oops. Sorry. Didn't mean to stick my nose in your business."

She was still quiet because he was right. Now she was seeing herself and her life from a different perspective, she didn't like the view. Somewhere along the line she'd lost who she was, and it was time she dug her background out of storage and put it to use.

Trouble was, first she needed to comply with Jason's wishes. Until Leo was found. Then...

Jason tried again, "C'mon, Katie, talk to me."

"I don't know what to say, Jase. Sometimes—" She stopped. She needed time to think things through. Make sure her decisions weren't emotional.

"Sometimes what?"

"Nothing."

"Interesting word, 'nothing.' It can be so meaningful, and yet, mean just that. Nothing. It can be nothing to eat, nothing to do, nothing to worry about, nothing to wear... Interesting picture, that..."

"Jason."

"Katie," he said, his voice dropping an octave. "Go eat some ice cream." Click.

She held the phone out in front of her and frowned at it. She was getting mighty tired of him hanging up on her. And his annoying habit of finishing off a conversation with a poke at her or a provocative comment was getting old.

Jason leaned back in his chair and took a long pull from a can of root beer, wishing he had something stronger. Juggling the investigation and a strong-willed, opinionated, independent woman was not an easy task, but he wouldn't change her for anything. He loved her. Even when she bordered on pigheaded and was almost impossible to manipulate.

Funny, her strength and determination were drawing him in harder and faster than he'd have believed possible, especially considering they were what drove a wedge between them years ago.

Had life experience changed him? Yep.

Law enforcement was eye-opening, to say the least. He appreciated every day now, every experience, and took nothing for granted because he'd witnessed too much. How the pull of a trigger, flick of a wrist, or glance at a text message could change lives, end lives, tear apart families, and create chaos in the calmest of situations.

The Jason who took life for granted was long gone, and in his place was a man determined to have a second chance with Katie. But first he had to figure out a way to keep her safe.

───

Kate told Zeke she had an important meeting that could potentially make her late for their flight, and sent him on ahead with his girlfriend, who had volunteered to drop them off.

Lying was starting to get easier, and Kate wasn't sure that was a good thing. But it was working so far, and once they were gone, she puttered around the barn for a while. Went in and out of every stall and checked each horse before she put in a call to her vet. She discussed the treatments and blood draws she wanted done in the morning, then added to the detailed notes she'd already left for Mark.

She glanced at the clock. Time to go.

Halfway to her car, she suddenly wheeled and went back into the barn. Marched directly to The Princess, put her arms around the big mare's neck and stood there for a moment, just drinking in the sweet smell, and the warmth of her hide.

After Kate stepped back and planted a kiss on the mare's nose, The Princess lipped at her pockets, making her laugh out loud.

"Mooch," she said, digging a couple of peppermints out of her jeans and handing them over.

"Be good while I'm gone." Kate gave her another kiss, then scooted out the door.

Once at the airport, she drove past the terminal and around to the general aviation area. Parked, and was soon hoofing it across the tarmac in the wake of a girl who introduced herself using a code word.

Kate eyed the plane. "One engine."

"Yes, ma'am."

"For such a long trip. What if something happens..." she trailed off.

The girl laughed. "There's an old saying that a second engine isn't good for much but to carry you to the scene of the crash."

Kate nearly turned and headed back to her car.

"There's no need for you to worry. This aircraft is sound. Solid. And will have us in Hamilton in just a few hours."

"Us?"

The girl opened the passenger door. "Hop in, I'll just do my walk-around."

She was the pilot. It took a second for that to sink in. She was putting her life in the hands of an eighteen-year-old girl.

Jason wouldn't put her in jeopardy, would he? She suppressed a shudder and figured out how the shoulder harness worked. Buckled in.

When the girl climbed aboard, Kate asked, "How old are you?"

A grin spread over the young face. "I bet you think I'm about twelve." She laughed. "I get that all the time. But for the record, I'm twenty-six, and I've been flying for ten years without any bumps on my record. I'm also security cleared to the highest level possible for a civilian, and can defend your ass if anyone threatens it."

Kate was impressed by the delivery as much as by the message.

"We good?"

"Yep," said Kate, and meant it.

"Great. Give me a few minutes to get us underway, and then we can chat." She passed a headset to Kate. "This will make it easier, but I'll be talking to the tower for a bit so stay quiet until we're clear of the airport."

Kate ended up enjoying the flight—and the young woman at the controls. Turned out she had quite a history, and had attended some of the most prestigious flight training programs. But besides all that, she was fun to talk to, and Kate was almost sorry when they landed. It had been a long time since she had a female friend.

Stepping inside the small terminal next to where they landed, Kate's eyes had barely adjusted to the dim light when she spotted Jason. Without a word, he took her hand and led her out to a sporty black car, and they had driven about a half mile when he suddenly cursed and pulled onto the shoulder.

He unclipped his seat belt, cupped the back of her head and brought her mouth to meet his in a kiss filled with fury and frustration. But something changed, and although his grip didn't loosen, his lips softened, and teased, taking a completely different direction.

When he let her go, she said, "Lucky for you we have a past and I trust you…or you would be in serious pain right now."

"We were being followed. Watched. Plus, we have a cover to consider." When she continued to stare at him he said, "You can't think I kissed you just because I wanted to."

"I can and I do."

"*I do*," he said. "Two interesting words. Together they can mean so much or so little... I do like watermelon, I do not like cantaloupe, I do, I do not..."

She landed a punch on his right shoulder, and he grinned. "What now?"

"You've become a very exasperating man."

"At least you've noticed I grew up somewhere along the way."

"Speaking of along the way, aren't we supposed to be going somewhere? Or do we just stay parked on the side of the road for the night?"

"Good point, Stanley." And he pulled back into traffic while making a mockery of trying to keep a straight face.

Kate refused to let her own laughter escape, so the rest of the ride was in silence.

She wasn't surprised when he pulled into the parking lot of the hotel they stayed at a few weeks earlier. They checked in quickly, and just like the last time, Jason asked for a different room than the one they assigned him, and they complied.

Kate went straight to the fridge and got herself a beer, raised an eyebrow at Jason, and he nodded. She put it on the table and went toward the window.

"Stop!" His voice cut through her, and she froze, didn't move when his hands landed on her shoulders and he muttered, "I didn't mean to scare you,

Katie."

She relaxed ever so slightly, and he drew her back into him, folded his arms around her, and rested his chin on the top of her head.

"It's not safe to be in front of the window."

She leaned into him slightly while willing herself to stay calm, and was almost successful. Until his lips touched the side of her neck.

She jerked away. "Jason, I can't do this."

"Sure you can. You can do anything. We both know what you're made of."

"Jason—"

"It's just a little cops and robbers game, Kate. Some sneaking around, a couple of white lies. It could be fun if you trust me." His tone turned serious. "We'll find Leo and have this thing solved before the month is over."

The thought of Leo made tears well up, and she blindly aimed for the bathroom and shut the door, creating a safe space where she could regroup. Resting her hands on the counter, and staring into the mirror, she filled her lungs with air and slowly blew out threw her mouth.

"It's me I don't trust."

Playing at romance and pretending had morphed into something real for her, and she suspected he was feeling the same way. And she'd had enough heartbreak. Wasn't looking for more.

Could she play along and still be able to walk away in the end? Damn good question.

———

Kate emerged from the bathroom about ten

minutes later with fresh resolve. From now on she was taking everything at face value and not getting caught up in runaway feelings. They were a waste of energy, and they had a man to find, a mystery to solve.

"You know way more than you've been telling me, and I don't appreciate being kept in the dark and used like a pawn. I have a right to know what's going on."

He sighed, and she got the distinct impression he was going to try and snow her some more.

"It's a long story."

"Apparently I have all the time in the world."

"Touché." He got comfortable in a chair by the window—which was now blocked by heavy drapes. "I already told you about what happened before I met you. About the night watchman."

"The one you found dead in a stall."

"And the missing horse, the one that should have been in that stall, had only arrived the night before, from Argentina."

Prickles danced across the back of Kate's neck.

"That's when I met Ted, my mentor, who was mostly trying to keep me out of trouble by giving me real goals to work toward while keeping me away from the case. Or lack thereof. But I couldn't seem to let go of the mystery of the dead guy. Kept working at putting the pieces together, and started coming up with ideas about him being murdered by gangsters and the horse's death being staged. What I didn't know at the time was how close to the truth I was." He took a swallow of his beer.

"Years later I discovered I'd unwittingly begun picking at the edges of a cover-up. Ted was taken out of the picture by shifting him out of one organization and into another one far, far away. But he was afraid they'd get rid of me in a less pleasant manner if he couldn't get me to shut up."

Having known the teenaged version of Jason, she could well imagine him refusing to leave the mystery alone.

"What I didn't know at the time was how the whole incident haunted Ted. Kept him trying to figure out the players and their motives. What he's never been able to come up with, though, is enough solid evidence to build a case."

Which is what they were still trying to do. "That's where I come in. Letting Rainbow ship to Toronto gives him an opening to smuggle something into Canada, and/or back into the States with her after the race. Then you'll be able to nail him."

He smiled. "I told Ted you were smart."

"But I'm not the only one, and I can't figure out why it's taken this long. Why not intercept one of his other loads over all these years?"

"Someone was in the way, but oddly, that person was also keeping others safe. Until recently. First Tanner, and now Leo…"

"There's more."

"Not that I can tell you yet."

At least he hadn't lied and said he didn't know. "What else *can* you tell me?"

"Your groom is a plant."

"Who?"

"Zeke."

"But he's worked for the outfit for years. Five or six at least."

"Deep cover."

"Wow. He's a damn good groom." A knock on the door startled her. "Now what?"

"Dinner. I ordered ahead."

Just like before, Kate hid in bathroom and Jason messed up the bed before he opened the door.

"Coast is clear."

She came out frowning at him.

"What now?" he asked.

"Coast is clear? That's the best you could do?"

"Sorry, I'm not too good at spy talk."

"What were you about to tell me about Zeke?"

He poured brandy into a pair of snifters. "No shop talk until after we eat."

Kate looked at the amber liquid. "Medicinal brandy for my frayed nerves, I presume?

"Actually, I was hoping to get you drunk."

Kate laughed. "The last time you tried that I drank you under the table."

"True enough, but at least you put me to bed."

"To the best of your knowledge." A grin escaped, and he frowned in return.

"What the heck is that supposed to mean?"

Kate laughed. "Supper's getting cold."

Jason's gaze stayed fixed on her face for an instant, then he shrugged and removed the metal cover from his plate.

When the aroma of Italian seasonings wafted through the air and her tummy growled in response, it occurred to Kate the last thing she'd eaten was a doughnut with her coffee around eight o'clock that morning.

They ate in silence, and when she finished her dessert, Jason pushed his cheesecake across the table.

"Want mine too?"

"Nope, eat it yourself. You ordered it."

"I also ordered an entire bottle of brandy I don't intend to finish."

"Cute." Kate rolled her eyes.

"A full stomach makes you pretty cheeky."

"I love food."

"Who'd know to look at you?"

She shrugged. "I'm usually either too busy or too tired to cook. And sometimes I just forget to eat."

"Not a terrifically healthy lifestyle."

"Healthier than in the old days."

"It must have been devastating to give up riding, but you'd be dead by now if you hadn't."

"How do you—"

"Keeping your weight down was costing you way too much, Katie. Hell, the last time I watched you ride, you could hardly make it back to the jocks' room you were so weak."

"You were there? Watching me?" She stared at him in disbelief.

"I came out for every race in the beginning. Was there for most of your wins, and was incredibly proud of you."

Jason had been there. Something warmed inside her. He turned the cheesecake over to get a forkful of crust, and she remembered how in the beginning, when money was tight, they'd shared that way. She ate the filling, he the crust.

"But once you started to get sick, I couldn't watch anymore. Tanner said he couldn't stop you, and I already knew you wouldn't give it up for me, so I walked away."

"Ouch."

Jason swirled the brandy in his glass, "Had to get on with my own life."

Ouch again. And, oh, what the hell, might as well be a glutton for punishment. "Is that when you got married?"

"Not exactly. I hadn't met Marcie yet, but by the time I did I wasn't bogged down by old baggage anymore."

"Another point to you," she muttered, then asked, "Why did you get a divorce?"

———

Jason told her the whole story. How they were instantly attracted to each other and he was swept up into her active social life. She took him from party to party, and they had a great time. They moved in together after just six months, and when Marcie became pregnant, there was no hesitation. They married and rocketed toward parenthood.

Marcie had the nursery fully decorated and equipped before she was three months along. Then she decided they needed a house of their own because she wanted lots of kids, and that was when Jason started getting nervous about the speed at which his life was changing. He started taking extra shifts so they could pull a down payment together, and wasn't home the night Marcie had the miscarriage. He wasn't there for her, and she was devastated by the loss. Inconsolable.

And no matter what Jason said or did, he couldn't reach her. Help her. And the marriage fell apart little by little until there was nothing left.

Marcie grew more distant, Jason worked longer hours, and one day when he came home from work she was gone.

Jason was sad but relieved, and their divorce was amicable.

"What about your love life, Kate? Anyone special?"

"No one willing to put up with me and my work for very long."

"So you've never had your heart broken?"

"Not lately. I thought you were going to tell me something important about Zeke."

Jason merely lifted an eyebrow at her abrupt change of subject. "Like I said before, he's a plant. I only recently learned he's connected to Ted, and working in your barn for the purpose of collecting information."

"Does he know you and I have a past?"

"No. Why?"

"I overheard something he said to Carol after we were here last time."

"What did he say?"

"He apparently misinterpreted my good mood after enlisting your help to find Leo, and I heard him remark to his girlfriend about how much happier the boss lady was since she got laid."

Jason nearly choked on his brandy.

"Funny," said Kate with a laugh. "That was my reaction too. Only I was choking on coffee and had to scramble to get out of earshot."

"You know what they say about eavesdropping. You'll never hear good about yourself." Jason wished he'd been a fly on the wall that day.

"I must admit I played into his speculation a few times after that, just for the fun of it."

"Cruel woman."

"Back to business. Why did Tanner have to die?"

He knew she'd circle back to what was important. "According to my source, he was suspicious of the deaths of horses in transit from foreign countries, and when he confronted Victor, they had words about the handler he was using."

All the color drained out of her face. "His name is Brett. I told Tanner I didn't like him and asked to fly with the horses going to England. He said he would talk to Victor." Kate shook her head. "I probably created the whole problem..."

Jason interrupted. "Tanner was suspicious long before that."

"How do you know?"

"After the night watchman's death in the barn all those years ago, Tanner stayed in touch with Ted because he, too, was convinced someone had gotten away with murder."

"Which accounts for you not being surprised when I phoned out of the blue asking for help."

"Katie, that call was the gift Ted needed. It gave him...us...a head start on Victor's next move." He hesitated. Needed to choose his next words carefully. "Ted didn't want me to tell you anything about the case. Told me to pat you on the head and tell you I would take care of everything."

Kate's jaw dropped, and Jason held up his hand. "He's concerned for your safety. But I told him you're too smart for that kind of ploy, and pacifying you could be hazardous to my health. He gave in grudgingly."

"Good thing."

"Now do you understand why I'm so worried

about you? Do you understand the danger? And that Tanner probably knew he was going to die?"

"I get it, Jason. More than I want to." She sniffed, and her eyes looked watery. "It has to be why he wrote his will. And everything I have is because he stuck his neck out to do what was right."

Jason held up the brandy bottle, and she nodded.

The silence growing between them was a comfortable one. They both had a great deal of thinking to do. Him, planning, and her simply digesting what he'd told her, which would take time. Something he hoped they had lots of.

CHAPTER 8

———

WHILE KATE WAS TRYING TO come to grips with what she'd learned tonight, wondering what Jason was thinking about was a waste of energy.

Tired of thinking, and feeling, she fished out the pajamas and toiletries from her bag and headed for the bathroom. Took her time, and wasn't surprised to find Jason sitting up in the king-size bed watching television when she emerged.

Kate slipped under the covers and propped herself up on an elbow. "What are you watching?"

"A commercial." His voice was deadpan.

He wanted to play games? Fine. "For what?"

"Soap, I think."

He pointed the remote at the TV and the room went dark.

"Tired?" Kate asked.

"The commercial was over."

She groaned. "You are such a smart-ass."

"Interesting subject, but I don't think you should go there," he said with laughter in his voice.

"Okay, I give."

"Great. You wanna fool around?"

"Jason!"

"What?"

"You're impossible." She turned away from him and lay very still.

He blew a breath on the back of her neck.

"Stop that." She tried to sound stern, but it had no effect. He edged closer and continued to blow but more gently.

"Jason."

He leaned close enough for her to feel his body heat. "What, Katie?" he asked softly.

"No point starting something we can't finish."

"Define 'can't.'"

"Can't. Won't. Whatever."

"That's not fair, changing words in midstream."

She flipped over to face him. Her eyes had adjusted to the darkness, and she could see his smile. Made it hard to keep sounding stern. "What do I have to do to make you quit this silliness and go to sleep?"

"You want details or a generalization?"

"Jason, go to sleep!"

"Only if you kiss me good night."

"Fine," she said, and gave him a quick peck.

His smile widened. "Now I get to kiss you."

"Who says?"

"I says?"

Yet, he waited. Didn't move even a hair closer. He wasn't the kind of guy to take without asking. She trusted him completely, and she was a glutton for punishment. But a kiss would make her want more, and she didn't dare go there...did she? "Okay, one kiss."

He leaned in until his lips grazed her cheek and

slid down the side of her neck, where he kind of nibbled for a second or two before saying, "You can breathe now."

Kate hadn't realized she was holding her breath, but now that she did, reality slapped her upside the head. She needed to put a stop to this now before she did something stupid. "I can't do this, Jase."

"Sure you can. Breathing is easy as long as you don't think about it," he said, and then sighed. "How about a truce, Katie? You turn over, I'll turn over, and we'll both go to sleep."

Disappointment mixed with relief. "Deal." She settled onto her side with her back to him.

Jason moved away, then muttered, "Oh, hell," and he was suddenly right there behind her, pulling her against him, saying, "Just shut up and go to sleep or I'll move in for the kill."

His warm breath on her neck sent waves of emotion through her, making her heart thump madly in her chest and heat pool in her middle. No way in hell she could fall asleep now, she thought, but his warmth and even breathing were like a drug, and she slipped into a dreamless sleep.

———

Jason smiled when her breathing changed and her body relaxed completely. He was glad he'd been able to tease away some of her sadness and worry. It would all come back when she woke up, but by then she would have a fresh mind to deal with it.

He thought about Tanner. The poor man must be turning in his grave while watching Kate live in the danger he'd put her right in the middle of. Ted had warned him he should have his affairs in order just in case he pushed the bad guys too far, but he hadn't anticipated Tanner unwittingly helping them by leaving everything to Kate. The way things worked out, he died so the game could live on, healthy and well.

But Jason was going to put an end to Victor's evil, somehow, some way, and then he and Kate were going to ride off into the sunset.

Right.

In his dreams.

Waking to the sounds of Jason in the shower had a bit of a déjà vu quality, and like before, she was quick to get her clothes on. But this time she was wearing jeans and a sweater, with her flak jacket and helmet by the door and her attention firmly on the television when Jason emerged. She couldn't afford for him to know what an effect he had on her. Hell, she wouldn't even admit to herself how badly she wanted his hands on her, his mouth…

Still without looking at him, she made her way to the bathroom.

Breakfast was waiting when she came out, and Jason sat to eat, but Kate hovered in the middle of the room drinking her coffee standing up.

"C'mon, Kate, eat something."

"I prefer to ride on an empty stomach."

His glance went from her to her gear. "I hate to break this to you, but we aren't going anywhere. Not for few hours at least."

Again he was taking control away from her. "But I told Zeke I'd be there to take Rainbow out this morning."

"You'll have to call him with a change of plans."

"And tell him what?" Her jaw was clenched.

"Tell him he was right. You needed to get laid, and you won't be coming to the track this morning," he said without expression.

"Why the hell did I tell you that? Like you needed ammunition."

When he laughed, she said, "I think I hate you."

"No you don't." He continued to smile. "Sit down and eat, Katie. It will make you feel better."

"I will feel better when I am damn good and ready," she said, grabbing her phone from the nightstand and calling Zeke. Halfway through explaining what she wanted done with Rainbow, Jason came up behind her, slipped his arms around her waist, and nibbled on the back of her neck.

Katie's voice cracked. "No, Zeke, I don't have a cold, I'm just..."

Jason nibbled the edge of her ear, and she coughed to clear her throat and finish her sentence, "...not awake yet. I'll see you tomorrow."

She disconnected, laid her head back against Jason's shoulder, and closed her eyes while continuing to revel in his touch. When she finally found her voice again, or a husky version of it, she said, "Zeke might have been right after all."

Jason turned her in his arms and looked deep into her eyes. "What are you saying, Katie?"

Focusing on his serious face took some effort. "That I'm tempted beyond belief," she said. "But I can't do this with you."

Like a coward, she bolted for the bathroom. Locked the door behind her and sat on the edge of the tub. Dropped her head in her hands. Took slow, deep breaths.

How the hell was she going to keep her sanity with him around? She liked sex, especially with Jason. But if she gave in, it would be a helluva lot more than sex for her, and there wasn't much chance he felt the same way. Sure, they could light each other on fire with little more than a look, but it wasn't enough. Not for either of them. And wasn't it time she told him that? They could do the "appearances" thing in public, but she needed him to back off when they were alone.

She strode out of the bathroom with her resolve firmly in place, ready to tell him what she needed… but he was gone.

There was a note leaning against her coffee cup.

Kate,

Someone named Max will be here at three to take you to your hotel.

Don't forget to make sure he's one of my people.

You're clear to go to the track tomorrow morning, and to fly home commercial anytime you like. Use your open ticket, but don't book ahead.

Jason

At first she felt deserted and a bit lost, but then she was angry with herself, because wasn't this the perfect solution?

Time passed slowly, but when the front desk called to say her driver was there waiting for her, she was somewhat reluctant to leave. She gave her head a shake and went down to the lobby. A chambermaid had been just outside her room and rode down with her. Kate looked at the woman, who simply nodded and said, "Nice day for a sailor."

Kate smiled. Sailor was the name of another horse from the past.

A big, burly man walked across the lobby toward Kate, and she was suddenly wary. He nodded and said, "I hear Dutchy was a roan."

Kate smiled, nodded, and was slightly comforted to know Jason was somehow still attached to her through his people.

———

The next morning Kate met Zeke at the front desk and found herself blushing when he shot an amused and speculative look her way. "Don't even go there," she muttered, and he grinned.

"Okay, boss lady, say no more... Say no more."

And the subject, which hadn't actually been broached, was dropped, and since they were only minutes from the track, Kate was soon distracted by the memories washing over her as they passed through the stable gate and down the main drive. Yes, it had seemed weird to have to check in and sign forms to be admitted into a place she used to call home, but now she was on the inside, surrounded by the familiar.

Some barns were still painted in the stable colors she remembered, others with a brand new look to go with new residents. Well, at least new to her, although they could have been here for ages.

Before she even reached Rainbow's stall there

was a chorus of hellos and shouts of, "Hey, Kate, where ya been?... Hey, Kate, lookin' good, girl... Hey, Kate, could you gallop a couple for me?... Kate, my God you look good, did you hear about... Kate, 'bout time you came home, girl... Hey, Kate, are you stayin' or just passin' through?"

Gawd, it felt good to be home. To belong somewhere.

Having decided to wait and take Rainbow out after the bulk of training was done for the day—so her friend Jim would be free to go with them—Kate hung out in the track kitchen, where she continued to feel the warmth of a welcome home. Every time she was left alone by someone going back to work, another old friend would sit down to chat for a while.

And later, when she rode the mare to the track, the camaraderie continued. Jim Fraser—one of her closest friends back in the day—was beside her on Anchor, and when she said how good it felt to be home, he asked, "Why'd you stay away so long, Kate?"

"Oh." She laughed. "Where do I start? Busy mostly, a ton of horses in training, racing in Florida in the winter, Kentucky and New York the rest of the time. Toronto just wasn't on the radar."

"I thought you might come home after Tanner died."

"Did you know he left everything to me in his will?"

"Sure. The grapevine is still damned efficient."

"Well, since we were already set up in Kentucky, it just seemed silly to move."

"But aren't Tanner's owners—*your* owners—

Canadian?"

"Sure, but their horses were mostly Ken-
tucky-breds, and the majority were willing to give
me a chance to continue Tanner's legacy."

"Must have been tough for you at the time.
Especially with no old friends to lean on."

She let her gaze travel across the infield to the
grandstand. "I'm not much of a leaner. And too
many friends in this business can be a liability." She
sighed. "For me, the hardest part of becoming a
trainer was cultivating the killer instinct. The drive
to be the best. It was different when I was a rider.
That competition was in the heat of the moment,
and during the short duration of a race."

She let out a long sigh. "With training it's more
constant. Like I still fight the desire to give in to
an agent when he wants to take the mount on
another horse instead of mine. I wasn't born tough
enough to be cutthroat."

"Thank God for that. And from what I hear on
the grapevine, you're a nice person in spite of the
business."

She grinned. "Yup, sweet as pie until you wrong
me, and then you need to hold on to your hat."

"You trying to tell me you still have a wee bit of
a temper?"

"Nothing compared to your wife," said Kate
with a laugh, thinking about the woman who had
been her best friend through the good times and
the bad—even though Kate pushed her away at
the end.

"My very own firecracker," he said. "And speaking of feisty redheads," he tipped a thumb toward
Rainbow, "this one worked herself into a fine tem-

per yesterday when Zeke took Anchor outside to graze. She stomped and fumed in there until your man had to bring the old horse back in. And then, when he stopped in front of her so they could sniff noses, she wheeled around and kicked the door. Talk about pissy."

Kate ran a hand down the mane glowing bright red in morning sunshine. "Temper she has in spades, but she's a real pushover once you get to know her. I just wish she'd put a little more energy into eating."

"I've got a pair of stalls set with a half wall between them if you want to try her and Anchor in them. Worked really well with a mare I had last year. Any time her world was disturbed even a little, she'd say no to her groceries. But every time the other horse beside her stuck his head into her feed tub, she would pin her ears and chase him away. Then stick her own head in the tub and eat."

"Might be just the ticket for this girl. Let's give it a try."

They'd reached the gate to the turf course, and Jim climbed down to open it for her. As Rainbow danced through the opening, Kate said over her shoulder, "We'll be back in a minute."

She set Rainbow into a powerful trot down the outside edge of the backstretch. The turf course was only available for horses preparing for one of the upcoming stakes races, and of the twenty signed up to use it today, she was the only one out there. What a wonderful treat to be able to ride without worrying about traffic.

Kate let Rainbow accelerate into an easy gallop, and when they got to the head of the home stretch she made a chirping noise and the mare gave her a lovely burst of speed. Wind whistled in Kate's ears, whipped tears from her eyes, and just a few lengths from the wire Kate chirped again—like shifting gears—and they sailed past the finish line on an effortless surge of power that had Kate grinning with a joy that came all the way up from her heart.

Feeling heart-whole and centered again for the first time in days, Kate was completely connected to the speed and drive of the powerful thoroughbred beneath her, and the adrenaline rush was amazing. This was what she lived for.

Rainbow eventually eased to a relaxed lope, then jogged to Anchor's side.

"It's a dirty shame you aren't about six inches shorter," said Jim.

Kate wished he'd leave it alone. The past was past.

"Five-three and a natural hundred pounds, you'd have been traveling the world, riding the best of the best. Watching you in the lane just now, I wasn't sure where you ended and the horse began." He shook his head. "Pretty as a picture, and your horse was doing everything she could to please you."

Kate didn't feel the pang that usually came with that kind of thinking. "It would have been great fun, but I get just as much from the morning workouts as I did from a race." The trick was to separate herself from her trainer duties to get those moments on the track that were just for her.

"What about watching your horses run? Do you get that glow when one of your charges wins?"

"Maybe not exactly the same as when I was on them, but great pleasure for sure." But the words sounded empty to her.

They rode side by side back to the barn, talking about the horses they trained and the racetracks where they'd run. Then Jim dug deeper with a question she didn't expect. "Why haven't you been back before now?"

Her chest tightened, then released when she accepted the honesty of her feelings. "I didn't want to confront the memories. Thought it would be painful."

"Guess you were wrong."

"Guess I was. Everyone has been so nice to me. Reminded me what family feels like." Something she didn't think she'd ever find again, but what if…

"You know, I've got about a dozen empty stalls in my barn. You could ship a string up here and commute. Our purses and our tracks are among the best in North America. Tell me you wouldn't love to run horses over that turf course."

"I'm pretty comfortable in Kentucky, Jim. It's home now. Where I belong. I'm not interested in relocating," she said automatically but in the back of her mind the possibilities jumped out at her and she needed to shake them off.

"Hey, why don't I take you and Jenny out for supper tonight?"

"Hang on." Jim dug his phone out and sent a text.

When the reply came he said, "Jenny wants you to come to our place instead. Hang out for a while, meet the kids."

"Only if I can bring the food," said Kate.

"Deal. I can pick you up after feed time, and we'll get pizza on the way home."

———

The wonderful chaos of children and laughter at Jim and Jenny's house had a slow twist of envy curling inside Kate because her life was so one-dimensional. When she wasn't at the barn, socializing with clients, or studying horse-related information such as past performances and bloodlines, she was sleeping.

Kate refused to let depressing thoughts ruin her visit, though, and took part in the fun, even helping tuck them into bed.

Once the kids were tucked into bed, Jim was yawning mightily.

"I'd better get you back to the hotel before I fall asleep too," he said.

"Kate can stay over, and we can visit for a while longer," said Jenny. "The guest room is all ready, and she can ride back in with you in the morning."

Kate was taken back to the times when Jenny made decisions for all of them, and she nodded. "Works for me."

"Catcha in the morning, then." Jim gave his wife a noisy kiss and disappeared down the hall, leaving the two women alone.

"More wine?" Jenny asked, and Kate nodded. She wasn't much of a wine drinker, but nobody ever said no to Jenny.

How much she missed her friend blindsided Kate. Reminded her how quickly they had become friends, almost sisters when they met. Kate was brand-new at the track, and Jenny had been there for years, a racetracker since she was a kid, moving from track to track with her parents. Kate wouldn't have expected her to be happy in any other setting, but look at her now. "This life really suits you, Jen."

She grinned. "Who'da thought?"

"You don't miss the track?"

"I still go in two mornings a week and work on a few horses. Feels good, and keeps me in the game."

"I'd forgotten about your massage business."

"You were preoccupied."

"Self-centered."

"You got so caught up in the whole reducing thing, it was scary."

"Nearly killed myself, and alienated the people who meant the most to me. I'm sorry about that."

"I have a confession," said Jenny. She was staring into her wineglass as though afraid to look up. Then she sighed. "I walked in on you one day when you were getting dressed. Saw you in nothing but your underwear, and it freaked me out. You were a skeleton, Kate."

Kate's memory of those days was murky sometimes. "Was that one of the times you yelled at me?"

"No. I backed out and closed the door before you knew I was there. Then I went to Jason and to Tanner, and even to the doctor in charge of the jocks' room. I begged them all to stop you, because I knew you wouldn't listen to me, and I didn't care if you never forgave me, because at least you'd be alive. I became a woman on a mission, determined to stop you before you either starved to death or were so weak you fell and were trampled during a race. But no one would, or could, help me."

"I wish it had been different. But I was beyond reach. Race riding was like an addiction, and I would do anything to get my next fix. No one could have helped me. But thanks for trying."

"You made it on your own. Well, after almost dying...but still. You did what you had to do, and you look damn good now. Strong, healthy." She squinted. "But are you happy?"

Was she? "Happy enough. I don't miss Tanner as much now, and I've sort of adjusted to Leo leaving me."

"I guess we never get back that crazy kind of happy we have when we're young."

"You did. I saw it tonight when you were passing out pizza to your kids. You and Jim have something special here."

She grinned. "We do, don't we? I hope you find the same one day, Kate, because even though it can be crazy and frustrating sometimes, my life is really awesome."

"Do the kids ride yet?"

"Yep. Let me grab my phone. I've got great pics." They *were* great photos, and Kate enjoyed seeing them, and hearing the pride and wonder in her friend's voice.

———

Jason let himself into Kate's room after the tenth time he'd called and she hadn't answered, and now he could see the dedicated phone he'd given her... on the night table. He dialed her personal cell again and it went straight to voice mail.

He slammed out of the room and marched down the stairs. How the hell had this happened? How did the two people assigned to her somehow miss her leaving the hotel? They were trained professionals, and she was a mere woman. Well, he thought, a little...or maybe a lot...more woman than most, but one civilian versus two pros. How the hell?

For all he knew she'd been kidnaped. More likely anger had made her reckless, and she'd slipped away just to piss him off.

She hadn't used her airline ticket, wasn't at the barn, or the hotel. Zeke hadn't seen her since early afternoon.

She'd fucking vanished, and when he finally found her, he would kill her with his bare hands.

He checked in again with Meyers.

"Any luck on triangulating her cell?"

"No dice. The battery must be dead."

He went back out to wait in his car. Dozed off sometime after three and barely woke up in time to see her hopping out of a black car at about four in the morning.

She strode into the lobby, and before Jason could catch up, the elevator door closed behind her. He took the stairs two at a time, and was on the fourth floor landing before common sense caught up with him.

What the hell was he thinking? She was a grown woman with every right to stay out all night.

Her safety was his only concern.

He willed himself to walk down the stairs instead of continuing up. Made his way back to the car yet again, and sat there for nearly an hour. Then, watching Zeke leave for the barn alone, Jason admitted to himself that he'd clearly been mistaken about how well he would be able to manipulate

Kate.

His cell phone signaled, and he stared at it for a moment before answering with a terse, "Hello."

"I'm leaving this morning."

He bit back everything he wanted to say. "What flight?"

"I thought you told me not to book ahead."

She had him there. Time to back off. Way off. Let her get on with her life.

"Jason—"

"Safe flight, I'll be in touch." He disconnected, and stayed right where he was until she climbed aboard the airport shuttle. He refused to think about how unhappy she looked. Followed her to the airport, where he got a nod from the agent assigned to stay on her tail until the flight departed.

She was someone else's problem now.

Jason had bigger fish to deal with. Like Interpol and Homeland.

CHAPTER 9

WITH A MAD DASH THROUGH the terminal, Kate managed to board the plane and flop into her seat just moments before the plane pushed back from the terminal, but unfortunately, while it *would* get her home by noon, she was going to be squished between two large businessmen for the next few hours. She reclined her seat, tucked a tiny pillow behind her neck, and closed her eyes to avoid conversation.

Jenny's barrage of questions the night before still niggled at Kate like a flock of goal-driven mosquitos, and now she had hours to think about them.

Was she truly happy with her life? What would she change if she had a magic wand? What did she want badly enough to make sacrifices for?

Huh. The only thing she'd ever sacrificed was her self-respect when she was dealing with Victor. And why? Because his cash envelope covered her payroll?

True enough, he had a few really nice horses like Rainbow, ones she would hate to give up, as well as her ten percent of their earnings.

But money was a funny thing. She'd worked

hard her entire life in order to make a good living. Yet, she rarely spent any of it outside of business. Didn't love shopping, didn't have a closet bursting with clothes and shoes.

Years ago, when Tanner moved his operation from Toronto to Kentucky, he'd insisted she get an apartment instead of living in a tack room. Said it was a matter of pride, which she didn't understand, but she did as she was told, and found herself a small, furnished studio to rent.

His makeover had also included her wardrobe. Out were the thrift store jeans and flannel shirts, and her new uniform consisted of black jeans, white shirts, and a red vest or jacket, all of which cost her a chunk of money it pained her to spend.

The last rule of appearance hadn't cost any of her precious savings, but did make her laugh. He insisted that her hair was never, ever, out of its braid. According to Tanner, she looked about twelve with her hair down.

Kate ran her fingers up and down the braid hanging over her shoulder.

Inheriting from Tanner had put her in a very comfortable position financially. She *could* make it without Victor's money.

In fact, she could walk away from the business and retire today if she wanted. But what would she do when she woke up at three o'clock every morning?

What did she want to do with her life? What direction did she want it to go? Jenny asked what she was passionate about. She had shrugged, not wanting to put it into words—not yet, anyway—but it was there.

She would willingly give up anything and every-thing to find Leo.

Even risk more contact with Jason…although she would have to work a lot harder to maintain her composure. But she could do it for Leo.

———

Kate wasted no time setting her plans in motion. Instead of taking back the figurative reins in the barn, she left Mark in command and went for real reins, enjoying time on the track with five or six of the horses every morning.

During the afternoons she worked at home, methodically clearing out the townhouse until there was nothing left but two full suitcases to take with her, three boxes for storage, and the furniture. Everything else—including the last of Tanner's things—went to a thrift store.

Next she worked on her storage locker. She sorted, boxed, and labeled the entire contents, loaded six boxes into a courier's van, and closed the door on the rest.

Then headed to the hardware store.

A few hours later, with drop sheets in place, she pried the lids off paint cans and set to work with brushes, roller, and masking tape. How hard could it be?

Three days later, the townhouse looked com-pletely different, transformed from a sea of off-white, burgundy and black, to a palette of grays and turquoise. She shopped for new bedding in snowy white with pale orange accents, and bought cushions in bright jewel colors to toss on the black leather furniture of the great room.

New towels hung on the bathroom and kitchen rails, and a couple of pretty scatter rugs looked great on the hardwood floors.

Painting the dark bedroom furniture the silvery tones of driftwood was the final touch, and she loved it. Couldn't believe she had pulled off the entire transformation so easily, and was grateful for all the inspiration she got from television programs.

She had no idea it would be this much fun to create her very own living space, and was almost sad when the project was finished.

Time to move on.

When she arrived at the training center the next afternoon, she stopped her car as soon as she could see her barn, and simply stared. It truly was Tanner's still. Hadn't changed since the day he died. Sure, the one small sign said, Kate Oliver, Trainer, but she could have Mark's name painted over hers and no one would even notice, because everything else was still the same.

But maybe not for long.

She drove on, parked, and helped out with the chores.

Once feeds were hung and the staff gone for the day, Kate opened trunks and barrels and went through all the excess equipment they contained. Made three piles: save, fix, and toss. She took the toss pile to the dumpster, and came back for the fix pile, which she loaded into a wheelbarrow and pushed to the tack repair shop located near the main security gate.

Back in the barn, she repacked the trunks with the gear she would need, then moved on to the feed room. There she did an inventory of extra tubs, buckets, and other equipment. She had enough there to set up for another twenty horses if she needed it. But adding to the barn wasn't on her list of things to do, and all the "doing" had taken its toll.

She headed for Leo's room and stretched out on the couch to contemplate her next move, and with the purring cat curled up beside her, she was asleep in minutes.

Until Caly's growl woke her.

Instinct kept her very still, with her eyes opening just a crack.

Terror froze the breath in her throat and nearly stopped her heart. The door was wide open, and a man was standing in the middle of the room.

She fought to keep her breathing deep and even. If he made a move toward her, she could heave the cat at him and make a dash for the door.

But he didn't move, but the scream froze in Kate's throat when he took one step back. Another. Then turned and closed the door behind him.

The hasp clicked into place, and she recognized the sound of the padlock being slipped through it. He was locking her in. Why? She heard the creak of the main barn door she kept forgetting to oil. What was he going to do inside the barn?

Her first thought was fire. *Oh, God, please no.* She'd been through a barn fire, and would never forget the terrified screams of the horses, the people shouting, pounding feet, crashing wood, sirens, smoke making the whole world black... She shook free of the memories, and a quick check confirmed she was locked in.

She grabbed Jason's cell and hit speed dial.

"Kate?"

Her voice squeaked. She tried again. "He locked me in Leo's room, and now he's gone into my barn."

Nothing but silence.

"Jason? Are you there?" His lack of response left her even more frightened until she could hear him talking urgently to someone in the background.

"Security is coming from the east gate, Kate. He'll be there any minute. Who locked you in?"

She could hear the vehicle approaching, and wished she had a window so she could see what was going on. She heard voices and jumped when someone pounded on her door.

"He's here," Kate was just approaching the door when Jason snapped at her,

"Lock it from the inside!"

Kate did as she was told.

"Now ask who it is out there."

"Okay." She cleared her throat and raised her voice to yell through the door, "Who is it?

"Bentley, ma'am."

"Don't open the door, Kate."

"Why?" Dammit, her heart was in her throat again.

"Wait until Max gets there. It'll just take a minute."

She was confused.

"Kate, did you hear me?"

"Yes."

"What's wrong?"

"Just a minor detail you seem to have missed."

"That is?"

"I'm locked in from the outside. And I have the only key."

"Oh."

"Can I send Bentley for bolt cutters?"

"Not until Max gets there. Bentley thinks you called Max when you found yourself locked in, and that's who notified the east gate for help." Which she could have, *should have* done herself. But then she was also *supposed* to call Jason if she was in trouble.

Kate could hear Bentley trying a multitude of keys for the lock. She hadn't given a copy of this one to the security office, though, so no way he would find a match.

"Kate, tell me exactly what happened tonight."

"I can't, Max just got here."

"Okay, call me when you get home. Max will be following to be sure you get there safely. And we'll keep you under full surveillance for a while."

"Lovely. Just when I was starting to enjoy myself," she muttered.

"Hang in there, Kate," Max's voice came through slightly muffled. "We just have to saw off part of the hasp."

"Thanks, Max."

"I'm hanging up now," said Jason. "Don't forget to call me."

When the door swung open, she tried to shrug the incident off to Bentley. Someone must have automatically locked the door at feed time, not realizing she had fallen asleep in there. And when she woke up, she panicked and called her friend Max.

Bentley shook his head, as though he thought

it was an awful lot of fuss over a locked door, and then he left.

Max stuck to her side while she checked out the barn, surveyed every stall and every door, looking for something amiss, but finding nothing. The horses looked calm and sleepy, which was good.

She stuck her head in the feed room and frowned. The lid on one of the bins wasn't fastened properly. Had someone opened it after she left earlier? She set the latches and shut the door, then turned out all but the security lights and closed the main doors.

Max followed her home, and came in to check the place out while she waited near the door until he came downstairs and nodded. Everything looked secure. She asked him if he wanted some coffee, and he said no, thank you, gave her a mock salute, and left.

The instant the door closed, Kate felt very alone. And cold. She wanted to get into a hot shower, but she'd seen too many horror films. Hands reaching through the curtain…blood running down the drain.

Oh, for heaven's sake. If the guy had wanted to kill me, there was more than ample opportunity tonight. She shook off the ridiculous fear and went upstairs, not stopping until she was in her bathroom. She locked the door, cranked the taps, and was soon under a hot spray, soaking in the heat without moving.

When the water started to cool, she climbed out and immediately heard Jason's cell phone ringing. "Shit."

She scrambled to dig it out of the pile of clothes on the floor and was slightly breathless by the time she was able to push the button and say, "Hello?"

"What's wrong?"

"Nothing, you phoned me."

"I know I phoned you, for crying out loud. I have been doing so for the past twenty minutes! And that other noise will be Max pounding on your door."

"Oh" She could hear it now. "What does he want?"

"You are going to be the death of us, woman." He took a deep breath. "Don't move. I'll call you right back."

Kate set the phone on the counter while she dried her hair. She saw the blinking light out of the corner of her eye and turned off the hairdryer.

"Hel-lo."

"Kate, what the hell is going on?"

"Nothing."

"You can't keep messing with me like this, because I always imagine the worst."

"I was doing nothing more than having a shower and drying my hair. If that is too out-of-the-ordinary for you, sorry, not my problem."

"A shower."

"You know, stand naked under a stream of hot water until you get clean and warm? I'm sure you've done it yourself once in a while. And then, wet hair? I used a modern convenience called a blow dryer to get it dry. Guess that's when you were trying to call back. Now I'm getting cold." She heard the bitch in her voice but didn't care, and he hung up on her without a word.

Once her hair was dry and she was tucked into bed with a hot cup of tea and a horse magazine, she started to feel bad about being snarky, but this alone and scared thing wasn't working very well for her.

She finished her tea, turned off the light, and slid down in her bed, trying to convince herself she was ready to go to sleep, but it didn't work.

She gave in to reality. Called him.

"Hello," His voice was sharp.

"I'm sorry."

He sighed. "So am I, but Kate, for crying out loud. I'm miles away, I know you're in trouble, and I feel helpless. Then when you don't call back, or you don't answer when I call, my mind launches into the gruesome possibilities."

"I really am sorry. But in my defense, I was scared half to death and then furious. Then I was cold and miserable. I figured a hot shower would put me in a better mood before I phoned you back. It hadn't dawned on me that Max would have told you I was home already."

"Truce?"

"Yet again."

"Smart-ass."

She smiled at his teasing tone. Snuggled deeper into the pillows.

"Now," he said, sounding businesslike all of a sudden. "Tell me exactly what happened tonight."

She sat up, propped against the headboard, and told him the whole story, starting at feed time when she was cleaning out the tack room and ending with the lid of a feed bin being open.

"I'm going to toss the contents of that bin, just in case he put something in it."

"Might have been a ploy to make you do just

that and feed from a different bin."

Well, hell. "Then we'll only use the unopened sacks and toss all the rest." Expense wasn't an issue if there was a threat to the horses.

"Before you get rid of it, pull a couple of samples from the top of each bin, and one from further down. Give them to Max, and he'll ship them to the lab for me."

She'd thought she knew what was going on. Victor using the horses for smuggling something. But it had to be more than that. More Jason wasn't telling her.

"Are my horses or my people at risk?"

"I don't know, Kate."

"Am I under house arrest?"

"Of course not. Just do me a favor and check in with either me or Max a couple of times a day."

"What about my trip to Toronto?"

"When?"

"Day after tomorrow."

"Kate..." Jason hesitated, and she have sworn she heard his brain clicking through files. Something was up. Was he going to try to stop her?

"I told Zeke I'd be there by Wednesday. Day after tomorrow, and I *have* to be there to run Rainbow on Saturday. No way I can, or will, no-show."

"Don't worry, you'll be there. Just call me tomorrow night, okay?"

"Okay."

Silence hung between them, and Kate closed her eyes. There was something he wanted to say or something he wanted to hear. She wasn't sure which. She continued to wait. Could hear the clock ticking on her wall.

But whatever it was went unsaid.

———

Mist lay over the infield like a soft blanket, the sun warmed Kate's back, and The Princess was on her best behavior. Life was good. For the moment.

Kate was learning to appreciate the little things, and today she got a bonus because it was work day for her favorite mare.

"You feel like stretching your legs a bit, old girl?" she asked, tightening her hold and getting a responding tug on the reins. The mare picked up speed.

"Go easy. Easy." But there was nothing easy about the way she bore down on the bridle, and Kate would have laughed out loud if she wasn't trying so hard to maintain a reasonable pace for just a bit farther.

At the head of the lane she let The Princess open up, and in two strides she was in full flight, eating up ground while the world around them disappeared, leaving nothing but Kate and the powerful mare rocketing into the clubhouse turn. That's when she slowed to a happy gallop, and by the time they made their way to the exit ramp The Princess was bucking and dancing, making Kate and everyone around them laugh at her antics.

Kate's intention had been to have a quiet talk with Mark on the way back to the barn, but The Princess was having none of it. She pranced and danced while Kate concentrated on not being unseated, and asked Mark if he could come over to her place around noon. They could talk in private then.

Several hours later, sitting in her living room, she told him her plan, and he was gobsmacked.

"Are you absolutely sure? I mean, for real, with-no-emotions-involved certain?" He shook his head. "You haven't been the same since Leo left. Are you—"

"I have never been more certain of anything in my life. And for the first time in many years, I am looking out for myself, and I don't care what anyone else thinks of me. Does that make any sense?"

Mark's chin came up. "I thought I'd gotten to know you pretty well over the last three years, but I never saw this coming."

She laughed. "Me neither." She sobered. "I can trust you to keep it to yourself?"

"Absolutely."

"Good. And in the meantime, even if Victor calls out of the blue and tells you to put a horse on a van to Timbuktu, just do it, okay? Then call me."

"I promise. You can count on me to be nice to Victor until December 31st. And after that I can send him packing, right?"

"Right. I'll call you from Toronto every day, as usual. Not that I don't trust you to do the job well, but for my own peace of mind—"

"The Princess will be fine. Whichever race you decide on for her, I'll make sure she's ready."

Kate's smile twisted. "Her division is so tough lately. I'm willing to wait for a softer spot. She's getting older, and I don't want her to have to run too hard."

"I understand."

"Thanks."

"Have a great trip. We'll be watching the race from here and cheering for Rainbow."

Kate shook his hand and couldn't suppress a grin. "I feel like a new woman already."

After Mark left, she got out pen and paper, wrote three letters, and put them in her briefcase.

CHAPTER 10

O NCE HER BUSINESS DOWNTOWN WAS
finished, she felt a little lost. There was nothing left to do but call Jason after supper.

Kate was driving slowly, trying to waste time.
She didn't want to go back to the barn any more
than she wanted to go home—until she looked
at her watch and got an idea. She pulled over and
made the calls.

When she got home, she emptied every bit of
food...which wasn't really a lot...from her cup-
boards and fridge, hauling it off to the trash bin in
the driveway. Then she went upstairs to finish with
her suitcases.

When Max arrived, Kate was sitting on the front
step with two tightly-packed bags beside her and
a very empty, impersonal home at her back. She
felt like an adventurer, heading out to discover the
world, which was exciting—and a bit daunting too.

Max smiled when he got out to open the back
of the SUV. "You look like you're running away
from home."

She shook her head. *Running to, not from.*

They talked about the upcoming race, and Kate

relaxed…until he drove right past the terminal and took the perimeter road. She slumped back in her seat. Of course he had called Jason. "I want to be mad at you for being a tattletale, but you were only doing your job."

He parked across from the building. "He said to take the same charter as last time."

"And I suppose you have to make sure I do."

"Yes, ma'am," he said, and, with one of her bags in each hand, escorted her to the small reception area, checked her in, then walked her out to the plane.

With her excitement returning, Kate remembered her personal vow to step outside her comfort zone. "Thanks for everything," she said, moving in a bit awkwardly to hug Max, and was surprised when he nearly squeezed the stuffing out of her.

Her pilot this time was a man in his thirties or forties who wasn't interested in conversation, so Kate concentrated on the scenery to keep her mind off of Jason—who she was certain would be picking her up when they landed in Hamilton.

At least this time she was ready for him and could probably handle whatever he dished out. These past few weeks of getting her life in order had taught her a lot once she gave herself permission to dream again. To want something simply because she wanted it.

She had a plan for after Rainbow ran on the weekend—a selfish one—and she was good with it.

Just as she expected, Jason was standing inside the terminal waiting for her. But in spite of being ready for the romance thing, she was dumfounded when he swept her up in his arms and planted a great, big welcome-home kind of kiss on her.

But she regrouped quickly and played along. Laughed up at him. Touched his face with her fingertips and tried to ignore the zing of something that felt like electricity.

Jason led her to his car, and they were soon on the road with nothing but silence between them. By the time they pulled into the hotel Kate was more amused than angry. Jason, on the other hand, appeared to be less than comfortable.

Instead of checking in, they went directly to the elevator and up to a room on twentieth floor.

"There's no bed," said Kate.

Jason pointed to double doors, and she opened them to find a classy-looking bedroom.

"I figured we needed a suite just in case you couldn't stand to be in the same room with me."

Really? Hmmm. She *would* be better off if she didn't have to sleep with him.

"As long as you don't provoke me, we'll be fine."

"We could start over," he said quietly and she stared at him in disbelief, which quickly morphed into resignation. She would never be able to forget they had a past, but she could cut him some slack. Was about to say so when he got a call on his cell and, without even a glance in her direction, went into the bedroom and closed the door.

He wasn't long, and when he returned she was getting herself a cider from the mini bar.

"Want something?"

"How about a beer?"

She handed him one, their fingers touched briefly, and she squelched a smile when he jerked away. He wasn't immune either.

"Why haven't you drawn the curtains?" she asked.

"The only way to see in here is to charter a plane."

"So I'm allowed to stand at the window?"

"Yup."

She walked over and looked out at the view. It wasn't much. Certainly no ocean or mountains or rolling fields out there. But she still liked having the freedom to look outside.

"What are you up to, Katie?"

She was puzzled at the sudden change in his voice. "What do you mean?"

"First you vanished on us that last night in Toronto, and now, according to my surveillance team you've been working like a dynamo. Cleaning, painting, sorting, throwing stuff out, and then today a trip to the lawyer."

"I'm not *up to* anything."

"Bullshit. It's my job to watch people and figure out what they're thinking and planning. I know for a fact you're up to something, and I want to know what it is."

"No."

Jason moved more quickly than she did and caught her by the arm. "If you run to the bedroom, I will follow you and get the truth my way. If you stay here, you can talk with your clothes on."

An empty threat. He'd never take. It simply wasn't in his nature, but her heart still banged against her ribs. A visceral reaction that made her question how much she knew about this man. Was he different from the guy she'd lived with all those years ago?

Would he go further than she believed possible? He would not hurt her, or force her. But there was something different about his face that made her pause.

She'd been in dicey situations before, and with people she didn't trust. She could handle herself.

She sat down on the sofa, and he sat right beside her.

"For starters, that last night in Toronto I stayed over at Jim and Jenny's so he didn't have to drive me home. And as for the renovations, I'm selling my place. Tanner's. I'm done with Kentucky. The Princess will be arriving here next week, and Mark will be in charge of the rest until the end of the year. Then he'll take over as trainer. I'll stay here until the end of the meet or until I find Leo, whichever happens first, and then I'm quitting." She looked him in the eye and dared him to disbelieve her.

"Quitting what?"

"Training horses."

"To do what?"

"I'm going to buy a little farm, raise a few foals, and do special care layups for very select clients. I'm through with the Victors of this world. I want my freedom back." Her voice cracked, "But I want Leo back first."

"Why, Katie? Why is Leo so important?"

The sound that came out of her was half laugh, half sob. "Leo was everything to me. He was the only person who could help me when I had to face the end of my dream. He took me for long walks in the sunshine, and nursed me back to heath as though I was a sick horse, and he brought me ice cream sandwiches hidden in a bucket of ice. He was like a father, a brother, and the family dog all rolled into one. Leo's love for me was unconditional. He could always see the good in me, even when I was hollow. He helped me to mend my heart and grow new drive. He taught me to always look forward and never over my shoulder." Her voice hitched. "I often wondered how he and I ended up together."

"I didn't realize."

"He was the first person I saw every morning, seven days a week. I could count on his smile as I walked into the coffee room just as certainly as I could count on the sun coming up in the east. And he was the last person I saw almost every night."

It was rare for her to let anyone see past her tough outer shell, but this was Jason, and he was one of the few people who would understand the joy of the friendship she had with Leo, and how his disappearance had such a huge impact on her.

She offered no resistance when he pulled her into his arms. Snuggled against him, soaking in his strength.

"Do you think he's okay, Jason? It rips at my heart to think about him in pain or waiting for me to find him. He has to know I won't stop until I do, but I'm terrified it won't be in time, because I'm not actually *doing* anything to find him." Yet.

His grip tightened, and something odd happened inside her, like a light dimming. Panic edged in. She shoved at his chest so she could look up into his eyes, and went ice cold.

"No."

"Katie."

"NO!" She wrenched away. Crossed the room. "No. I don't feel it. I would have felt something." She spun and stared at him. "You're wrong. It's a mistake. He *called* me." And she had a plan. Was going to take off to Alberta after Rainbow's race. Go to High River and find Leo. She was sure that's what he'd meant on the phone, was that she could find him there.

She went to the window. Leaned her forehead against the cool glass. "That was the call you just got?"

"The confirmation."

"I should have gone instead of running to you. Should have *done* something."

She had to ask, even though she didn't want to know. "When?"

"Less than two hours after he called you. But he wasn't identified until today."

She couldn't think. Couldn't feel anything but cold.

She turned and found Jason standing right there, close enough to touch, but there was a vast distance between them. Like a deep, dark, valley.

"I don't know what to do," she whispered. "What should I do?"

"Nothing, baby. Come here." He held his arms out, and she stepped into them automatically. Let him take her to the sofa, and hold her while her mind raced in a million directions. Things to do, not do, stuff she wanted to say to Leo. Needed him to know before he left. But he was gone. Dead. Someone had killed him.

Wait. Had Jason said?

"How? What happened to him? I should have…"

Pressed against Jason's chest, she felt the thumping of his heart and the rumble of his voice when he said, "There was nothing you could have done. Nothing."

"I loved him so much." She shook her head, swallowed the ache of tears. "So d-damned much."

He pressed his lips to the top of her head. "I'm so sorry, baby."

That's when she broke. When the tears poured, and her mouth opened as though horrible pain would come out in a scream, but instead her body was wracked by silent wails. Pain tore into her, through her, and was ripped from her. And in some corner of feeling there were Jason's hands rubbing, soothing, until she was finally spent. Nothing left but the horrible ache that was her present.

He pressed his lips against her forehead, then wrapped her up even tighter and just held on. She was cried out. Hollow. Empty. Her fingertips had been tingling, but now she couldn't feel them at all. She shook out her hands, trying to get circulation going.

"Numb."

Jason took them between his and rubbed, then planted kisses on her palms.

She slid her fingertips across his rough jaw. Glanced up, and their eyes met. His dark, shadowed, and hers looking for something she could hang onto, something real, and then she lifted her mouth to his. Seeking comfort, begging to feel something other than pain. And they were swept up in the storm.

Kate was lost in him. Wanted to crawl inside his

skin. Tugged at the buttons on his shirt, but he grabbed her hands.

"Katie, stop." His voice was rough and gravelly. "You don't want to do this."

Yes, she did. She kissed him again, and heat started to replace the cold inside her. Heat she craved. Needed. "Please, Jason," she said between kisses. "Please love me."

He tipped her over, and his mouth burned a trail from her mouth down her neck to the place he'd stamped as his own years earlier. Where the touch of his mouth made her groan every single time. He pushed the collar of her shirt aside and the roughness of his stubble against her throat had her arching under him, pulling his mouth to hers, and the world dropped away.

When the brightness of morning filtered under the edges of the curtain, Kate rolled over to find herself alone in the big bed. She listened for the shower but heard nothing. Didn't want to get out of bed to look for him, because in the light of day she knew it would be over. She closed her eyes and sighed.

"That wasn't a happy sound," his voice came through the doorway and he followed, wearing only a towel, and she couldn't help but smile at the sight of him. Cleared her throat so she could get words to form.

"I thought you'd run away already."

He came to the side of the bed and leaned down, placing a hand on either side of her while he kissed

her gently. Looked deep into her eyes and said
softly, "I will never run away from you, Katie."

He lay back down beside her, pulled her into
his arms, and held her for a long time, his fingers
fiddling with her hair.

She lay still against him, wondering what to
say, how to move forward without awkwardness.
"What are the plans for today? Am I allowed to go
to the track?"

"I think we should stay here until checkout time,
and then I'll take you to your hotel." He rested his
chin on the top of her head. "Do you need to call
Zeke?"

"What time is it?"

"Just after six."

Kate forced herself to move away from him and
scurried to the bathroom, refusing to think about
how she looked in retreat.

"Nice ass for an old gal."

She muffled a snort and shut the door firmly
behind her. She looked at herself in the mirror and
turned to look at what he'd commented on. Obviously he likes muscular women, she thought as she
reached to turn on the shower. She stepped in, and
while hot water poured over her skin, she thought
about what the future held for her now she didn't
have Leo to look for.

The pain in her chest when she thought of him
was eerily familiar, like when she'd lost Tanner, and
years ago when her parents were killed. She wasn't
a stranger to grief. It changed her each time, and
now she wondered who she would be when she
finally got over Leo.

After her parents died, Kate was high and dry.

Suddenly without a home, and her future as Kate Oliver DVM evaporated. Without funds for university, there would be no vet degree, no moment of triumph to share with them when she accepted her certificate.

Instead, she arrived at the backstretch gate of the racetrack she'd once attended with her dad with a hundred dollars in her pocket, a small suitcase of her personal belongings, and a determination to get a job working with horses.

Years later, Tanner's death left her with everything she would ever need and a ton of responsibility. As she knew he would have expected, Kate stepped up to the plate. Carried on his legacy with Leo at her side.

But now? Now there was nothing left. Nothing to hold onto, nothing tying her down.

She didn't need the sting of hot water on whisker burn to remind her of Jason, but it was timely. They just had one night, and she didn't dare wish for more. It was enough. A memory to hang onto on long, quiet nights.

Was she foolish not to want more? Let things progress and maybe...? Nope. She stuck her face into the spray. No way in hell she was ever getting attached to another human being. Not going to endure another loss. Not now, not ever. Her heart just couldn't take it.

She would savor their one night together, and know he was healthy and well somewhere, living a life he enjoyed.

Jason stood outside the door. He wanted to go in and join her, but did he dare? No. Better to let her lead, and not risk scaring her away.

He ordered breakfast for them instead and it was sitting on the table by the time she emerged from the bedroom wrapped in a fluffy terry robe, with her hair swinging free.

Jason set his newspaper aside and smiled. "You look about twelve with your hair like that and your face all shiny."

"Twelve could land you in jail, my friend."

"Cheeky, too."

Kate sat down and poured coffee from a big silver thermos, and sipped while pushing the bacon and eggs around her plate for a while, but in the end ate only a piece of toast.

When he couldn't stand the silence anymore, he asked, "Are you okay?"

"Yup."

"No regrets, Katie?"

"About last night? Nope. I told you I wouldn't. I needed you." She looked at him steadily, as though nothing at all was wrong, but he could see the sorrow in her eyes, and then she sighed.

"I regret not asking you for help as soon as Leo went missing. I knew in my heart, right from the first morning, that something was terribly wrong."

"You can't do this, you know. You can't blame yourself."

"Why can't I, Jason? Maybe I could have saved him."

"Katie, it was way more than you could fix."

"What does that mean?"

He couldn't hide everything. "Do you know

who Leo was before you met him?"

Kate started to respond, and he was certain she was about to say yes, then changed her mind. "No."

"I do."

"Meaning?"

"Meaning that Leo put his life at risk the day he walked into Tanner's barn."

Kate simply waited for him to continue.

"Leo had been after Victor for a very long time, and I'm only telling you this because I need you to be afraid for your own life."

Her eyebrows lifted.

"After retiring from the FBI, Leo worked with the RCMP in Canada and with Interpol. He agreed to go undercover in Tanner's barn for as many years as it took to finally figure out what was going on there."

"And they killed him."

"He went into this knowing he probably wouldn't come out alive. He had a death wish when he signed on."

Her eyes filled with tears. "His wife died before he went to work for Tanner. He had nothing to lose. And he phoned me to say goodbye before they killed him."

It had to be said. "He wasn't murdered."

Her eyes opened in shock, and then she frowned.

Jason swallowed, hating that he had to finish this. "He took his own life, Katie."

She leaned back, face blank. Stayed very still. "No. He wouldn't do that."

"I can only assume he knew there was no way to get out alive." Jason's eyes didn't leave hers. "He never gave up any information."

She sat frozen, working over what he'd just said. It was as though her mind was refusing to let anything in. They were just words, and she was confused for a moment. Why would Leo be willing to die? Why would he give up on her finding him? What would make him choose death? What could have happened to change...

And Jason's word sank in, and images began to tumble over each other. Leo's face twisted with agony, and Leo crawling, trying not to scream as they swung at him again and again... Leo being tortured... Her stomach knotted, and bile rose up the back of her throat.

She scrambled to get to the bathroom with Jason right on her heels. He held her hair while she retched and when she sat back against the tub, he gently wiped her face with a damp cloth. He left her for a minute and returned with a cup full of ice chips.

"Hold one in your mouth. It'll help." The ice melted and slowly slid down her throat a drip at a time until she felt able to get up.

Jason helped her to her feet and held her still in front of him. "Are you okay?"

Kate gave him a weak half smile and turned to the sink to find her toothbrush.

When she emerged, all evidence of breakfast was gone, and she wandered the room, uncertain what to do next.

"Katie." She looked at him. "Come here."

She obediently walked over to stand in front of

him, and he drew her down onto his lap.

She rested her cheek against his chest. She was finally empty. Her mind had nothing left to work with, and the awful images had somehow been tucked away out of sight.

Life was so hard sometimes.

———

Jason stroked her hair while she slipped into a healing sleep, and held her for a very long time before he got up and carried her to bed. Tucked her in, robe and all.

He spent the afternoon on the phone with Ted and several Meyers agents, and by the end of the day decisions had been made, and Interpol was putting their people in place.

Jason was sitting at the table working on his laptop when Kate finally emerged, barefoot, wearing jeans and a T-shirt, her hair still swinging free.

Their evening passed pleasantly. Old friends talking about things they had done over the years. Jason told her bits and pieces of stories from cases he had worked on, and when he asked her about her horses, she told him about The Princess and how much she loved the mare. How she'd breed her in the spring instead of putting her back in training. "Maybe I'm destined to breed a Derby winner since I can't ride one."

"You really love the racing game."

She shook her head "No, I've been driven. There's a difference."

"How so?"

"Two months ago I could have recited the past

performances of every horse in my barn, their bloodlines back four generations, and exactly what mix of grain went into their tubs at night. But if you asked me what color my bedroom walls were, I would have been stumped.

"My barn has dozens of beautiful flower pots hanging from the eaves because they're tended by gardeners every single day. But the last of Tanner's house plants shriveled up and died in my living room and I never even noticed."

"Maybe you just need to scale back your work and have some fun, Katie."

Her smile was wry, "Work is all I know. Understand. I don't know how to have fun anymore, Jason. But worse than that, I didn't even realize it."

"What changed?"

"I went to dinner at Jim and Jenny's house. Did you know they have three kids?"

"No kidding. I bet they all have red hair."

"They do. And her temper, too." Kate laughed. Jenny's red hair had been the brunt of many jokes back when they were young.

"Do you want kids someday, Katie?"

She shook her head, "Definitely not. But I would love to have a life like hers. She knows exactly who she is, and that she's loved and needed twenty-four hours a day. If she goes to the bathroom, somebody notices she's missing."

"I bet she would love to have a bit of the freedom you have."

"I don't think so. There's something very peaceful and complete about her."

"You need to take a good look at yourself, Katie. You exude confidence. You're strong, capable, have a solid sense of reality, yet you're beautiful and soft, too."

"Thanks, but if I disappeared off the face of the earth tomorrow, only a handful of people would notice I was gone."

"I would notice."

"That's one."

Jason gave her a dirty look. "So I'm chopped liver."

She grimaced "Not what I meant."

"It's what you said." He went to the window. Stared out at the dark sky.

She joined him. "No stars. We're supposed to get rain tomorrow."

He pulled her around so he could nestle her back against him. Rested his chin on her head and wrapped his arms around her middle.

"I don't know how to help you, Katie."

"You already have." She hesitated. "More than you will ever know."

"Cliché."

"True."

"You never phoned Zeke."

"I know. I just couldn't seem to face any more reality today."

Jason smiled. "Reality isn't all it's cracked up to be. But fantasy. That's something else again."

Kate twisted around to look at his face and, as she suspected, he was grinning at her.

"What kind of fantasy did you have in mind?"

"Is that an invitation?"

"Maybe."

"Close enough for me," he said and pulled her with him to the bedroom.

CHAPTER 11

———

KATE WAS BARELY ONE STEP into the lobby of her hotel when reality slapped her, hard and fast.

Victor's voice and presence filled the space, and there he was near the front desk, ranting at Zeke.

When the younger man spotted her, she shook her head and waved him away, and he slowly edged toward the hotel's restaurant with Victor in tow—still talking.

Kate slipped into the stairwell, and was startled when Jason came in right behind her. "What are you doing?" If Victor caught sight of them together, would it put Jason in his crosshairs like the others? She could only pray neither one of them had been seen.

"When you were halfway through the door you froze like you'd seen a ghost. What's wrong?"

"Victor was there, harassing Zeke." She frowned. "You didn't know he was here. Why is that? Why don't you have surveillance on him? Someone to keep you informed of his whereabouts?"

"Because he isn't working alone, and if one of his people picked up on surveillance we'd be toast, and starting back at square one again. Where is he now?"

"Zeke walked him into the restaurant."

"Good. Don't move."

Jason left her there, and Kate called Zeke on his cell.

"Hi, sound surprised that I'm not there yet. Then tell me where you are and that Victor is with you, waiting for me." She could hear Victor blustering in the background while Zeke followed her instructions.

"Good work. Tell him I'll be there soon. Twenty minutes tops."

More Victor grumbling.

"Okay, now please, don't let him out of the restaurant for the next ten minutes, no matter what, and I'll see you in a bit."

Kate stepped out of the stairwell just as Jason reached for the door. He scowled, and she held up her cell phone with a smile. "Handled."

She checked in, and they rode up to her room together.

"Thanks for running interference," she said.

His expression was a bit grim. "You managed just fine on your own."

"I've made a career out of ducking Victor, and my help knows how to play the game." She hesitated. "It's both weird and good to know that Zeke gets what's going on and won't ask awkward questions."

Once in her room, she got to work messing up her hair, pulling strands to hang around her face, then pushed them aside so it looked like there had been a vague attempt to fix the mess.

She studied the contents of the mini bar for a minute before selecting a tiny bottle of scotch, cracking the seal, and swallowing a good mouthful, barely managing to stifle a cough and gasp.

"What the hell are you doing?"

"Trying to kill myself. What does it look like?"

"Kate."

"Okay, trying to look..." she hesitated. "Like I've just left someone's bed."

Jason gaped at her.

"What? It was supposed to be my cover, wasn't it?"

"For sure. But straight scotch? What the hell was that supposed to do?"

"It makes my face flushed."

He put his hands on either side of her face. Waited until her eyes met his, and smiled. "The look you wanted has been on your face for hours. You didn't need the scotch." He lowered his mouth to hers, and she groaned, tipping her head to avoid contact. Tried to back away from him, but he wouldn't let go.

"There is not a man alive who wouldn't know by the look on your face that you have been loved, very recently."

Loved? Nope. No way. It was sex. Just sex and nothing more. It couldn't be love. "I've gotta go and rescue Zeke before he punches Victor."

They walked together to the elevator, and when they stepped in, Jason pushed the button for the first floor instead of the lobby. She raised an eyebrow, but he didn't explain.

When the door opened, Jason led her to the stairwell, and they walked down to the lobby level.

He stopped her before she could open the door. Took her by the shoulders and looked her right in the eye. "Phone me as soon as you get back to your room, okay? I need to know everything Victor says."

"Sure."

"And for the sake of your cover," he murmured as his lips met hers. The kiss was sweet, tender, and she drew strength from him, then wanted more. To hell with Victor. She leaned in, but Jason—always the responsible one—put space between them with apparent ease, and his expression was cool when he opened the door for her.

With an odd ache in the vicinity of her heart, she walked into the restaurant, where at least Zeke looked very glad to see her.

"Hello, Victor. Sorry I'm late," she said, not that she needed to apologize since they hadn't actually arranged to meet.

Victor looked her up and down. "I've been trying to reach you since yesterday when your man said you came up here. Where the hell have you been?"

"Visiting a friend."

"Who's looking after all my horses while you're gallivanting around?"

"Oh, Victor," she said with a smile. "The Kentucky barn is in Mark's capable hands. He'll be following my training schedule and detailed instructions, and we're in constant contact."

He looked like his head was about to explode. "I pay you to look after my horses, and I don't mean by telephone!"

How had she tolerated him since she took over

from Tanner? And why now that she *had* to get along, did she suddenly have a backbone and want nothing more than to tell him to take his fucking attitude and get out of her life?

She dragged in a breath. "Victor, I am on call twenty-four seven. But I have friends here, connections from back in my riding days, and I treated myself to a visit with one."

"Well your *riding* career is long over, so you'd best put your energy into the business at hand."

"Have you had supper yet, Victor? Would you like to join us? The food here probably isn't up to your standards, but it's edible."

He sneered. "Eat here? I think not."

"Is there some business you still want to discuss? Or are you going back to your hotel now?" She took great pleasure in nearly dismissing him.

"I will see you in the morning." He shoved back, and was almost to the door when he turned and sneered, "Unless you're otherwise detained."

"You okay?" asked Zeke.

"Better than." She grinned. "Fiddlesticks."

"What?"

"A trick Tanner taught me years ago. When Victor's being obnoxious, just start repeating the word over and over in your head. Eventually the ridiculous sound will force you to smile, and poof, your anger will vanish, and as a bonus, your smile will probably annoy the hell out of the asshole."

"A well-directed fist would be my choice."

"But then he'd have you hauled to jail for assault."

"Good point. But—"

"How do we get some service in here? I'm starving."

Zeke waved at the waitress. "Victor scared her away a while ago."

Kate apologized to the server for her business associate's bad manners, and then she and Zeke ordered.

Over supper he told her Victor had come to the barn that morning and instructed him to give Rainbow a special herbal mixture to help her breathe better. "I told him she was within days of a race and I didn't know if the mixture could have something in it that would show up in a drug test. He freaked. Said he would never drug a horse blah, blah, blah. I stood my ground and phoned Mark. He talked to Victor and told him the same thing. Then Jim came over to see if he could help me out, and Victor ran him off."

"Why didn't you call me?"

"I didn't want to bug you?"

"I could have defused him and saved you a lot of aggravation."

"I know, but Mark said you left town last night, and when you didn't come to the barn I thought..." He hesitated and looked down at the tablecloth."

"What did you think, Zeke?" She waited for him to look up, and she pinned him with a stern look, even though she knew the color had risen in her face.

"I thought you could use a break from the jerk," he said but then grinned as if to say he knew damn well she had been in the sack with someone.

Luckily their meals arrived, and the subject was left to die a natural death.

After supper, Kate asked Zeke if he would mind loaning her his car—she wanted to run to the store and pick up snacks—but he hesitated.

"I need it to go back and check Rainbow. I don't trust Victor. He'll probably put his magic potion in her feed."

Kate dug out her phone and called Jim. Asked him if he had anyone who could sit with her mare until the race Saturday, and he said he would call the agency he used and someone could probably be there within the hour.

"Perfect. I'll be there to meet him."

"I'll come with you so he knows who I am when I arrive in the morning."

"Good idea."

When Kate and Zeke arrived at the barn, it was quiet except for the contented munching of hay. Kate went into Rainbow's stall to check her over, and was pleased she didn't look like she'd lost any weight. Zeke had managed to keep her eating with the help of Anchor and the half-wall between them. As predicted, every time he tried to reach into her feed tub, she chased him out and ate the feed herself.

Kate lifted a handful of grain from the tub and smelled it. Then she stuck her tongue into it to taste for bitterness or anything foreign. It seemed fine, but just to be certain she dumped the mixture in a manure basket and asked Zeke to get her some plain oats instead. Hiding a drug or poison in plain oats would be like adding salt to raw rice. It would simply fall through and lie on the bottom of the tub.

When Kate heard a car pull up, she went out to meet the security guard, a pleasant older man who reminded her of Leo. She swallowed hard and introduced him to Zeke, Rainbow, and Anchor. She gave him her cell number and Zeke's, told him she would pay him fifty dollars cash each morning—over and above his wage—and bid him good night.

On the way back to the hotel Zeke asked Kate if that fifty would come out of her own pocket.

"Not a chance. If I have to protect Victor's horses from anyone, including him, he'll get the bill at the end of the month."

"And he won't argue?"

"Sadly, no. He is arrogant enough to think his bill should be high at all times. He only grumbles that I must be cutting corners if it seems too low."

"The man is an idiot."

"But a very wealthy one who signs our paychecks."

"I still don't get why you let him talk to you the way he does."

"Fiddlesticks."

"Yeah, yeah, but at the end of the day, is it really worth it?"

"Sometimes yes, sometimes no." Kate studied Zeke's face in the light from the dashboard and wondered exactly how much he knew. Did he just monitor and report? Or did he know exactly what was going on?

"You're a good trainer, Kate. You don't need him and his money."

Not going there. "What time are we going to the track tomorrow?"

"Meet you in the lobby at five."

"Okay."

They said nothing more until they got off of the

elevator on the tenth floor.

Kate asked what room he was in.

"Ten oh two. You?"

She nodded the opposite direction. "Ten twelve."

Once Kate had washed and slipped under the covers, she called Jason. She told him why Victor had been ranting at Zeke, and that she'd hired a security guard for her horse. She was surprised when he simply thanked her for the update and said goodbye.

But it was good. No strings. Would have been perfect if she was still planning to take off right after Rainbow's race to try and find Leo. But now emptiness was all she could see stretching across the days to come.

No dreams, no goals, nothing to work toward.

———

Saturday dawned slowly, with the sun struggling to penetrate ominous black clouds. Kate couldn't believe the change. When she'd galloped Rainbow the day before, sunshine on the morning dew created a sparkling blanket over the turf. Made her feel alive again, and rejuvenated by the elements after a long and sleepless night.

But today, watching Zeke walk Rainbow around the sawdust ring outside the barn, she could almost smell the rain about to fall.

Half an hour into Rainbow's walk the wind suddenly whipped up, sending people and horses scrambling for cover. Within seconds, raindrops were pelting the ground as hard as hail, and thunder rumbled in the distance just as Zeke got the mare safely tucked into her stall.

A storm in southern Ontario could last five minutes or five hours, and it would only take about an hour of hard rain to change the turf course from firm to yielding—which was not optimal for Rainbow—but there was little Kate could do besides cross her fingers and hope.

Back at the hotel she showered and dressed in her racing clothes—black pants, white shirt, red leather jacket—twisted her tidy French braid into a knot at the base of her neck, and slipped into her well-polished black boots. With a bright red raincoat over her arm, she headed out, and noticed a man suddenly sliding down low in the driver's seat of a car parked just a couple away from Zeke's rental. Her heart skipped a beat, but she continued on undaunted. It was probably one of Jason's men.

She kept an eye on her mirrors and felt relieved when she wasn't followed out of the parking lot.

Shrugging off the funny feeling in her gut, she went straight to the barn to check on Zeke and Rainbow. Finding everything quiet, she left them and drove over to the grandstand. She'd been invited to join some old friends in the dining room, but had to go to the turf club for a quick visit with Victor first. He would pout if he thought she was at the races and hadn't acknowledged him.

When she arrived he was busily stuffing his face in the usual revolting manner, talking to her with his mouth full, telling her Zeke was way out of line suspecting him of doping his own horse. Kate stroked his feathers by explaining how it was her fault because she'd given Zeke such strict instructions about the mare's feed, and told him she was the only person, bar none, who could make any decisions about Rainbow.

Victor only grumbled for a little longer before Kate excused herself, saying she would see him in the saddling paddock later.

Hours later, in the saddling paddock, Victor was strangely tense. He stood off to one side, away from Kate, and she was puzzled by the change in his usual pattern, but shrugged it off, more concerned with Rainbow's behavior.

Muscles rippling while she danced at Zeke's side, Rainbow's eyes were bright and clear, and she looked ready to take on the world. Kate couldn't have been more pleased.

Heading for where she would leg up her rider, Kate was surprised to see him having an animated conversation with Victor who then shook his hand and hustled off into the crowd on the other side of the fence.

Jake made his way over to Kate.

"Hey, Jock," he said, making her grin at the memories. He'd been kind to her back in her riding days.

"Hey, Jake. Was Victor giving you a hard time?"

He glanced around. "Are you in on his plan?"

"What plan?"

"That's all I needed to know."

Before she could ask what he meant, the call came for "Riders Up!" Kate put her hand down to leg Jake up onto Rainbow, and once he was in position, she patted his boot. "Safe trip, my friend."

Kate was slightly concerned about whatever Victor was up to, but she knew Jake would give Rainbow an excellent ride. He breezed the mare a few days earlier and had a good feel for her ability, personality, and attitude.

He'd have studied the charts of her past races and figured out for himself how this one would set up. He would know where she should be placed in the early stages of the race, and he was well aware of her ability to close hard. Once she turned for home, she was like a missile locked on target. Rainbow knew exactly where the wire was, and would give everything she had to get there in front of the other horses. Jake's only job at that point would be to steer and stay on board.

When Kate left the paddock, Victor suddenly appeared at her side, bumping into her in the crush of people, and grabbing her by the arm. "Are you coming up to sit with me?"

"You know me, Victor. I need a quiet spot to watch alone. I'll join you after for celebration."

He was obviously displeased with her response, then oddly remarked on her jacket having something on it. He brushed at it for a minute, then said, "Oh, well," and stormed off.

Kate lifted her arm to look and see what Victor had been fussing about and saw the corner of a mutual ticket sticking out of her pocket. Kate slid it out far enough to see it was a hundred-dollar win ticket. She stuffed it out of sight. Annoyed because he *knew* she was superstitious and *never* wagered on her horses. But dammit, she wasn't going to let him ruin this last race for her.

Kate looked around for a good vantage point, finally opting for the outdoor box seat section, where she could see the starting gate off to the right and the finish line almost directly in front of her. Light rain had chased most people indoors, so Kate had the area pretty much to herself, which was perfect.

As luck would have it, the sun peeked through a hole in the clouds and warmed her face while she watched Rainbow dance beside her escort pony. But once they made their way through the narrow chute from the main track to the turf course, she stopped prancing and focused on the starting gate with her game face on.

This was it.

CHAPTER 12

FOR A MOMENT KATE WAS sad, because this was the last time she would send Rainbow to a race. But shaking off her gloom, she savored the moment, committing the entire picture to memory. Every little detail.

This is mine, and nobody can take it away from me. I am the only person here, and it's you and me, girl. Make me proud, Rainbow. Show them what you're made of.

The horses were loaded into the gate and dispatched quickly, without incident. There was a bit of jostling for position going into the turn, and Jake let the mare settle in behind the first four horses. She was moving easily and relaxed in the backstretch, until another horse came up alongside of her just before the big sweeping turn for home.

Suddenly competitive, she bore into the bridle and Jake let her open up a notch. *Good move, don't fight her.* Halfway around the turn there was a challenge from the inside, and Jake had trouble on his hands. Rainbow refused to be steadied, fought for ground, and was finally given her head.

She sailed past her rivals and was two lengths in front when she turned for home. Kate's heart was in her throat and tears ran down her face as she cheered them on, hoping, praying she could out-run any latecomers, and that's when it happened. A dark brown horse burst from the pack and began to close in on Rainbow. Advancing stride by stride. Drawing alongside.

Jake was on his belly urging Rainbow on, and even though it looked like she was giving her all, she managed one last surge of power at the very last second and it looked like the two horses crossed the line as one.

The photo sign flashed on the infield tote board.

Kate shot down the stairs to the wide apron between the grandstand and the track. She was almost positive her mare's nose had been in front, but they were going so fast.

When she reached the trackside gate the security guard gave her a thumbs-up and the crowd sent up a cheer at the same time.

She glanced at the board.

It was official. Rainbow had won.

Kate let out an undignified whoop, and laughing, was swept into a double hug from Jenny and Jim.

The jockey's valets arriving to unsaddle gave her high fives. And as the riders brought the horses back they, too, shouted their congratulations.

"Nice work, Jock!"

"Well done, Kate!"

"You could have rode her better than Jake!"

"Way to go, bug girl!" That one made her laugh. Bug, was the slang for an apprentice rider, and back in the day, when she'd been race riding, there were often articles about her with titles like, "Bug-girl takes Toronto by storm." Ha ha, in today's climate, they would probably have called her a bug-rider, not girl. So much in the world changed, while still more stayed exactly the same.

"Welcome home, Kate!"

The faces and words kaleidoscoped, and then Rainbow and Jake were there. Zeke led them across the tracks to the famous infield winner's circle—a spot Kate had only dreamed of in her riding days. The presentation of a trophy in *this* winner's circle meant you were on top of the game.

Victor was already there waiting, and looking a long way from happy, but at that moment Kate didn't give a hoot. This was a once-in-a-lifetime moment for her. She had not only come home a winner, but she'd done it in style. What a perfect way to close out her career.

Jake jumped off Rainbow and threw his arms around Kate. "Well done, girl. She couldn't have been any more ready."

"Perfect ride, Jake. Tried to harness her power, and when she objected you gave in." The mare reached over and rubbed against Jake's shoulder. "I think she likes you," Kate grinned.

Jake had to hurry back to the jocks' room to get ready to ride the next race, but just as he left, he reached up as if to kiss Kate on the cheek and whispered in her ear, "Come to the room."

He was gone in a flash, and Kate wondered if she had imagined the tension in his voice. She shook her head and turned to talk to Victor, who had just been interviewed by the local television station.

"Well, Victor, you were right, and I was wrong."

He scowled. "About what?"

"The race. I said she should stay in Kentucky,

and you said she could win here." She held out her hand. "Well done."

His hand was limp in hers, and her stomach suddenly churned with unease. Kate shoved concern aside, but Victor's silence on the walk back across the track together was hard to ignore.

Kate paused for just a moment to watch Rainbow walking toward the barn area with Zeke and one of Jim's hot walkers. She would love to be with them instead of with Victor, but when they reached the grandstand he strode away from her without a word. Cut through the crowd, headed for the exit.

Sour old thing.

"Hey, Kate, come on!" Jenny grabbed her by the arm. "It's time for champagne, and you're buying!"

Kate laughed. "I'll be there in just a bit, I have to tend to a little business first. Go ahead and start without me."

She made her way to the jocks' room, and walking through the glass doors into the lounge, she was greeted by a sea of smiling faces. Again they were congratulating her as though she was still one of the family. And it felt damn good.

"Looking for Jake," she said.

"Hey, Jake," someone yelled. "Put some clothes on! There's a dame out here wants you!"

There was lots of laughter, and Jake emerged wearing green silks, whip in hand, looking like he was ready to ride the next race. He pulled her into a deserted hallway and handed her a mutual ticket. A one hundred–dollar win ticket on the horse that lost the photo to Rainbow.

Jockeys weren't allowed to bet, so she knew he

hadn't bought it himself.

"Your owner gave this to me in the paddock before I got on the mare."

Kate was stunned. If someone had caught Jake with the ticket, it could have cost him his license. Especially if the photo-finish had gone the other way. "Can I keep this, Jake?"

"What are you going to do with it?"

"I'm not sure, but I have to do something."

"Can you keep me out of it? Just say I passed it to you in the paddock, thinking it was for the horse I was riding?"

"Absolutely. I would never put you or your career in danger. You're family."

He kissed her on the cheek. "Thanks, Kate. I knew I had to tell you. That guy is trouble."

"Not for long, Jake."

They called him from the weight room and he grabbed her hand. "Get upstairs and celebrate, girl. You earned it." When she turned to go he gave her a pat on the butt, and she grinned instead of being insulted. "Careful, pal. I'm not one of the boys anymore."

"I'll say. You've got an ass now."

She made a mock swing at him and he scooted away laughing. It was nice to be reminded what it was like to be part of a brotherhood. One of the guys. A respected member of a closed shop. At least a dozen of the men in this jocks' room would comfortably slap her ass, just as she would do the same to them, because permission had been granted. Any of the others tried it? One of the newcomers she didn't know? She'd deck them.

Kate stuffed the mutual ticket deep in her pocket

and went upstairs to celebrate with her friends, and by the time she got to the backstretch, Rainbow had been bathed and cooled out in the test barn, her blood and urine samples taken, and she was safely tucked back in her own stall with Anchor watching over her.

Zeke was crouched beside her left hind, putting on the last of four bandages.

"How is she?"

"Everything looks good so far. I gave her a good rub and did her up 'cause I didn't know when you'd be back. You want the wraps off?"

Kate shook her head. "No need. You know what you're doing. I'll see how she is in the morning when she goes out to walk." She looked around for Rainbow's feed tub. "Have you mixed her supper yet?"

"Nope. I have her oats steaming, though."

"Give them to Anchor. I want her to have plain dry again tonight."

Zeke sent her a questioning look, but she gave no explanation.

"Has the vet been here yet?"

"Banamine is already on board." Kate believed in her charges getting an anti-inflammatory injection to make sure they had a pain-free and restful recovery from racing. Precautionary, and maybe unnecessary, but it was her thing.

"Good. Put some extra electrolytes in her water bucket and liquid vitamins directly into her mouth instead of into her feed."

Kate waited while he finished putting the mare to bed and then, just before they left, she went into the stall and gave Rainbow a big hug. "Thanks, my girl. You have no idea how much I needed that."

Anchor was hanging his head over the separating wall. Kate gave him a hug too.

———

Back at the hotel they had dinner together, and Kate put her happy face on. Told Zeke stories about the riders from back when she was one of them, and she had him laughing through most of the meal. When she couldn't keep it up any longer, she begged off and headed upstairs, leaving Zeke to finish their second bottle of champagne.

When the phone in her pocket vibrated for about the twentieth time, she still didn't answer. But once she was tucked into bed, she called Jason.

"Where the hell have you been?"

"Celebrating."

"You couldn't pick up? Just once?"

She had her answer ready. "Nope. I didn't want to think about Leo."

"And no chance you wanted to think about me."

Surprised, Kate didn't know what to say. She closed her eyes and swallowed hard.

Something in Jason's voice changed. "Where are you?"

"In my room." She hesitated. "Safe from the world."

"What does that mean?"

"Nothing special."

"Kate, what aren't you telling me?"

"Nothing."

He sighed. "Okay, I give."

Taking a page from his book, she said, "I gave at

the office."

"What, exactly?"

Keeping up with the banter she said, "Wouldn't you like to know?"

There was silence for a second, and just then someone tried to open her door.

"Jason," she whispered.

"What, Kate?"

"Someone is trying to get into my room." She slid out of bed and looked around frantically, but the best she could come up with was a boot. She stood behind the door, heart hammering, boot held ready to swing, heel first.

"Don't move. I'm on my way."

"Great, what do I do in the meantime?" she whispered urgently.

"Stay very quiet. I won't be long," he whispered back.

Kate's heart was banging double-time, her muscles tense and ready. Had to be ready. Then the door handle turned down and she held her breath.

Slowly, ever so slowly, the door swung inward.

She had to wait until she could see her target so her blow landed where it could do the most good. No point swinging blind.

Jason peeked around the door with a huge grin on his face.

"Oh!" She swung the boot and nailed him in the shoulder. "You bastard! You scared the freakin' life out of me!"

He grabbed the boot and hand, twisted her arm behind her back, and effectively pinned her body against his. "Payback's a bitch." His mouth came down hard and fast, capturing hers for just an instant before backing her toward the bed.

She got in one good punch with her free hand before he grabbed it too and held it behind her.

The anger on his face was something she wasn't prepared for. And his voice carried just as much emotion. "All you had to do was answer your phone. But no, you had to dish out a little torture. Prove you were in control again."

"Have I mentioned lately how much I hate you?"

He dropped her unceremoniously onto the bed, and stood over her. "I don't think so, but you can start now. I'm all ears. By the way, congratulations. Your horse ran a great race."

Kate jumped to her feet, smoothed a hand down over her thin nightshirt and grabbed her pants.

"Modesty, Kate?"

I have no intention of getting dressed for you," she said, scowling and digging into the pocket. "Victor tried to get the rider to throw the race and implicate me. And Jake." She handed him the mutual ticket. Then she got the other from her jacket.

Jason looked at them and then back up in question.

"Victor gave one to Jake in the paddock before the race."

"But your horse was number three and this is for number seven."

"Precisely. I believe it was his way of asking Jake not to win."

"And the other ticket?"

"He slipped it into my pocket just as the horses paraded onto the track."

"Damn the man. Just when I start to figure out

his game, he throws another curve." Jason set both tickets on the table and stared at them until Kate continued.

"If we hadn't nosed the seven out for the win and someone had caught Jake with that ticket, he could have lost his license. Race fixing is considered the worst possible offense a jockey can commit, and even if my mare had been beaten honestly, the suspicion would have always been there."

"And you had a ticket too so it would look like you were in it together."

"Exactly. Could have cost me my license as well." Which didn't really matter anymore. "Betting against a horse in my care is illegal."

"Why didn't Victor want to win?" he asked.

"Or, from another perspective," said Kate, "why did he want to ruin two careers?"

———

Jason hadn't wanted to point that direction, but she went there herself. Would she realize it might mean she was in a whole lot more trouble than they had thought?

No way he could leave her tonight, but if he stayed, how the hell was he going to keep his hands off of her? Rock…hard place.

Dammit, he wasn't a horny teenager anymore, but suddenly remembered those days vividly. He'd wanted her. Always wanted her, no matter what. Sure, he loved her too, but his feelings then had nothing on how he felt now.

When had her strength and tenacity become just as compelling as her smart mouth—and legs that went on forever? Her independence and loyalty moved him in a way he'd never been moved before, and there was so much more—besides the fact he could make love to her for hours on end.

They hadn't been together all that much, but it was as if his feelings, untended and unencouraged for years, had been growing in spite of the neglect. Even when he was buried in a busy career. Immersed in the world of law enforcement and all the secret other things he'd been involved in with Meyers Security.

Which reminded him of the day they crossed paths some years ago, and he gave her a Meyers card so she could always reach him. If she ever needed him, he would move heaven and earth to get to her...and that was before Tanner's death and the sudden realization that she could be in mortal danger.

Maybe the feelings he had that day should have been a warning of what was still there under the surface, in the dark shadow of his heart.

Kate was one helluva woman, and he wanted a forever with her.

He shook off the distracting thoughts and concentrated on the here and now, the reality of Victor wanting to harm Kate. Jason would let her have tonight in peace before he impressed upon her how dangerous Victor was. That's when he would tell her about the safe house where she could stay until this whole thing came to an end. She would be safe there for as long as it took...but first, to get through tonight.

He grabbed pen and paper from the desk and settled back against the backboard, listening to

Kate's ideas about Victor's motives, writing notes until she finally wound down enough to fall asleep.

Then he made plans for the morning. He had to leave for a couple of hours, but he had a man to leave at the entrance to make sure Kate and Zeke got to the track safely, and chances were she would hang around there until nearly noon. He'd be back well before then, and be ready to move her to the safe house.

He sent a text to Meyers requesting a float plane for the trip—there were no roads into where they were going, and although they could go in by boat, he was opting for a flight instead.

When it was time to go, Jason had a bitch of a time making himself leave. He wanted to stay, to hold her forever. He stopped that thought with a hard *no*. There was a job to be done, even if there was something scraping at the back of his mind like a warning. He needed to get over it. He was a professional. Couldn't be giving in to a foolish emotional attachment. At least not yet.

Not until he had her safely squirreled away in the house on the lake.

He shot a text to the man in the parking lot, then headed down to meet with him. Gave him the scoop and made sure he understood he was to sit there until she came out, then follow her to the track. No losing her this time—not that this guy had been part of the other inept team, but still worth the warning.

Was he happy about leaving someone else watching over her? Of course not, but there was no work-around, so he'd have to get over it. And he'd continue to puzzle over whatever it was she still wasn't telling him, because sure as shit, she had something up her sleeve.

Maybe Jenny knew.

———

Kate was glad Jason wasn't there when she woke up. It would have made things a whole lot harder. And although she wished she'd kissed him good-bye, there was no time to grieve for what might have been.

After making a small pot of coffee, she set to work. Phoned the transport company she preferred to use in Kentucky, and then Mark. Confirmed the van would be there at one o'clock to pick up The Princess and Caly. She asked him to load them himself and not tell anyone where they were headed. She reminded him that everything for the cat was set and ready in Leo's old room, and all Mark had to do was open the can of tuna and put it in the far corner of the carrier, close the door after she went in, and fill the water bottle.

Kate let him know she was going out of town with friends for a few days, but Jim would be there to receive the ship-ins and care for them until she got back from the cottage at the lake.

Mark wished her bon voyage, shared some comments about Victor and how nice it would be for her to get away from him for a few days, and she was laughing when she hung up.

Next she called Zeke to check on Rainbow, and once she knew the mare was good, both physically and mentally, she told him about her trip and said Mark would phone in a day or two about shipping

Rainbow and Anchor back to Kentucky.

Kate sat back and closed her eyes for a few minutes, then took out a page of hotel stationary and wrote a detailed explanation of horses' coming and going. She told Jim she had promised Caly to Jenny, so it was up to him to take the cat home once she was off the horse van.

The next letter was the tough one. There was no easy way to say it. So she stuck to the bare facts.

Dear Jason,

It is time once again for me to move on. With the loss of Leo, my last tie to Tanner's barn has been severed, and I've decided to take the advice Leo gave me so often. I am going to keep my eyes firmly fixed on the future, and not look back.

To truly live, I will have to let go of Kate Oliver the trainer and discover who I really am. I want to learn to have fun again, and maybe one day I will find what it is that Jenny has.

I wish you health and happiness, and truly, I could not have survived Leo's death without you. I have NO regrets. Thank you for being there when I needed you.

Yours forever,
Katie

She slipped both letters into envelopes, along with a check for Jim to cover her horse expenses, and one to J.K. Investigations, Jason's company.

Her original plan had been to go to High River. But with Leo dead, what was the point? She would shed her old life like a snake sheds its skin, just as she had so many years ago, before she'd met Jason. She would be new and whole, and her life would be very different once again.

———

Kate called for a cab to meet her at the service entrance of the hotel. Dressed in blue jeans and an old brown sweater she'd stolen from the coffee room at her barn, she stuffed her hair up under one of Tanner's ball caps and left her luggage in her room. Crept down the back stairs to the employee locker room she'd already scouted out and pulled on a set of overalls and a big jacket with HOTEL MAINTENANCE across the back.

She marched across the loading dock to the waiting cab and paid cash for the ride to a shopping mall a few miles away. It was early, but there was a discount store that opened at seven, so she was golden, and twenty minutes later she left through the busy exit beside a coffee vendor and within spitting distance of a bus loop, wearing khaki shorts and jacket, with a brand-new knapsack over her shoulder and a money belt hidden under a gray shirt.

She hopped a bus into downtown Toronto, got off near a big hotel, and walked into the lobby where a rental car agency was located. Soon she was driving herself to see Jenny, who was very surprised to see her.

"First, the business part," said Kate, handing her the two envelopes. Then she mixed truth and lies into a viable story.

"I'm having trouble with Victor, and the police are going to deal with it eventually, but in the meantime, things between Jason and I have gone sideways, and I need to get away from him and do some thinking." So far, mostly truth.

Then came the lies. "I've rented a cottage in lake country, and I'm just going to veg for a couple of weeks. Think about my life, what I want and don't want, how to let Jason down easy."

"But—"

Kate shook her head. "It would never work. I'm just not relationship material. But I do want to hang here in Toronto again, and The Princess and Caly will be arriving some time tomorrow. You don't mind taking care of Caly for a couple of weeks, do you? She could just hang out in the guest room, and since I've stayed in there once she'll recognize my scent and all…"

"I can't wait to meet her."

Relief washed over Kate. One less thing to worry about. She held out the letters. "The one for Jim is just about the mare, and Caly arriving, and some details about The Princess. Plus a check for expenses."

"You don't have—"

"Yeah, I do. This is short notice on all fronts, and besides, I always pay my way up front. Friends or not friends."

Jenny nodded.

"You're bound to hear from Jason after I'm gone, so you can give him this for me, okay?"

The expression on Jenny's face said she had plenty of questions, but, in totally non-Jenny fashion, she kept them to herself, and for that Kate was grateful.

But when Kate was ready to leave Jenny hugged her and said, "I know something's wrong, and it only hurts a bit that you won't confide in me, because at least you're trusting me with this much."

Oh, hell. "Confiding in you could put you in danger." Shit. She shouldn't have said that. "I really can't say anything. I'm sorry."

Jenny hugged her one last time. "Call me sometime and let me know you're okay."

"I'll see you in a couple of weeks, Jen."

"No. You won't," she said, and Kate wasn't surprised by how intuitive her friend was.

Without another word, Kate left. Drove to the airport next and left the rental car in a long-term parking lot, bought a return ticket for a flight to Montreal, slipped into a restroom to change her clothes yet again, then left the airport, grabbing a cab close to customs, blending in with bleary-eyed travelers swarming out the doors, blinking at the bright sunshine.

This time her destination was a small roadside car lot where she paid cash for a plain, gray late-model compact.

She pulled in at a giant electronics store nearby, considered laptops, but settled on a tablet and added it to her knapsack, along with a simple flip-top prepaid phone.

It was nearly noon before she completed her intricate plan and was finally on the highway headed west.

Tears blurred her vision for a while after she turned off Jason's cell phone and pulled out the battery. Its constant vibration had been a steady reminder of what she was leaving behind.

He would thank her for this someday.

CHAPTER 13

———

LESS THAN TWENTY-FOUR HOURS LATER, somewhere in downtown Winnipeg, the air felt terribly hot all of a sudden.

"Last chance. You're absolutely, positively certain?"

Kate met the young woman's gaze in the mirror. She was holding up a pair of scissors, and Kate's hair had been put in one long braid in preparation.

"I want it gone. He forbade me to ever cut my hair, and he would never dream of looking for me with short hair. It's the best possible solution. It'll make it easier for me to disappear."

When she arrived she'd hung a story on the two hairdressers alone in the shop, minutes before closing time. Told them she was running from an abusive husband whose brother was a cop, so she couldn't trust law enforcement to help her.

She still felt a twinge of guilt over her cover story, because she didn't like making the police force look bad, but she needed a good excuse not to call them.

"I'm through with being a boring farmer's wife. I want it short and bright."

"Your wish," she said, began snipping above the elastic at the base of the braid, and moments later she held it up like a prize. "This is going to make someone an awesome wig."

"Perfect," said Kate. "You'll be able to send it to the right people?"

"Yep, leave it to me." She turned Kate away from the mirror. "I don't want you to see it until the makeover is complete, okay?"

"I'm game," said Kate, and what totally surprised her is that she was excited to see what they had in store for her. The only clue she got along the way was the hot pink nail polish applied to her finger-nails and even her toes while she waited for a timer to go off and the hair color to progress. That was the only moment her excitement wavered, but not for long. Pink hair might be kind of fun.

The process was slow, but they filled the time with their bubbly chatter, and when they were crestfallen by her refusal to have her makeup done, she gave in best she could. "Okay, but just lipstick and a little eye makeup, but no heavy foundation or powdered stuff."

Three hours after she walked through the door, they made her close her eyes while they led her to stand in front of a full-length mirror.

When she was told to open her eyes, she was truly amazed. The girl in the mirror looked fresh out of high school. Black hair with dark pink high-lights, cut close to her head, and the top stood up in gentle spikes.

Deep pink lipstick matched the hair, nails, and tank top she was wearing. Her eyes with not much more than charcoal and purple shadow under drastically waxed brows looked remarkably huge.

Not a single person in her past life would be able to pick her out of a crowd. Hell, she thought, I could probably sit beside them on a bus and not be recognized.

She laughed out loud and then shot a glance at the beauty shop owner. "I have to look a little bit serious when I go job hunting. I don't suppose you have any fake glasses that would make me look a tad less like a schoolgirl?"

"There's a dollar store just down the way. You could probably get something there."

"Great. I can't tell you how much I love what you did for me today. I feel brand new," she said with a grin, and was almost giggling by the time she left. It was the best money she'd spent so far. For less than two hundred dollars, boring old workaholic Kate was gone and young, energetic Amy took her place behind the wheel.

Kate continued driving west, doing a little shopping along the way until she finally had almost enough clothing to fill the small suitcase she bought in Winnipeg. And she was gradually less startled by her reflection in the mirror.

Arriving in Danston, Alberta on day three, she stayed in a motel close to the fairgrounds for just one night so she could check out bulletin boards and such in the shops around the area. She found a publication geared to ranchers and horsemen and spent the evening poring over it and making phone calls from her room. She checked out at dawn, now southbound, and stopped at several boarding stables and a couple of ranches.

By the end of the day she had two jobs, and one

of them came with a small room to live in over the barn. At six am she would feed there, and then muck fifteen stalls. At noon, she had to drive thirty minutes to a private facility, where she would clean paddocks and move sprinklers until about four.

The work was relatively easy, and the long hours kept her tired enough to sleep at night. On Mondays she only had the morning job, and when her stalls were finished she would drive north to an internet café on the outskirts of Danston and check on the news, searching for anything about Victor being busted, but nothing so far. Not that it mattered. He had no reason to come after her.

She'd been tempted to email Jenny just to say she was okay, but resisted opening a door to the past. She was safe, and happily settled in for winter in the frozen vastness of southern Alberta.

It was a long, cold winter, and working conditions were often a lot worse than unpleasant. Winds could howl for days, pouring frigid air through the very soul of a person while snow drifted up against every door or gate you needed to open.

Yet, when the sun shone on a quiet day, the change was absolutely incredible. Snow glistened on the ground and ice crystals danced happily into the heavens, while the horses bucked and played, making everyone laugh out loud.

In December Kate finally committed to a full-time job at a boarding stable. As caretaker of forty horses, she had the farm truck to use as she wished and living quarters above the arena. Her wages were small but sufficient.

The stable catered to kids, and there was an entire swarm of young girls and a couple of boys, all terribly devoted to either their own horses and ponies or the school horses.

The place was quiet on weekdays up until about three-fifteen, when the first kids arrived from school. Then there were scheduled riding lessons with three different instructors until seven o'clock at night, and the barn was closed by eight. Although Kate enjoyed the quiet time with the horses, she loved the energy of the happy, horse-loving kids.

And weekends were pure bedlam. From eight in the morning until eight at night the place was wall-to-wall children ranging in age from five to fifteen. Except, of course, if there was a horseshow to attend.

Then the walls reverberated with energy, and everything was crazy for an hour or so in the morning while she got the exuberant youngsters, ponies, and horses on their way, all spit and polished. While they were gone, quiet hung slightly uneasy in the air, waiting for life to return. And it always did with gusto. There would be ribbons and trophies and stories galore while the place teemed with excitement.

Mondays were peaceful. A designated day of rest for the horses. No kids were allowed at the barn, and Kate only had to feed in the morning, then the rest of the day was hers.

She spent those afternoons at a different internet café a short drive away, checking on the headlines, looking for news of Victor. She eventually got to know a few people there, and even lucked into someone with a connection, and before too long she was proud owner of a fake Alberta Driver's License with her picture and the name Amy Long printed neatly underneath.

Besides the café, the busiest spot in town was the craft store, because it seemed like most people had hobbies to help get them through the never-ending winter nights, and they loved to talk about their latest projects. Kate listened to stories about everything from wood crafting, wire wrapping, and rock painting, to scrapbooking and quilting.

With a need for something to help keep her thoughts at bay, Kate decided to try making a quilt herself. She thumbed through a book on the subject while in the store, but found the instructions somewhat overwhelming. Could she do it without a book? A quilt was just squares of material sewn together, after all.

The fabrics in the quilting section didn't do much for her, so she wandered until she found fleece in three pretty blues. She bought half a yard of each, a package of needles, and a spool of thread, to begin what would be a long winter's project.

Her goal was two or three pillow covers, but every time she went to town, she saw more fabrics which sparked her imagination, and by springtime, a beautiful blanket of a brilliant combination of happy colors was draped over her bed, and she loved it. Not so much as one dull color in the mix.

Spring didn't happen until nearly the end of May, then summer followed quickly on its heels, and everything at the stable changed.

Half the kids moved their horses to summer homes and pastures, while the other half seemed to become permanent residents at the barn. Kate finally gave a few of them jobs mucking stalls, picking manure out of paddocks and moving sprinklers.

They seemed much happier with responsibilities of their own, and to help to fill their days she began teaching horsemanship classes in the afternoons when it was too hot to ride. The surprise was how much she enjoyed them herself.

Kate had begun to find contentment.

In early July, Mary Dixon, a barrel racing champion from Wyoming, brought her horses to stay at the boarding stable during the week of the Danston rodeo. She preferred to keep them away from all the noise and excitement of the fairgrounds so they could rest and unwind while she could also ride without the distraction of the crowds.

Kate knew nothing about barrel racing or rodeos, but recognized Mary as a very competent horsewoman, and enjoyed the stories she told of her years on the rodeo circuit. It sounded comparable to what horse racing was like for Kate in the beginning. Lots of camaraderie and a real sense of family among the competitors.

Two days before the barrel racing finals, Mary's best horse, Oreo, suddenly had swelling in his ankle, and Mary feared he wouldn't be able to compete. When Kate had a look at the leg and said she could probably get the swelling down, Mary gave her permission to try anything she thought could help.

Armed with ice packs and heated pads, Kate set to work, alternating hot and cold treatments, and rubbing methodically to help flush away any irritation. She worked on him every few hours, and before she called it a night wrapped his legs in big, soft, quilted bandages.

When Mary arrived around eight in the morning to find Kate leading Oreo around a grass paddock, she jumped out of her truck and ran to the fence. Kate turned the horse and trotted him straight up so she could study his action.

"Amy, you fixed him!"

Kate laughed, "It was pretty superficial, and came out just the way I hoped." She opened the gate and walked Oreo toward the barn.

"You must have magic in your hands, girl," said Mary laughing. "This means I still have a shot at the championship?"

"Possibly. The problem being he'll need protection. Supportive bandages just in case there's something cookin' in that ankle."

"Can you put those on for me before we leave?"

"I wish, but they need to be tight, and shouldn't be on for more than about thirty minutes. An hour, tops."

Mary grabbed her arm. "Then come with me. You can help Oreo and spend a day at the rodeo. We'll have great fun."

"I can't. I have work here."

"I'll talk to the owner, pay for someone else to be here."

"I don't think—"

"You'll love it! I promise, Amy. Heck, you might even meet a nice cowboy." She grinned. "Come on, please do this for me... I'll pay you handsomely."

Kate frowned. "Bribery won't help. Begging, however..." she couldn't help but laugh. "That's something else entirely."

Mary hugged her. "Thank you so much, Amy."

Kate finally extricated herself from the joyous woman and said, "Just one rule."

"Anything!"

"We have to keep it low key, really low key." She took a breath. "I'm hiding from an abusive ex, and there's no chance he would be at a rodeo, but someone he knows could be. I've done a great job of avoiding him for over a year now, and I would dearly love to keep it that way."

Mary had sobered instantly. "Oh, God. I promise. Maybe it's not worth taking the chance."

Kate shook her head. "I'll make sure no one will recognize me."

She touched up her hair, put on the glasses and the deep pink lipstick, then when she was almost ready to leave, she went back into the bathroom and added the eye makeup just to be on the safe side. She knew there was little possibility she'd see anyone from her past, but being careful was never a bad thing. She had a nice, simple life, and wanted to keep it that way. No excitement, no intrigue and, most of all, no more dead people to mourn.

When they pulled through the gate at the fairgrounds Kate slid a glance at Mary. The woman had her game face on. Gone was the pleasant, chatty person Kate spent time with the week before. Today she was a serious competitor, and there were thousands of dollars on the line...not to mention the points toward another championship title.

Kate smiled to herself and thought back to the similar days she had in the racing world. She shook off the memories and took a good look around while Mary negotiated the sea of livestock trucks and trailers.

Once they were unloaded and Oreo was settled into a stall next to Mischief, her backup horse, Mary went off to find the supplies Kate asked for. Stretchy bandages with sticky backing were the best way to give Oreo support and protection without hindering his movement in any way.

Sitting on a bale of hay in front of the stalls, wearing the cowboy hat Mary had given her, Kate put it to good use, tipping it way down over her face so she'd look like she was sleeping. From under the brim she had a bit of a view to each side but couldn't see much straight ahead. She crossed her arms over her chest, stuck her legs out in front of her, and hoped she looked like a boy sitting there.

By the time Mary returned, Kate was hungry and decided to go along with Mary's idea and find one of the pancake breakfasts happening on the grounds.

Mary nodded. "Your ex wasn't a morning person?"

Kate shot her a look but made no comment, and their day passed pleasantly. When it was almost time for Mary's first run. Kate carefully applied the bandages to Oreo's legs and then slipped a pair of black neoprene boots over them to keep the support wraps out of sight.

She went to the edge of the arena to watch them, and was pleased to see he was moving fluidly and not altering his upper body to compensate for a problem in his ankle. Mary was beaming when she came back to the stall.

"Nice run," said Kate, taking Oreo into the stall to remove his boots and bandages. She didn't want anyone to notice that he had on what looked like something worn by racehorses at thoroughbred tracks. No need to send out clues.

The final barrel run wouldn't be until nearly

nine o'clock that night, so Mary and Kate took a walk around the grounds. There were booths offering everything from soft foam cowboy hats to very fine bronze sculptures.

They snacked on corndogs and curly fries, and Kate bought several flavors of homemade fudge to take home with her.

The evening performance was the grand finale, and Mary was quietly walking Oreo around behind the arena, his bandages neatly hidden under the boots once again.

Kate slipped into a spot at the arena fence so she could watch Mary's run and see the time clock as well. If she came in under fifteen seconds, her competition could not beat her. If she was over fifteen seconds, it wouldn't be decided until the last girl rode.

Kate held her breath when Mary and Oreo dashed in, aimed at the first barrel. A left turn, a right turn, another right turn, and then a deadly fast gallop to the finish line.

Fifteen and three one hundredths of a second. Four riders had a chance to beat her. Kate stayed and watched every one. The third girl hit two barrels, and while they were being reset, Kate glanced at the sea of faces in the grandstand.

Her breath caught in her throat and her heart nearly bounced out of her chest. She tipped her head forward to hide her face for a moment and then slowly turned sideways to take a second and third look at him from under the brim. She turned on her heel and plowed her way through the crowd to get back to the stall where Mary waited with Oreo.

Kate dove under the horse, pulled off boots and bandages with clammy, shaking hands. She peeked over the stall door, but saw no one moving toward them from the grandstand. Didn't think he'd seen her, but couldn't be sure.

"Amy?"

"He's here. I'll meet you in the truck whenever you're done." And with that she melted into the crowd of cowboys and horses in the aisle between the stalls. She used every tactic Jason taught her nearly a year ago, and when she was fairly certain no one could be watching her, she opened the door of Mary's truck, and threw herself inside as fast as she could. Had the interior light given her away? She huddled on the floor under the steering wheel, where it was less likely she'd be spotted by someone walking by. Even if they flicked a light inside.

She pulled out the cell phone and the battery she still charged every night. Made the call.

"Kate?"

She was shaking and trying hard to keep her voice calm. "I just saw Victor sitting in the grandstand at the Danston rodeo. One section over from the chutes on the east side. Four rows up from the bottom. White shirt with blue piping, light brown leather vest, and cowboy hat.

"Did he see you?"

"I don't think so."

"Kate, are you safe?"

"Hopefully."

Kate squeezed her eyes shut then and did something she really didn't want to do. Disconnected and turned the phone off. A single tear slipped down her cheek as she tried to swallow away the lump in her throat. Like ripping off a Band-Aid. The sting would dissipate.

Cramped and unmoving, she would stay on that floor mat all night if she had to.

Over and over in her mind she replayed the details of the face, and was absolutely certain it was Victor.

The truck rocked, and the thudding let her know Mary was loading the horses, so it was time for Kate to slide over to the passenger side.

When Mary climbed in she whispered, "Just hang on, Amy. I'll get you out of here." She started the truck and wound her way out of the parking lot. Once they left the lights of the city she asked, "Are you going to stay down there the whole way home, Amy?"

"I think so."

"Wow, he must have been some monster. I am so sorry I put you in danger. I had no idea."

"Don't worry, I'll be okay," Kate said.

"Is he from around here?"

"No, he's from the east, which is why I didn't think there was any chance he'd be there today."

"What will you do now?"

Kate took a deep breath while tears stung her eyes. "Move on. Find another safe place. Not a big deal."

They were silent for the rest of the trip, obviously each lost in their own thoughts, until they turned off of the highway and Kate asked Mary to watch the mirrors carefully.

"Not a headlight in sight since the last cutoff," she said. "But I'll keep an eye open."

When they slowed to turn into the driveway, Kate slid up onto the seat and banged her elbow on an enormous trophy.

"Oh, Mary you did it! And you never said a word."

"I was too scared for you to even think of mentioning it."

Kate shook her head silently. It was strange to think that once again the bastard had taken the pleasure out of something very special.

Nine hours was too fucking long, but aside from teleporting, there was no way to get to her any faster. Jason had been following a lead, a possible sighting of Kate at a racetrack in Florida when her call came. And now he was cooling his heels at the airport. Turned out Meyers couldn't get him to Alberta any faster than he could get there on a commercial flight, and that news had him nearly snapping the head off the ticket agent who asked if he was checking luggage.

He needed to get a grip, but what he needed more was to get to Kate and keep her safe from Victor. Had the bastard tracked her there, or had he accidently ended up where she was? Jason could only hope and pray for the latter, and that Victor hadn't seen her.

Adrenaline surged at the thought of Victor's big, beefy hands on Kate…

Jason brought his heart rate back under control by replacing the image with one of Victor on the ground facedown, hands secured behind his back.

Better.

And when Jason got his own hands on Kate? Hell, he was likely to throttle her. What was she thinking, taking off like that, putting herself in danger by cutting off all contact to the one person committed to keeping her safe? Did she not trust him to take care of her?

Trust and caring.

Was that the root of the problem? Did she not trust him? Was she trying to shake loose of him? Was her goal to put distance between them because she didn't have feelings for him anymore?

Did she think they had nothing but chemistry?

When the speakers clicked, he assumed they were about to announce boarding and was on his feet instantly, heading for the passenger bridge to the aircraft before a single word was said. He'd already gotten clearance due to his security pass, and he needed to get to Kate, to tell her he loved her, then get her home where he could keep her safe. Then he'd drag out of her the reason why she'd kept fucking running, kept putting herself in worse and worse danger instead of calling him for help.

That night, after the horses were tucked into their stalls and Mary had left for her hotel, Kate walked out to the hayshed where her car was stored and removed the Ontario license plates, took them far out into the back field, and buried them.

Then, back in her room above the riding arena, she went through her things and packed the knapsack with her tablet, a couple of changes of clothes, and of course, the makeup kit, leaving behind most of her belongings and a note to the stable's owner explaining there had been an accident at home and she had no choice but to leave immediately. She promised she would be back or in touch by the end of the month, and asked that in lieu of her last two weeks' pay, would she be able to leave her car in the shed for another month or so.

Kate sat in the dark, wishing she could stay here, where she'd begun to build a comfortable new life. She ran her hand over the brightly-colored quilt, thinking about the peaceful hours spent stitching squares together. She'd become very handy with a needle and thread.

She scolded herself when a tear slipped down her cheek.

Glancing at the clock, and wishing time would move more quickly, she came up with something she could do to help pass the time. Over the next few hours she used scissors, needle and thread to create pockets in her panties.

She used the silky fabric from one pair to create a thin pocket in four others. She worked swiftly in the glow of a tiny flashlight, and was pleased with her accomplishment, because now she would have a safe hiding place for her single piece of ID and her money.

An hour before Mary was due to arrive, Kate slipped down the stairs and, in the dark, went from stall to stall, dropping in morning hay and rubbing the heads of a few of her favorites.

As promised, Mary arrived at four o'clock in the morning, and without a word between them, they hooked up her trailer, loaded the horses, and drove away, Kate once again on the floor mats of the pickup.

CHAPTER 14

Summer 2017

AFTER ABOUT TWENTY MILES ON the highway, Mary finally broke the silence.

"Every car that has showed up in my mirrors has continued and passed right on by. I truly don't think we've been followed, Amy, so why don't you get up from there?"

Kate climbed onto the seat, and a good deal of the tension faded when she saw nothing but open highway in front of them and behind.

Mary glanced over. "Instead of getting out in Lethbridge, why don't you come home to Wyoming with me? Or at least cross into Montana before you go off on your own. You could disappear in the States a lot easier than up here."

"I don't have a passport."

"Pop the glove box and see if my sister's is in there."

Kate dug around and came up with a US passport. Opened it. The picture looked nothing like her. But heck, she looked nothing like her own passport photo, either. "Not a very good likeness." But Mary's sister had green eyes, and Kate took that as a sign from the universe that she was meant to take the chance and cross the border. There would never be a better opportunity.

"They get so wound up checking the livestock paperwork that they never pay any attention to mine, and I'm sure it would be the same for you. I think it's worth a try, and you can come and stay at my ranch for a while. He'd never find you there."

"My brother-in-law is tight with a gang, and they have connections everywhere. It's risky enough for you to be helping me get away. You have to drop me off somewhere as though I was just hitching a ride. I don't want them to make you a target too."

"I'll be on my way to another rodeo within a week and safely tucked in among the guys again. Kinda like having twenty or thirty big brothers, so no need to worry about me," she said with a grin.

"Sounds nice."

A couple of hours later, as they approached the border crossing, Kate took long, slow breaths, working hard at looking relaxed. She didn't want to be a blip on anyone's radar.

They opened up the trailer so the inspector could look at the horses, make sure their markings matched what was written on their health papers. Then he said, "Drive around to the right side of the building where there's some shade, ma'am. I'll bring your paperwork out once it's processed." He left with all their paperwork, including passports, attached to his clipboard.

The waiting was hell, but finally, *finally* he came out of the building, walked straight to the passenger side of the truck, and Kate nearly swallowed her tongue. She was busted.

He pinned her with a look and she met it head on. Didn't flinch.

He handed over the paperwork with a curt, "Good to go," and walked away.

Even though Kate felt like they had been under scrutiny for an hour, the whole process took less than twenty minutes before they were through, safe and hassle-free.

As the truck picked up speed on the open highway, she laid her head back on the seat and let the tension of the past twelve hours drain away. She willed each and every muscle to relax, and drifted off to sleep.

Jerked awake by a hand on her shoulder, she glanced around, totally disoriented. Had no clue where they were.

"You want something to eat?"

The sign she could see through the windshield said, Gas, Food, Dew Worms.

"They have good sandwiches. Want one?"

"Sure. Whatever you're having. And something with caffeine in it." She managed a sleepy smile, and reached into her pocket.

"My treat," said Mary, hopping out.

It was late afternoon when they pulled into the fairgrounds on the outskirts of a good-sized town in Montana. They unloaded the horses and got them settled into stalls for the night before driving to a local motel. The lady at the front desk knew Mary from previous trips, and asked Kate if she ran barrels too. Kate said she hoped to be as good as Mary someday, but for now still had her training wheels on. The woman smiled and nodded as though they saw plenty of wannabe rodeo cowgirls around here. Did give Kate's hair a funny look, though.

"You know anything about coloring hair?" Kate asked Mary when they got to their room, and she laughed.

"Honey, I can barely be bothered to wash out the dust. Let's see if we can find somebody who can help you."

They found a tiny beauty shop in the strip mall just down the street, and two hours later Kate's hair was boyishly short once again, and a deep, rich, reddish brown.

Over a quick meal at a local diner they made plans for the morning, then crawled into side-by-side double beds.

Mary fell asleep quickly, but Kate wasn't so lucky, and with increasing edginess knew it was time to make a move. One that would get her a hell of a lot farther away from Victor in a short time, and would also protect her friend.

Kate worked and reworked her plan until it finally seemed to be flawless. She wrote Mary a quick note by the light of the television, thanking her, wishing her luck and happiness, and reminding her to be careful.

Leaving behind her boots, jeans, and pink lipstick, Kate slipped out the door, used the pay phone in the diner to call for a cab, and got the driver to drop her off at the bus depot. From there she made her way to the airport, where she boarded a flight to Los Angeles.

In a hotel room back in Danston, Jason shot both fists into the air. "Yes!"

He had her now, and his heart beat double-time. She'd crossed the border less than twelve hours ago.

He grabbed his phone and while waiting for the call to connect, zoomed in on the video to get the plate number.

"Jason." Eve Meyers was all business.

"I've got her crossing the border into Montana this morning. Need you to run a plate number for me."

He gave her the details, and within seconds she had a name and address for him.

Jason plugged it into his map.

"Do you have a plan?" asked Eve. "Need backup?"

"There are a couple of routes they could take if they're headed for the other woman's home. But could just as easily be on their way to another rodeo."

"Hang on," said Eve. "Let me put her into the system and see what pops."

Jason studied the map while he waited. Decided on the route he would take if he was in their shoes.

"She's entered in a Wyoming rodeo in a week, and it's only a few hours from her home, so I'm betting home is where they're going now."

"I agree."

"As for transportation, flying means you'll still have to backtrack three hours to her place." Computer keys clicked in the background. "But I can get you a charter at first light which puts you at her ranch by noon. Or you can get a car now and be there only a couple hours later if you drive straight through."

No way he could sit here all night worrying about Victor getting his hands on Kate. This was the first solid lead on either of them in months, and Jason was not about to let the chance to get her to safety slip through his fingers.

"If I stay on the ground, I'm free to change direction if anything new comes in, and it can't hurt to travel the same route they're taking, either, just in case." Of course he could end up on a completely different route. Would they be driving straight through? Or would they have stopped for the night? If they stopped, he might even catch them still on the road.

Or he might miss them altogether.

"Car will be there for you in about twenty minutes," said Eve. "Meantime, I need the ID video sequence for our records."

"Sending now. And she's not hard to spot. Look for the pink hair."

Eve laughed. "Your lady is creative."

Oh, she was that. He ran his hand over the multicolored blanket he'd taken from her room. Could almost feel her energy in it.

Jason was nearly holding his breath as he drove through the rustic gateway and wound his way down a long, dusty lane to a house and outbuildings. Mary's pickup truck and horse trailer were parked near the barn, and the ramp was down and the side door open, as though she was still in the process of unloading. But there was no one in sight.

He stepped into cool darkness of the barn, and when his eyes adjusted he realized there was a woman facing him, holding a very large, unfriendly-looking dog by the collar.

"I'm Jason, a friend of Kate's."

"Uh, no Kate here. You must be in the wrong place," she said, looking convincingly confused.

"Kate was with you at Danston the night you won the championship, and she crossed the border with you yesterday morning."

Her demeanor changed. "I gave a lift to a groom by the name of Amy. She lit out last night, from the motel. Took half the contents of my wallet with her."

He caught a flicker of something in her expression that made him hopeful. "Please, Mary, she's in deadly danger, and I have to find her." He took a step closer and the dog's lip curled while a low growl rumbled from his throat. Jason froze in his steps. His voice softened. "Please help me find her before it's too late."

She shook her head. "I truly know nothing more. She told me she was running from her ex-husband and didn't want me to know where she was going. Said it would be easier for me that way."

Mary took a deep breath and pinned him with a look he'd bet many men would back away from. "If you're the guy she's running from, you need to back the hell off. She was scared half to death that night at the rodeo, and that's just wrong. You need to get on with your own life and let her have one of her own."

Jason knew when he was beaten. He would have

to track Kate from a motel somewhere between here and the border. "For the record, I'm not her ex-husband, nor am I the guy chasing her."

She wasn't buying it.

"All I can say is thank you for helping her, and if you ever hear from her, just tell her to use the damn phone and call Jason." Should he give her a code word too? No, Mary could describe him, and Kate would know.

She nodded. "I can do that."

"If anyone else comes looking for her, you need to be very, very, careful. Trust your friend there to protect you, and then call me immediately. Please?" He handed her his card and headed for the car now baking in the sun. If he was lucky, Mary had used a credit card for the motel, and that at least would give him another starting point, because even though not everything she had said was truth, he believed her that Kate had taken off in the night.

The question now would be her next destination.

———

When Kate landed at LAX, she knew she needed money if she was going to play tourist for the summer, and she needed a way to get into her bank accounts.

Without a credit card, renting a car was out, so she headed for Vegas by bus. When she got there, she contacted her lawyer in Kentucky. He wired funds within the hour, and she was soon on a bus back to California.

The next morning, while she ate breakfast in a San Diego hotel room, Kate accessed the internet and googled secluded cottages for rent. Fell in love with a listing on the Oregon Coast. She used Mary's sister's passport to secure the reservation, then grabbed a shuttle to the airport. First a flight to Seattle, then city buses for a while before boarding one to a town farther south. It took all day to get where she was going, and while she knew the excess travel exposed her to video cameras and too many people, it was still worth it to make sure her trail wasn't easy to follow.

Watching the sun rise from a rustic porch overlooking the Pacific Ocean, she breathed easily for the first time in weeks. Hell, maybe months. The cottage was tucked in among huge trees, the nearest neighbor was about half a mile away, and there was an old cat who happened by to welcome her. According to the website his name was Stanley, and although he had a home of his own, he often stopped by to visit.

Also according to the website, there was a telephone, as well as internet access. She paid to have the pantry and freezer stocked before she arrived, and would never have to step a foot off the property until her lease was up on the first of September.

Kate followed the rodeo circuit results on the internet and was pleased to see Mary was still doing very well. She finished in the top three at every rodeo, and had won several. The day before Kate was to leave her refuge, she sent Mary an e-mail, and was surprised to have it answered in minutes.

Mary told her about the visit from Jason, and said that she liked him, unlike the older guy who had bugged her a couple of times at rodeos, asking about her friend with the pink hair. She had told him the truth, that the girl took off in the night without paying her half of their gas and motel bill. When he pressed her even more for information, Mary's cowboy friends intervened and the man went away.

The following morning her horse had a badly swollen leg and couldn't compete. The vet told her something had been applied to his leg that burned the skin, but he would be all right once the swelling went down and the skin healed.

Kate felt sick to her stomach from knowing that because of her Victor had injured an innocent animal.

She had to let Jason know, but stared at the cell phone for a couple of minutes before putting in the battery and hitting speed dial.

"Kate, where the hell are you?"

"Doesn't matter. I'm leaving now anyway. You need to contact Mary. She had a run-in with Victor." She pressed the power off button, dropped the battery out.

With her meager belongings already in her knapsack, she closed up the cottage and hiked to the stop where a bus passed only once a day.

She boarded with a heavy heart. Her momentary contact with Mary and Jason made her lonely, and she wanted so badly to quit running. She wished she could put her arms around The Princess's neck and inhale the rich, horsey scent that always managed to make her whole. She missed the mare almost as much as she missed Jason. And Jenny.

Changing buses in Portland, she continued north

into Washington State and finally arrived at the Canadian border, where the borrowed passport once again got her through. She thought about that. Wondered what she would have done if she didn't have it. Not crossed borders, obviously, but there were plenty of places to hide in Canada, and now she was certain Jason knew about the passport, this had to be the last time she used it.

———

Jason was standing outside a cottage on the coast of Oregon when his phone beeped with an incoming call from Meyers.

"Yep."

"Got a hit on the passport," said Eve. "Crossed into Canada just south of Vancouver yesterday."

"About freaking time she headed home."

"Yeah. Bad news, though."

His heart stopped. "What?"

"There was a shadow on the alert when we got it. I tried to follow it back, but it's from offshore and I can't identify the source."

"Victor is into international shipping. Has offices all over the world."

"Interpol is on it, but thought you needed the heads-up."

Victor was just as close to finding her as Jason was, and that made his gut churn. "How fast can you get me to Vancouver?"

———

Instead of riding the bus all the way into Vancouver, she got off at the first stop, a village just minutes north of the border. It was surrounded by small farms with lots of horses and cattle in the fields. As good a place as any to try to find a job. One she could do, at least, because even though working with horses would make it easier for Victor to find her, what else could she do? She had no experience at anything else.

At least with horses she could find jobs where no one would ever see her. Small farms were the best, but bigger stables needed more help.

In a tiny motel room she put some thought into the Victor problem—she'd refused to think about him during her stay in Oregon. Was there really anything to suggest he was actively searching for her? When she saw him at the rodeo, he seemed to be there as a patron...so just a chance encounter, right?

But he chased down Mary. Opportunistic because he saw her at the rodeo? Or had he been actively searching? Why?

She weighed the odds carefully, and in the end found a job posted on a bulletin board at a tack store. A working couple needed someone to do feed, turnout, and stalls at a private barn five days a week.

Kate met the couple on a Sunday and started work on Monday. They worked in the city, and were gone from seven in the morning until seven each night. Kate would care for their six horses on the weekdays, and have the place to herself, which was perfect.

Then she found a basement suite to live in, right on a bus route. Her landlords were a happy pair of elderly immigrants from China. They spoke no

English, but communicated very well using nods and smiles.

They were the perfect landlords, because not only were they kind and friendly, but Victor would never get information about her out of them.

———

Kate had been working at the stable for just over a week when she got a strange note from the owner.

A big, burly guy was here last night. Flashed a badge and a photo of you. I said we'd never seen you before. Please stay late tonight so we can talk.

Kate's stomach did a backflip with a twist. Had to be Victor. Which meant he *was* actively searching for her, and that couldn't be a good thing. Not by any stretch of the imagination. So now what? Run? Call Jason?

But if Victor believed what the owners said, wasn't she safe here? Why run? Why do anything besides be very careful until he moved on?

She got her work done and hung around for a while, but got antsy once it was dark, left them a note that she'd come and see them before they left for work the next day.

Heart in her throat, she shoved the battery in Jason's phone just in case, and headed home. She'd gather her few belongings and hit the road tonight.

She kept her eyes peeled while she rode the bus past her stop. Saw nothing to account for the feeling of dread in her gut.

She pulled the cord for the next stop. Got off and hesitated. Was there anything in her suite she couldn't do without? Not really, but was she over-reacting? Did she need to run right this minute? Wouldn't it be better to get her things, make a plan, be smart about what she was doing rather than reactive?

Walking quickly through the dark, empty car-port, on her way to the basement steps, a shiver ran up her spine.

A heavy hand landed on her shoulder.

She twisted, spun, broke his hold, and jumped down the two steps. Got her key into the lock, but he grabbed her. She swung her pack at his head and kicked backwards, but he somehow got her turned around and used his body to pin her against the door, wrapped a hand around her throat and squeezed hard while staring right into her eyes.

With one hand tearing at his cruel fingers, she used the other to dig into her pocket and hit speed dial on the phone, just as she'd practiced a million times.

Victor let go of her throat to drive a fist into her face, and her head lolled back. "Time for you to pay for siccing the feds on me, you little bitch," he said with a snarl.

She dragged the phone out of her pocket and held it behind her back, nearly dropping it when he swung at her again, and she fought the bright lights, the threat of total darkness.

She groaned and forced words from her throat. "How did you find me in Vancouver, Victor?"

"My people have been tracking you for months."

"Are you going to kill me like you killed Tanner?"

His laugh was evil. "You eager to die, bitch? You

will, but not here. The last thing I need is your body showing up too soon. You and I are going for a long drive first."

Kate was trying to think fast and find a way to stall when she heard a car pull into the driveway. Yes! Hope bloomed, gave her new strength. "You're about to get busted by my upstairs neighbors, Victor so I suggest you let me go."

His hand closed around her throat again, and his laugh was sinister. "You'd like that, wouldn't you? Then you could run to the feds and tell them where I am. Do I look that stupid? Open the fucking door, and we'll just go inside for a minute."

Kate fumbled the key into the lock, and he shoved her inside the moment the door opened. Backed her all the way to the kitchen and opened drawers until he found a knife. Skimmed it across her throat, and she felt a sharp pinch, but the smell of her own blood jump-started her into high gear.

She twisted her head to one side and bent her knees to dip down quickly and away from the blade while shooting up a hand to protect her throat.

It worked.

Spinning on her heel, she headed for the door, and grabbed the cordless phone from the table on the way by.

She pushed speed dial for 911, wrenched the door open—

And he grabbed her by the hair.

He lunged for the phone, and she dropped it when he latched onto her arm.

She kicked the phone across the yard just as he began swinging at her with the knife. She tried to run, but his grip was relentless, and he kept slashing at her, making contact again and again but she didn't feel pain, just cool air on her skin.

She let out a scream, and his fist drilled into the side of her head once, twice, again and again. And she fell, and kept falling until darkness enfolded her.

———

Kate woke up in the dark, in the back seat of a car, with the metallic taste of blood in her mouth. She lay very still while she took stock of the mess she was in. Victor was at the wheel, and it was very dark outside. No streetlights, which meant they were far from the city she'd been living in. A rural destination meant there was little or no hope of having easy access to law enforcement. She was really on her own this time, and she had nothing but the clothes on her back, and, tucked in an underwear pocket, two hundred dollars and a fake ID card.

This was the reality she had feared for months yet constantly told herself would never happen. She was in Victor's hands, and there was no longer the slimmest doubt.

He wanted her dead. And he was more than capable of murder.

There was absolutely no point in trying to reason with him. Not that she wouldn't beg for her life if it came to that, but it was better to use her head to come up with alternatives. Like what?

The sound of a train whistle seeped past her thoughts. Was there a chance he would have to stop at a crossing?

She shot a glance at the door close to her head. It looked normal, like it would open from the inside. She checked the lock, saw it was one to pull near the handle. She slipped one hand toward it, then the other. The train whistle sounded again. That meant another crossing.

Oh please, she thought.

"Shit," Victor muttered, and the car lurched forward, picking up speed. Kate braced herself and held her breath until he suddenly slammed on the brakes and ground to screeching, bone-jarring halt.

She had the door open and was running before she'd even finished thinking it was what she needed to do.

CHAPTER 15

———

Fall 2017

IN THE PITCH BLACK OF night she ran faster than she had in her entire life, trusting her feet and instincts to keep her safe. Stayed alongside the rumbling freight train at first, knowing there would be fairly open ground and hoping her eyes would adjust to the endless dark.

Then she saw...almost felt...a gap in the trees, veered left, and found herself in a clearing where a derelict house sat, dark and empty.

She ran past, into the woods behind it, stumbling on underbrush and fallen branches. But still she ran and ran. And ran. Her lungs were screaming for air and her legs were on fire with pain, but she ran on, certain if Victor was behind her, she could outlast him on foot. And with the noise of the train finally leaving the air still and calm, she could hear that no one was behind her.

When she reached the edge of a deep ravine, she decided to rest. Picked her way down to the bottom and found a good spot to tuck in among a pile of boulders.

She stayed there until the faint light long before

sunrise gave her a good glimpse of her surroundings. Victor or one of his henchmen would be trying to find her soon, and while hiding among the rocks worked well in the dark, daylight would expose her, so she needed to move now. Right now.

She was working her way up the side of the ravine when an idea came to her. Could she get up a tree? Up high in the branches where they'd never see her? Never even think to look? She loved climbing trees as a kid, just hanging out up there, watching the world go by or her mom looking for her.

Kate searched for just the right tree, and it took every ounce of her strength to get up among the highest possible branches. That's when the stinging pain in her middle warned her to check out her wounds. None were overly deep, but a few still oozed blood. She pressed the decimated shirt against her skin to make it stop, and hummed her way through the worst of the pain.

Thankful for the watch on her wrist, she counted off the passing hours until she heard a noise and sucked in a hard breath. The crunching of twigs grew closer and she hoped she was up far enough to be hidden, was thankful she wasn't wearing bright clothing.

Someone was on the far side of the ravine.

She crouched down among the branches, waiting, waiting, hoping whoever it was wouldn't look up. And then a black bear ambled past the bottom of her tree.

She clamped her jaw on the slightly hysterical laugh bubbling up her throat. Didn't need the bear's attention any more than she needed Victor's.

Two hours later she was so cramped and sore her

muscles were spasming, and her head was pounding so hard she started to wonder how smart this idea was. She tried her old mantra to help her cope, but *fiddlesticks* just didn't seem to have any impact on her uncomfortable situation.

It was nearly noon when Victor and another man came by. They went down into the ravine where she'd spent the night tucked among the boulders, and she was bone-meltingly relieved she hadn't stayed there. Then they walked the top of the ridge looking under bushes. Suddenly the stranger said, "Wait, I hear something." They went very still and quiet.

Kate held her breath and prayed, searching the forest floor below her, and she had to choke back a laugh when she spotted the bear. She waited, hoping, and before too long she heard the sound of panicked men racing out of the forest.

"Good on you, bear," she whispered to the wind. "And thanks."

Kate spent the rest of the day wishing for the darkness of night and contemplating her next move. She could hear the trains passing, but they always seemed to be going very fast, and there would be little chance of flagging one down.

She didn't dare to go to the highway, because Victor was bound to have someone patrolling, watching for her. The only safe time to travel was at night, and the best course would be to follow the train tracks. Eventually they would lead to civilization.

Climbing down from the tree was extremely difficult, and when she reached the ground she leaned heavily against the trunk until she could get her bearings and balance. Her legs were heavy, but she took a deep breath and started out in the direction of the tracks, always alert for the sound of water, because thirst had been dogging her for hours, and she knew dehydration was as nasty a foe as Victor.

When she reached the tracks she went left, certain from watching the path of the sun during day that she was pointed south—which meant she was headed in the general direction of Vancouver, or the US border, depending on where the hell she was.

At three o'clock in the morning, exhausted, with her knife wounds on fire and her head feeling like it might explode, she finally found water. Dropping down beside the tiny creek and using an old beer can she'd come across, Kate drank and drank and drank.

She had hope now.

After a while she moved to a wide rock, where she sat and rested for a bit before pushing on. When she started looking for a tree to climb at sunup, she had a terrible time finding one suitable. The trunks were either very wide with no low branches for climbing, or too thin to support her, so she kept walking.

The sun was fully in the sky before she found a tree she could hide in, shoved the can of water into the front of her pants, and climbed to a safe perch. The day was incredibly long, and she had to work hard to stay awake and not plummet to the ground.

On the third night, she had to cross a large railway bridge on the outskirts of a small town, waiting until about two o'clock in the morning before there was an opportunity to cross without being picked out by headlights from a nearby highway.

It took Kate a week to reach a railyard at the edge of a large city, and she was staring at the bright lights when a yellow car suddenly appeared. *Security*, was printed in bold, black letters on the door.

Kate's heartbeat echoed in her ears while she waited, and a very young officer got out of the car.

"You're on private property."

"I'm sorry, I must have lost my way," she mumbled and he shone his flashlight into her eyes and blinded her momentarily.

The beam played over the rest of her and she saw shock on his face. She must look like hell, dirty, beaten, her coat all sliced up, bloodstained…

He activated the mic on his collar and said some numbers into it, then asked her if she would like to sit in his car for a minute. She couldn't think of an answer, and he led her by the arm to the passenger door, where she sat on the front seat with her eyes closed and legs still stuck out the door.

"I'm going to call an ambulance for you," he said, and Kate's mind clicked back on.

"No."

"But you need help. There's blood."

"It's old. I'm fine."

He shook his head. "You don't look fine."

She took a deep breath. "Look. The guy I'm running from is connected, if you know what I mean. What I could really use is a ride to a women's shelter, somewhere I can be safe until I can regroup."

He studied her like a bug under glass for a minute, then pulled out his cell phone and made a call. Then another, but this time got out of the car to talk, and Kate got ready to run. She could go back the way she'd come, get lost in the forest, find a house, steal…

The young man got back in the car. "There's a place you can go, but I can't send you in a cab because the address is secret. Someone is going to come and get you in just a bit, okay?"

It sounded too good to be true.

"How do you know about the place?"

"Part of my training. They give us some special numbers we can call when people need protection. There's kind of a network you have to get connected into. Like you phone one number and they give you another, then someone calls you back."

Sounded plausible, and Kate was desperate. If it turned out to be a trick and she was being delivered to Victor, she'd just find another way to escape. Or would it be better to contact the police here and now? If only she still had a number for Meyers.

"You got data on that phone?"

"Yep."

"Maybe you could get a contact number for Meyers Security. They would help me too."

"Look, if you don't go to the safe place, I really do have to call the police. I can't stretch the rules too far."

"Please," she begged. "Just a quick Google search so I can call them later?"

He sighed. "Miers, right?"

"That's it."

He keyed it into his phone. "Nope, nothing."

They must be secret, not available to the web. "Wait, there's another. J.K. Investigations."

"Headlights," he said, pointing to the security gate along the way. "That will be your ride." He put the car in gear and took her to meet the person tasked with getting her to a safe place. Or at least that was what Kate chose to believe. For now.

The people at the shelter were so kind, and a doctor came to treat her wounds, check her out. He hooked her up to an IV, and once two bags of fluid had run into her veins Kate was feeling much, much stronger.

She had been there for two days when she gave in and tried to call Jason. She googled the number for his company, but when she called she got a recording that the number was not in service and that horrified her. What if something had happened to him? What if he, like the others, was dead?

She was on her own. Didn't dare even call Jenny, because what if that pointed Victor her way too?

Kate talked to the staff at the shelter about making a run for it to Alberta, and a plan was set in place. Getting a bus out of Vancouver would be a risk, so instead a volunteer would drive her to a town called Kamloops, three and a half hours away. From there she could get a bus to Calgary. They gave her money and personal items for the trip, and wished her well.

Kate was still a bit numb when they reached Kamloops. Not being able to reach Jason when she decided it was time was a game-changer. She was truly on her own now.

She thanked her driver profusely and walked into the bus station. Went straight to the ladies' room and stared at herself in the mirror. She didn't look all scary and gaunt anymore, and maybe out here in the wilds of British Columbia she could find some work after a while. But first a place to stay.

Motels turned out to be higher priced than she'd expected, and her funds wouldn't last long, so she put in a call to her attorney to get more money, but he didn't answer. She looked at the clock and called herself an idiot. The time change made it well past business hours in the east. She'd have to wait and call him on Monday.

With the weekend stretching in front of her, she grabbed a book from a shelf in the lobby and curled up in her room, trying to get lost in a story to keep thoughts of Jason and Victor at bay, but it didn't work.

She thumbed through the magazines about the area, and stumbled across an ad for a livestock auction which was going on the next day. A perfect place to look for a job.

She caught a bus partway, then walked the rest. The parking lot was teeming with stock trailers, and just inside the main door she found bulletin boards covered with colorful papers advertising everything from horses and ropes to rabbits, dude ranches, and stud managers.

A girl standing close by asked if she was looking for a horse to buy, and Kate said, "No, I need work." She shook her head. "I've got lots of experience, but every ad says I need to have my own transportation."

"My cousin needs farm help, and there's a room in the barn you might be able to live in."

Kate turned to the girl. "Is your cousin here? Could I meet him?"

"Her. And she's just over there. Come on."

Kate rode out to the farm with Alison and Pam. She was shown the room in the barn, and gladly accepted the job. She wouldn't make a whole lot of money, but for a while she could be safe. She explained about her abusive ex, and they assured her they would tell no one she was there.

———

Jason was halfway between Toronto and home when his cell signaled an incoming from Meyers Security. He quickly pulled to the shoulder. "Clear," he said, which meant he was in a secure location and able to speak freely.

"Good news, bad news," said Quinn Meyers.

"She's alive." In his gut—hell, his heart—he *knew* she was alive, but he still needed to hear it.

"Yep."

Relief brought an easing of worry, a lightness rapidly tromped on by the trepidation marching up his spine. "What's the bad news?"

"We don't know where she is."

Fuck. He should be used to this by now, because whenever they managed to get a lead on her, she was gone before they got there. But this time, dammit, this time would be different, because that, too, he knew in his gut.

"Tell me what you know. All of it." Because as good as the Meyers agents were, Jason was the one who understood her. Was most likely to predict her behavior accurately. Maybe his insights hadn't helped so far, but still.

"She was picked up in West Vancouver some time ago. The private security company patrolling a rail yard found her walking the tracks. She was mildly hypothermic, seriously dehydrated, and possibly delirious. When questioned, she said she was running from an ex-husband. She convinced the guard to help her get to a battered women's shelter without notifying any authorities.

"Before the ride came they tried to get a contact number for Meyers, and also tried to reach you through your website.

"This same guy was approached by Victor last week, looking for Kate. Rubbed the guy the wrong way, and he thought about when they were trying to reach Meyers and tried again, this time with various spellings, and came up with us. Called me this morning."

Months ago. Fuck.

"Funny thing, they got a not-in-service message when she tried to call you. That was when your system got hacked and we were certain it was Victor."

"He was making sure she couldn't reach me. He knew way more than we thought, dammit."

"How long ago?"

"One week after Victor grabbed her."

"What the hell? We had her ID posted in every conceivable system, and they missed it?"

"Private security, women's rescue-type shelter. They wouldn't be privy to the postings. And their focus is on keeping domestic violence victims safe. Hence she slid beneath the radar."

"This is bullshit." But he understood. Had been hired by victims trying to escape abusive relationships. Applauded the people who went to such lengths to protect those trying to have a new, better, safer life.

Jason rapped the heel of his hand against the side

of his head a couple of times. "Okay, then what happened?"

"I did a video conference call with the safe house group, and they finally told me they took her as far as Kamloops, where she planned to get on a bus to Calgary."

"But Calgary is one of the places Meyers has eyes on the bus station, right?"

"Affirmative. She never arrived there."

Jason glanced at his watch. "I'm an hour from the airport."

"Take your time. We've got you a seat on the next commercial flight, red-eye out of Toronto, which puts you in Vancouver at six tomorrow morning. Angie will meet you there with the Steed."

Having a skilled pilot and the high-speed, high-tech helicopter at his disposal would be worth the wait. Not like he had a choice. If Meyers said this was the best alternative, he would just have to sit tight for twelve long hours. But... "There wasn't a flight out of Ottawa or Hamilton?"

"Nothing. Even sending Angie to you now in one of the jets would only make an hour's difference, and then you wouldn't have the helicopter at the other end."

Good point.

"And," said Eve, "by the time you land, we should have a better handle on where to start the search."

"She'll be rural. Working on a farm or ranch. Horses are what she knows."

———

Riding the western perimeter road to check on

fences, Kate was enjoying the squeak of dry snow under her horse's feet, the puffs of steam from his nostrils, his sweet scent mixed with that of the pine trees, and the glorious sparkle of ice crystals in the air.

She looked forward to this ride every Monday, even though it was mostly to check for damage from weekend hunters—or poachers—stirring up wildlife. Spooked elk and moose could take out a wide swath of fencing, but today all was well.

She could have turned back, but decided to ride all the way to the far end of the field, hoping to spot a deer. She'd seen several black-tailed does at the edge of the pines the first time she made this ride, but none recently.

About twenty feet from the end of the pasture Kate decided there was no game to be seen, and it was getting too cold to linger, even with the added warmth of the crazy outfit she wore.

The outer layers belonged to a bull rider—an old boyfriend the girls ran off the ranch some years back—and the rest came from the local thrift store. The jacket, flak vest, and chaps were about three sizes too big, but she layered up under them with sweaters, sweats, and leggings.

The first time she tried the outfit, the girls said she looked like she was bubble-wrapped. They had a good laugh, and, aside from being a bit awkward for mounting, Kate found the peculiar outfit kept her warm for longer than anything else she'd tried, so it was a win.

But it was getting late and time to return.

She nudged the horse into a right turn to get them pointed toward the warmth of the barn and home.

And was suddenly jerked from the saddle.

Flying backward through the air, she heard the gunfire booming and echoing through the valley and her horse made a mighty leap forward.

She hit the ground in a heap, somehow face-down in the snow.

Years of falls had taught her to stay still and take inventory before trying to get up, so luckily she hadn't moved yet when she heard the sound of a vehicle.

Horrendous, dull pain in her chest made breathing hurt to the point that she was trying not to inhale at all, and then her brain kicked into over-drive. Gunshot. Hunters. Then, hard on the heels of that, *Victor*.

She didn't move a muscle. Heard men's voices, and then three things happened simultaneously. This time the hard blast to her body came at the same time as the gunshot and the sound of gallop-ing hooves on hard ground.

The engine sound faded away. Were they gone? Or waiting? Watching to see if she got up? The only cover was the pines, and she'd have to wade across the field of ass-deep snow to get to them.

Home was acres of open pasture and two hills away, and someone could be waiting over the first rise, or the next one, to pick her off. And maybe this time they wouldn't hit the flak jacket under the big winter coat.

She was crazy lucky that bull rider vests had thin layer of Kevlar to prevent a bull from goring a rider—the same stuff used in some bulletproof vests. The girls had jokingly said it would protect her from angry bulls and nearsighted hunters. Little had they known their theory would be tested.

While she lay there on the frigid ground she thought about Jason, and Jenny, and The Princess. The horse she'd been on today was nothing like the fiery mare. He was a plodder, but reliable, and she could only hope Alison or Pam would spot him as soon as they got home. The barn doors were closed, so he should be hanging around the outside, waiting to get in for his supper.

And, lucky for Kate, they had a rule about leaving a note before she rode off, so they would know what area she was riding, just in case. Kate had thought their overly cautious rules endearing, but now she was just damn glad, and nearly frozen solid when Alison rolled up on a four-wheeler, jumped off, and crouched at her side.

Kate stayed very still, and whispered, "Someone could be watching, and I need them to believe I'm dead. Stick your hand under my throat like you're looking for a pulse."

"What the fuck?" She ripped off a glove, and her hand connected with Kate's skin.

While Alison did as she was told Kate said, "You're going to turn me over and look again for a pulse, then act like I'm dead and load me into the back of the machine. When you get to the house, put me in the bed of the pickup and drive me to the hospital, but when you're halfway to town, call the cops to meet you there because someone has been shot."

Kate didn't know the science, wasn't sure if rigor should have set in yet, but betting Victor didn't either, she was stuck with looking limp and lifeless, eyes wide open, and feeling bad while Alison struggled to lift her.

The ride over frozen rutted ground was painful, but Kate maintained, and was eventually hauled into the back of the pickup.

Town was thirty minutes away, and Kate had trouble resisting the need to move, to get into a less awkward position, but with the enemy out there somewhere, she maintained. Sprawled on her back.

The two police officers and emergency room staff joining Alison and Pam to lean over the edge of the pickup to stare at Kate contributed to the blinding mix of chaotic energy she was swimming in. Emotional responses ranged from fear and impatience to anger and disbelief while Alison quickly and quietly explained the situation.

"And we were followed the whole way here. Headlights suggest a pickup, but it was too far back for me to tell for sure. When I pulled in here, it hung back. Didn't drive past. Not sure exactly where it is now."

A nurse appeared in the doorway with a gurney, and the two officers unceremoniously dragged Kate onto the tailgate and then heaved her limp body onto the gurney for the nurse to wheel through the doorway into the emergency ward, not stopping until she reached a small examination room. A doctor and the two officers followed and carefully closed the door before anyone spoke.

"It's okay, you're safe now. We're here to help you." Kate wasn't certain who the speaker was. The only thing she knew for sure was the gender. Male.

"C-c-c-cold. C-can't see." Kate's voice was scratchy and barely audible at first.

The person leaned over her and gently touched her face. "At all?"

"B-blurry since k-keeping them open on the back of the quad. W-wanted to make sure I looked d-dead," she said through chattering teeth while the clothes were stripped from her and replaced with warm blankets.

Her eyes were examined and some kind of drops put in. The burn was like liquid fire, and she gritted her teeth and wiggled her feet frantically while waiting for the pain to ease, and when it finally did, she let out a long, slow breath.

"That was fun," she said in a voice suddenly deeper than it had been a minute earlier, and a nurse—she presumed—put a straw to her lips and told her to take slow sips.

"Can you tell us exactly what happened?" asked a man at the foot of the bed.

"You're law enforcement?" she rasped.

"RCMP. Sergeant Baker, and Corporal Duncan is with me."

"Lisa," said the female shape beside him.

Kate told her story, beginning to end, and then begged them help her escape again. She explained the ideas she had come up with while playing dead for hours, and they agreed to help her with at least some of them. The male officer used his radio to call for the coroner, and the female used a hospital landline to contact a pilot friend and make the rest of the arrangements.

The doctor checked her over and decided that, aside from major bruising, she was in pretty good shape. Photos of her fully dressed had been taken when she arrived, and as soon as they stripped the clothing off of her, the police bagged her parka and flak jacket with the bullet holes and burns to hold onto for evidence, and that's when the coroner arrived.

He entered the room with stretcher and body bag in tow, completely unaware of the setup. When he saw Kate sitting on the edge of the bed, he apologized and started to back out, but the doctor quickly stopped him. They closed the door, and Kate, whose vision was already improving, explained the plan to him. He smiled and said he had never done much acting before, but was glad to help catch the bad guys, then left to get his paperwork completed.

Lisa, the female police officer, came back into the room at that point, and things happened quickly. She informed Kate they had modified her plan just a little. She dropped a set of scrubs on the end of the bed and stripped out of her uniform. Put on the scrubs.

"You put on the uniform," she said.

When Kate pulled on the pants, she felt a lump in the pocket, and dug out a wallet. Held it out to Lisa, who said, "We don't exactly look like sisters, but just in case this plan backfires, my ID and credit cards could be the help you need. Use them any way you have to, and send them back to me by courier someday."

Kate was stunned. She stared at a total stranger sticking her neck out in a major way for someone she had just met. A single tear ran down her cheek. "Why?"

"Let's just say I believe you. And I can't imagine being in your shoes. And if you won't let us protect you here, maybe this will help."

Kate wrote down her lawyer's phone number and explained that he would reimburse Lisa for everything. Then she wrote the name Meyers Security. "Please call them and let them know everything that's happened. They'll need to know if you have Victor, or, if not, at least that he was here."

"Any other messages?"

"Just that I'll be home as soon as it's safe, and—"

The door swung open, and the sergeant came back in with the coroner. They helped Lisa get into the body bag on the stretcher, and something inside Kate snapped. "No. Stop. Wait. He'll kill you." She grabbed Lisa's hand and swung on the two men.

"Fake it. Use a bunch of sheets or something instead. Please!"

Lisa took a firm hold of Kate's arms. "This is what I do. I'm a cop. I'm wearing full body armor, and I've got another vest to protect my head, see? And we know, based on what happened to you, that he's using tame ammunition, so our armor will do an even better job than yours did."

The sergeant lowered the other vest over Lisa's head, and she said, "Everything will be fine. Rick will get you safely away from here, then they'll roll me out, and there will be dozens of officers ready to grab your Victor. Trust us, okay?"

Kate swallowed hard and blinked back her tears. She nodded, and the sergeant—Rick—gently but firmly pulled her away from Lisa.

Once he had Kate's full attention, he said, "Here's the plan. We're going to hurry out to the cruiser like we've had a call. When we head through the doors to the parking lot, put your hand up, pretend you're squeezing the button on your microphone, and then duck your head and talk into it. That will hide your face a little more than the hat already does."

Kate did as she was told, and their departure was swift and silent. Within just a couple of minutes they were speeding away from the hospital with lights and siren going while Kate said a silent prayer for Lisa's safety.

Rick filled the short drive to the airport with questions about Victor, and in minutes he was driving through the security gates and right out to a small airplane sitting on the tarmac.

The pilot was a friend of Lisa's and she he was going to fly Kate to Vancouver.

Rick shook her hand, wished her luck, and she jumped out of the car and ran the few steps to the plane.

CHAPTER 16

December 2017

KATE LANDED IN VANCOUVER JUST shy of six am, and hit the ground running. Hopped on a shuttle to get her from the south terminal, where the small planes came in, to the main terminal for a flight to the US.

"What airline, ma'am?"

"Ugh. Well, I'm not sure yet. Ticket was being bought while I was en route, and my battery has died."

"Where ya headed?"

Shit. Hmm. Say something, anything. "Chicago."

"US Departures, Level three. But I need to swing through arrivals first to pick up someone who's been waiting awhile. You could get out there and just scoot up the escalator since you have no luggage."

"That works. Thanks."

When she hustled through the busy exit, she homed in on the first flight status board she saw to find out what was leaving next. She'd buy a ticket on the first one available.

Her stomach twisted. Top of the board was a

Toronto flight.

Should she? Did she dare?

No. She couldn't put Jenny and her family at risk. Something Victor had said to her the last time they were together on a racetrack echoed in the back of her mind. They'd been in the winner's circle, and, after an enthusiastic hug from Jenny, Kate had turned to say something to Victor. He said, "I didn't know you had a sister."

"Jenny's just a friend, but as close as I've got to a sister."

"Good to know. Not much a person wouldn't do to keep their family safe, is there?"

That moment was a huge part of what drove Kate away from Toronto. Hoping distance from them would keep Victor from targeting those she loved.

No, she couldn't go to Toronto. Not until she knew Victor was in jail. That's when she realized the board she was looking at was arrivals, and the Toronto flight she was looking at was due to land in twenty minutes, not take off.

She hustled to the escalator and rode up to the departure level, found a status board. At the top was a flight to Las Vegas leaving in thirty minutes. That would do.

With Lisa's uniform and ID, plus a story about picking up a prisoner in Vegas, Kate was able to quickly purchase a ticket, breeze through security, and clear customs with enough time left to stop at an ATM and put five hundred cash in her pocket—thanks to the officer's bank card.

Jason deplaned quickly and grabbed a shuttle to the south terminal, where Angie would be waiting with the Steed. Used to be he loved any chance to ride that amazing bird, but today he just wanted to get to wherever Kate was as fast as he could.

He hopped on board the chopper and, without even a hello, Angie shoved a black helmet at him, saying, "On. Now."

While she flicked switches and did all the complicated things it took to get the sleek black helicopter off the ground, excitement built. They had to be hot on Kate's trail, but he didn't dare ask Angie what was up. Not until they were out of the crowded airspace.

He watched seconds and minutes tick by on the digital clock, and eight minutes went by before she finally spoke. "A call just came in to HQ from the RCMP in Kamloops. They have Victor."

"Great." And it was, but he'd been hoping Angie's excitement was because they found Kate.

"When Eve asked them why Meyers was being notified, they would only say they got a tip that we would want to know. They asked us to send someone right away."

His smile grew. "Has to be Kate. She must be there." But why hadn't she called? Was she hurt?

"Eve asked if their tipster was Kate, and they confirmed. Said she wanted Meyers to know she is okay, and would be home as soon as Victor was caught."

"Which he is." Hope bloomed.

"Apparently she left before the capture."
Fuck.

———

Kate worked out a plan, which she then executed with the same kind of confidence she had when dealing with a powerful horse. Believing what she was doing would work was key.

Using Lisa's ID and credit cards, she rented a car, went to a big discount store to buy a carry-on-sized bag—motels frowned upon women with no luggage—and filled it with the bare essentials. She did a cash from credit withdrawal for a thousand dollars, then bundled up all Lisa's things and sent them to her by courier.

With almost fifteen hundred dollars and a car, she should be good until news of Victor's arrest showed up on the internet. But just in case he had partners or anyone else still out searching for her, she kept moving.

By noon she was headed south. She tried to do touristy things along the way, but failed miserably. It was dinnertime when she cruised into Phoenix, but she wasn't hungry, nor did she feel like stopping for the night, so she kept on with her plan, and was soon on Interstate 10 headed west.

Twelve hours after landing in Vegas, she parked in the long-term lot at LAX and hopped on the shuttle for a prestigious Los Angeles hotel. There she used the guest computer in the lobby to access the internet. Found nothing about Victor's arrest, so located a cheap motel close to a library and used public transit to get there.

Two days later, when there was still no word of Victor's arrest, she could no longer assume she was safe. He must have gotten away. She took a bus to the John Wayne Airport and used a pay phone to call her attorney, because she would need more money if she had to stay in hiding, and getting jobs hadn't worked well so far. But not only was there no answer, the voicemail box was full.

A sudden prickling at the back of Kate's neck set her into action again. Something definitely off there. What if something had happened to him? Something being Victor...

Time for another change.

Kate got her hair bleached blond and cut very short again. Then she made her way to a strip of motels just off of Interstate 5. They were the cheap but clean type meant to attract people passing through the area. She paid for three days in advance, explaining that she was meeting her sister here and they were driving to San Francisco together. She asked the desk clerk if there was a library close by, was pleased to find one just a short bus ride away, and was able to access the internet.

Kate searched the Kamloops TV station and newspapers first, then all Canadian news sites, but found no mention of Victor's arrest. Nothing at all, in fact.

She continued calling Dan's office, but to no avail. She called information for a new listing just in case he had moved, because, heck, she'd been gone for over a year. But there was nothing.

She changed motels every three days, and each day, when she was at the library hoping for news, she also researched other things, like hostels, women's shelters, thrift stores, and the Canadian Embassy.

When her money was almost all gone, she bought a three-dollar knapsack at a thrift store, packed in her meager belongings, put the last of her cash in the pocket sewn into her panties, and disappeared into the streets of Los Angeles.

First she stayed in hostels, and while watching an older woman sitting in a corner talking to herself, she realized it was the perfect way to keep people at bay. And when someone was too persistent, she only had to yell, "Quit touching me!" for people to avoid her like the plague.

For the next few weeks she was an avid student of human nature. She studied both the interactions and the avoidance tactics of others, realizing she could learn as much about people as she had about horses by quietly observing their behavior.

When the money finally ran out—except for her emergency five-dollar bill—she headed for a women's shelter. Walked past, hesitating at the doorway for just a moment, and then went on by. She saw a lineup for a soup kitchen on the corner and looked away. She didn't want to do that. Didn't want to see anyone so helpless.

She crossed the street and kept walking, circling, learning her surroundings. By evening she would have go to the shelter. No way could she stay on these streets after dark.

The next time she stopped in the doorway, a gray-haired woman at a desk inside said, rather firmly, "We fill up quickly, so if you want a bed, you'd better make up your mind."

Without a word, Kate went in. Was handed

a form to fill out, which she did quickly with a made-up name and next of kin. Kate didn't think who she was or wasn't would matter to anyone here. She was led to a large room with mattresses lined up on the floor and handed a blanket and a face cloth.

She looked around at the strange collection of women, mostly old. She counted the beds. There were twenty-eight. She counted the women. There were seven beds left. Kate lay down and covered her head with the blanket.

It was hard to believe Victor had driven her this far down.

Over the next few weeks Kate learned what it meant to survive by a thread. She struggled with her loss of control every day, refusing to give in and line up at the soup kitchen for free food. Instead she waited until they were about to close and then slipped in for last-minute leftovers.

Every morning she walked for two hours to a library where she could check for news of Victor. And then she walked back to the shelter.

She passed a small diner on her journey, and after nearly a week, she stopped and asked if she could wash dishes in exchange for food. The old woman behind the counter looked at her thinness and agreed.

Every day Kate stopped on her way back from the library, washed the morning dishes, then left with a huge sandwich in her hand. And it was enough to sustain her. She didn't have to go back to the soup kitchen anymore, and she could continue to silently shake her head at the volunteers offering to help her "get back on her feet." They were kind, and meant well, but she had a destination, a home to eventually go to, or at least a place. Others needed the help far more than she did.

For weeks Kate's routine never varied, and she kept to herself. In the beginning she took in everything, and found herself worrying about some of the women, wondering what would happen to them. Kate would eventually go home, but what about them? Did they have family somewhere? Did anyone in this world care where they were? Was their homelessness a life sentence, or a choice?

Mental illness was clearly the common thread, but some, she suspected, had run away from their pasts, barely escaped with their lives. And Kate soon learned that it was easier to ignore the odor of an unclean body than the pain in their eyes.

She often wanted to reach out, comfort a human just as she would a sad-looking animal, but she never did. Personal space was all any of them had left, something no one dared encroach on. As small as the mattresses were, each one had a very large, invisible barricade around it.

And Kate's sleeping place was no different. It was where she crawled so far inside herself that sometimes she didn't even notice if someone spoke to her. She eventually cared less and less about everything, including herself. Even sleep didn't help her anymore, and had become as elusive as her ability to concentrate. She moved through her day in a state of halfness. Half there, half nowhere. Lucid thoughts were becoming less frequent, and she followed patterns with very little deviation.

Every day, during her long walk to the library, her thoughts were like a mantra. *This could be the day. Today could be the day.*

Yet, when the day finally happened, when she spotted what she'd been hoping to see for months, she experienced no emotions whatsoever. Stared numbly at a photo of Victor under the headline, "Smuggling kingpin charged on three continents." The story went on to say that, in total, there had been forty-seven people in six different countries arrested over the past few days on various charges. Victor had been in custody and held without bail on an attempted murder charge since his arrest last December in Kamloops.

Kate looked at the day's date on the article. February 17, 2018. She had been safe from Victor for a very long time. She tried to count the weeks and gave up, somewhat certain that it was more than eight.

The only thought which stood out clearly in her mind was that after the fancy detectives and agencies had failed for nearly two years, the little town of Kamloops scooped the bastard up with nothing more than a decoy in the coroner's wagon.

She walked back to the shelter as usual, stopping at the diner to wash dishes. She asked the old woman if she could spare a few dollars instead of a sandwich today, and was given a scowl. Kate explained that she had to go home and needed bus fare. The woman nodded and handed her six dollars. Kate thanked her and left quickly.

She couldn't believe it was over. She was so tired of running.

When she got back to the shelter, Kate lay down on her mattress and stared up at the ceiling, wondering if she could ever be normal again. She couldn't remember what normal was.

With a knot growing in her chest, she rubbed the place on her thigh where Jason's cell phone used to press against her while it waited in her pocket, and she started to cry. She rolled over and hugged the blanket to her stomach while she silently sobbed out her sorrow for what was gone. She wept for Tanner, and Leo, and Jason. She cried for the loss of her innocence, her assumption that the world was as it seemed.

She didn't know if she could ever learn to trust again.

Katie cried until she had no tears left and could feel nothing but emptiness. She was so very tired of being alone.

When she woke up hours later, it took a while to remember why she felt different, and her belly was emptier than usual. All stuffed up and her blanket soggy from crying, she went to the bathroom to clean up, and stood in front of the mirror asking herself what she should do.

She could quit running and go home...if she had one to go to. She felt the tears start to sting her eyes again and stared at her herself until she got a grip... scolded the woman in front of her.

"You look like you've been kicked to the curb one too many times." She studied the hollow blackness under her eyes and the jawbone jutting out under her ears—like back in her rider days. Collarbone, ribs, and hipbones poked at the inside of her sun-beaten skin, and knobby knees made her legs look misshapen.

Leo's voice echoed somewhere in the back of her mind, "If you were a horse, I'd take you for a walk in the sun and let you eat some green grass."

She swallowed the self-pity and dug for some courage. "In the morning I will take my life back, and I promise to only look forward."

She went back to lie on the thin mattress one last time, staring up at the ceiling. Every now and then a single tear escaped, but was quickly swiped away.

The next morning Kate looked the gray-haired woman behind the desk right in the eye and spoke clearly, "I won't be back today." The woman merely nodded, and Kate walked out the door to begin her journey to the airport.

Four hours later she was standing just inside the international departure terminal, wondering what to do next. She looked at the board and saw there were no Toronto flights leaving in the next few hours.

She watched people being hugged by friends and family. Happy faces and sad ones swam past her.

Kate used to have people, too. Friends.

She stared at a bank of pay phones. She had less than a dollar left.

Kate dialed the operator, asked to make a collect call, and then closed her eyes while she waited for a voice on the other end.

"Yes!" said Jenny when the operator asked if she would accept a collect call, then, "Katie? Katie, where are you? Please don't hang up, Katie! Talk to me. *Please say something!*"

Kate almost didn't recognize the feeling of the smile spreading across her face. "I would if you'd shut up and give me a chance."

"Oh, God, Katie, *please* come home. It's over."

"I know."

"So come home, Katie."

Kate swallowed, "I need your help, Jen."

"Name it. What do you need? What can I do?"

Kate's voice was quietly apologetic, "I don't have plane fare."

"What airline? I'll phone and buy you a ticket right now, but where are you, for heaven's sake?"

"Los Angeles. LAX."

"Honey, give me a number to call you back, and *promise* me you'll still be there when I do."

"I'm at a pay phone, Jen, at the airport."

"What's the number on it?"

She looked it over. "There isn't one."

"Okay, don't move. Just wait for ten minutes and call me back."

Kate hung up and watched the clock. She waited for twelve minutes and placed another collect call.

"Katie, I can't get you a direct flight until tomorrow morning. Will you be okay till then? Or do you want to try a route with a stopover?"

"Morning will be fine, Jen."

"Are you near the ticket counter? I need you to go there so they can give it to you when I call them back."

She looked around and recognized the name of the Canadian airline on a sign. "I'll go there now."

A young, uniformed man was on the phone, watching her approach for a moment, then looking past her. Kate stopped in front of him and waited. He continued to look past her, then said into the phone, "I'm sorry but I don't see her yet. Could I put you on hold for just a minute?"

He put down the phone and looked at Kate. "Ah, can I help you?"

"You have a ticket for me."

He looked surprised and asked her name, then, obviously startled by her answer, he picked up the phone. "Yes, ma'am, she's here. Yes, ma'am." And he passed the phone to Kate.

"Katie?"

"Jen."

"Katie, you have a ticket for tomorrow morning, and I was wondering... I mean... Is it okay...? I can get a flight out of here tonight and meet you at the airport."

"Why, Jen?"

"Katie, don't take this wrong, but you sound awful. I would really like to come and fly home with you. I promise not to ask any questions or bug you, but..."

"But what, Jen?"

"But I'm afraid you'll panic and somehow not get here. There. I said it, and I'm not sorry."

"You are such a worrywart, Jennifer. But I wouldn't mind it a bit if you came to fly home with..." Her voice faded away. And she turned her back to the young man at the desk.

"What's wrong, Katie? Are you okay?"

"I don't have a home anymore."

"You have one with us until such time as you are driven out by my noisy children. I will have the spare room ready for you just as soon as I can get Caly off the bed."

Kate smiled again, and she recognized it this time. "We can share. Trust me, I won't need a whole lot of space."

There was an odd beeping noise on the phone, and Jen said, "Katie, that's someone calling, probably one of Jim's owners, so I have to go."

Jen promised to see her the next morning at the airport.

When Kate hung up, for the first time in forever she was warm inside. She was going home.

CHAPTER 17

February 2018

JASON LANDED AT LAX JUST before ten, and when he stepped off the jetway, the first person he saw was Kate, sitting in the departure lounge less than twenty feet in front of him…and if he hadn't known her back in her riding days, recognition might have taken a helluva lot longer.

Without taking his eyes off her, he made the promised call. "I've got her. I'll call you back." He clicked off in the midst of Jenny's questions. Couldn't deal with anything but what was right in front of him.

She was pale in spite of a deep tan. Her eyes dull, and surrounded by shadows. Long arms and legs stuck out of beat-up shorts and a thin tank, and her hair was short…and white.

He swallowed hard. This was not going to be the reunion he'd pictured while fighting Jenny over who should fly down and bring Kate home.

The woman he was desperate to yell at and demand answers from wasn't here. Neither was the one he hoped to sweep up into his arms and declare undying love to, the woman he had planned to keep in his bed for at least a week.

All the thoughts he had and the plans he made on the long flight went right out the window. He crouched in front of her, and when she started to jump up he clamped his hands on her knees to hold her in place.

"Katie."

Her eyes locked with his, and she blinked twice, then breathed out a single word, "Jason."

She touched his face, and he took her hand, drew her up and right into his arms, held on, savoring the feel of her, celebrating the end of a long, hard fight to get her back.

Kate burrowed against him, silent, still, with her arms curled up between them and her face tucked into his throat.

After a minute he leaned back so he could see her face. "You okay?"

Was she? Kate wasn't sure.

All she knew for certain was that she was safe now. Victor was locked up, and Jason was here to take her home. She could stop running. Stop hiding. Stop being in control for just a little while. Instead, she would allow herself to lean. She closed her eyes and sort of drifted. Safe.

"Kate?"

His voice registered. Low, smooth, but then there was an announcement blaring. Time to go. Get on the plane. She opened her eyes and held up the ticket she'd been so afraid of losing. "Time to go home."

"Not yet. We're going to a hotel and get you checked out first, then we can fly out together tomorrow." He took the ticket from her hand. "You won't be needing this."

"But…"

He led her to the counter and said, "I'm afraid we have a problem. Kate is too ill to fly."

"Oh, but…" The agent's voice trailed off when she looked at Kate, and something like pity flickered in her eyes. Kate stared at the floor.

She cleared her throat. "Thank you. There is someone on standby who will be very grateful. It will just take me a minute."

While they waited, Jason handed Kate a half bottle of water from the case at his feet, and she took a sip. Another, and as her parched throat eased, she drank the rest.

"The ticket has been cancelled, and the account credited with the full amount, minus booking fee. Kate?"

Kate looked at her, and she smiled. "You have a year to use the credit."

They were soon out in the bright sunshine, climbing into a cab which Jason directed to an airport hotel. Then he handed Kate a bottle of juice and made a phone call.

"It's on speaker," he said.

Jenny's voice filled the cab. "Jason, don't you dare hang up on me again. Where's Kate? Is she okay?"

"I'm here, Jen." She took another small swallow of the juice she wanted to inhale in one gulp. But she knew better.

"Are you okay?"

Jason answered for her, and she was grateful.

"She's been through hell, but she'll be okay. Just needs a good night's sleep and a couple of solid meals." The understatement of the year.

"I want to hear it from her."

"Jen, I'm okay. Just tired and hungry." Jenny had been there for her. Had bought her a ticket home, no questions asked. "Thank you for being the best friend ever."

"You start talking sappy and you'll be scaring me."

Something like a rusty laugh came out of Kate, along with words she'd said a million times over the years, "You're such an idiot."

"Jason," said Jenny. "Take care of her and call me tomorrow."

Twenty minutes later they were in a hotel room, and Jason was on the phone again.

"I've got her, but she's dehydrated and bone-fucking-thin." He frowned. "Sort of disconnected, but lucid."

Bone-fucking-thin? She glanced down at her legs. At least her daily long walks had helped her keep some muscle.

"Apple juice so far, two bottles." He opened the minibar and poked around. "Nope."

If she had the energy she'd grab something to eat—anything—out of the minibar. Or even a soda. But getting out of the chair seemed like too much work.

"Okay. Okay. Yep, hang on."

He held the phone in front of Kate long enough for her to know he was sending someone a video and although she'd always hated having her picture taken, she couldn't be bothered to object.

"Yep. Thanks. ETA?"

He put the phone back in his pocket. "Eve is sending someone to help."

"Help?"

"Get you hydrated, and give you one of her special tonics that will get you back up and running faster than plain food."

"I'm tired of running."

He pulled a chair over so he could sit right in front of her.

"Why, Katie? Why did you keep running away from me?"

She took another swallow of the juice.

"What the hell were you thinking, Kate? Did you get some perverse pleasure from being in constant danger and knowing you must be driving me insane?"

She shook her head wordlessly, and he sighed. His voice softened. "Do you remember the day you called Meyers to ask for my help? Did you know that was all it took to hook me all over again?"

A lump filled her throat, and suddenly it was all too much. Tears spilled over and her shoulders began to shake.

"Aw, Katie." He pulled her into his lap, and held her while all the horrors, all the fears, and all the uncertainty boiled up and out of her. She hadn't shed a tear since the day she left Toronto. Had held it all in until she didn't have to. Stayed strong until now.

When she finally ran out of tears, he mopped her face.

"I'm sorry. I didn't mean to scare you."

"He nearly killed you, more than once, but you

kept running instead of calling me for help."

"I couldn't..." she trailed off and sighed.

"Couldn't what?"

"I couldn't lose you too."

"*You* pushed *me* away and then bolted."

Kate took a deep breath and tried to get up, but Jason maintained a gentle, implacable hold for a second, then set her back in her own chair. Put his hands on her knees.

"Make me understand why."

She gazed into his eyes for a moment, and then back at his hands. "Because I love you."

"Look at me and say that again."

Defiance crept into her voice. "Because I love you."

He shot to his feet and marched to the far side of the room. Turned and stared at her. "Then why on God's green earth did you leave me? Why couldn't you just stay put and let me love you. Keep you safe?"

"It was easier to walk away than lose you."

He threw his hands up. "Why would you lose me?"

Kate mustered all her strength to get out what she needed to say. "I just would. It's the way my life is. And I knew I couldn't possibly survive the pain of your death, too, so I left rather than having to spend the rest of my days knowing you were dead because of me."

Stunned was the word she would use to describe his expression. He really didn't get it.

"Everybody I have ever loved has died on me," she whispered, "I've survived the losses so far, but your death would...kill me."

"So you took control and made it comfortable for yourself. Did you ever think about how I was feeling, Katie?"

The juice must have been the reason she was starting to feel so much better. She drank more.

"Yes." And she was feeling a bit pissed off now too. "And I thought that if you were just having some fun with me, it wouldn't be a big deal. And if you weren't simply keeping me busy as Ted had asked you to, and you did have deeper feelings, you would still be better off if I left before it was too late." With that outburst, her new energy evaporated. She leaned back and watched him pace, then stop in the middle of the room.

"It has always been too late for me. I've loved you from the first moment we met, and I have never, ever, stopped." He sat back down, took her hands and said, "You're as much a part of me as breathing is."

He pressed kisses to her knuckles. "How can I convince you not to run away from me again? Make you believe we are meant to be together and nothing will happen to me."

He drew her into his lap again, and her heart soared. She was ready to believe.

"Just love me, Jason..." and she leaned forward to touch her mouth to his, slip her fingers up under his shirt, and she reveled in his warmth.

Jason pulled just far enough away to look into eyes he knew well, but not at all. "What will be different this time, Kate? Will it ever be more than physical?" He gently brushed his lips across hers. "Will I ever have your heart?"

Could he not see that he did have her heart?

"Why do you trust me when our skin is touching, but not when we have our clothes on?"

A flicker of something like panic had her saying, "I don't know."

Bullshit. "Sure you do. What happens when we make love, Kate? What is it that you can't face afterward?"

Kate wanted to give him the answers he needed, but she had never been able to put her feelings into words, expose who she was deep inside. She closed her eyes. "I..."

Jason's touch changed, and she knew he was backing off. "What do you need from me, Kate? What will help you right this minute?"

"Patience?" She opened her eyes but didn't look at him. "Wait for me. Help me learn how to be who you need without losing who I am."

"Whatever you need, I'm here for you." He pressed a kiss on her forehead.

"When I knew you were at the other end of that stupid little phone—just in case I was in more trouble than I could get out of on my own—I could handle anything. But when I lost the phone, it was like hell came and got me. I was so terribly alone. Wishing every night I could feel safe again."

Jason squeezed his arms tighter for just an instant. "You *are* safe, Katie."

She looked into his eyes. "I know, but could you just hold me forever anyway?"

"On one condition."

She waited.

"Would you stop changing your hair color?"

She laughed weakly. "I just wanted to know if blondes really have more fun."

There was a soft knock on the door, and they both jumped.

"Help's here," he said.

Eve's associate turned out to be a sharp-eyed, middle-aged woman of color who obviously *believed* in color, and wore it well. Her dress was sunflower yellow with royal blue trim, and her shoes a delightful emerald green. Her hair wasn't much longer than Kate's and was worn proudly natural with one tiny braid and beads to match her outfit.

"I'm Doctor Price," she said, and proceeded across the room with a suitcase in tow and a multicolored bag draped over her shoulder.

"I'm Jason, this is Kate."

Her businesslike expression softened when it landed on Kate. "I'll unpack my supplies while you climb into bed. You'll need to sleep for a few hours after I'm done."

In a far corner of Kate's mind she balked at taking orders from a stranger, but the kindness in the doctor's eyes convinced her to do as she was told, and while she stripped off the weary shorts and tank, Jason handed her a pair of soft cotton pajamas from his bag. She raised an eyebrow and he shrugged.

"Jenny," he said, by way of explanation.

Dr. Price sat on the edge of the bed to take Kate's blood pressure and temperature. Used a stethoscope to listen to her heart and lungs, then inserted an IV needle and withdrew a vial of blood, which she set aside. She passed Jason a bag of clear fluid, primed the line, and hooked it to the needle in Kate's arm.

"This will take a minute," she said, taking the vial of blood to where she had set up some kind of machine on the table.

"What are you doing?" Kate asked.

"Running some quick tests so we can fine-tune your infusion. This way we can make sure you get exactly what you need, and nothing you don't."

Her phone rang a minute later, and she answered with, "Eve?" She nodded. "Perfect, thanks."

She returned to Kate with a bag full of supplies. "Good news is, you're basically healthy, just depleted, so we'll fill you up with all the good stuff. How long have you been starving yourself?"

"What?!"

"You're extremely underweight for no apparent reason, so you haven't been giving your body the calories it requires. How long has this been going on?

"I ran out of money about six or eight weeks ago."

"Good. Short-term is easier to reverse than long." She touched Kate's shoulder. "I'm sorry for what you went through, and I'm going to help you feel strong again, sooner rather than later." She started injecting things into the fluid currently dripping into Kate's vein, as well as a second bag.

"Special concoctions per Eve Meyers," said the doctor. "Guaranteed to have you back on your feet in no time. And it will go quicker with a second line."

Kate soon had fluids flowing into both arms, and that's when Dr. Price said, "I would like to examine you. Perhaps Jason could give us some privacy?"

He raised his eyebrows first, then they came

together in a frown that almost made Kate laugh as he headed for the door. "I'll be right outside."

After the door closed, the doctor smiled at Kate with genuine warmth. "Anything you'd like to ask me? Tell me?"

Kate shook her head.

"Nothing you're worried about?"

"Nope."

"Use any sunscreen in the last couple of months?"

"No."

"Then I'll just take a look." She checked Kate's arms, legs, chest and neck. "No sign of trouble, but keep an eye on your skin."

"Question."

"Shoot."

She tipped her head toward the bags now hanging from a lamp at the side of the bed. "How long does is this stuff supposed to last?"

The smile lit her face again. "Feeling it, are you?"

"My mind is almost clear for the first time in weeks, and I feel sort of light."

"Eve is a genius, and capable of amazing things. You're very lucky to be on the receiving end."

"I'm grateful. Very grateful."

"Should I let Romeo back in before he wears a path in the carpet out there?"

Kate laughed, and it almost sounded normal. "He's afraid I'll run out on him again."

"Will you?"

"No, the murderer I was running from was caught, so everything's okay now."

Dr. Price pressed her lips together, then twisted them around a bit as though trying not to put a thought into words.

Before opening the door for Jason, she said, "There will always be something to run from—unless you don't. Which makes it wise to remember an important fact. Those who love us are stuck living with the choices we make."

———

After the doctor left, Jason watched Kate while she slept.

She had better color now, and of course, the tension was gone while she slept, but the shadows would be back as soon as she opened her eyes. Living with endless fear and profound loneliness must have changed who she was.

She would put on weight and get physically strong again, and her hair would grow. The short tufts of white would… He frowned. Maybe the white was natural. Shock and stress. One of the Meyers children ended up with a white streak in his hair months after his heart stopped and he was brought back to life.

Hair mattered for nothing, and if hers stayed white it would be a badge of honor. One she could wear proudly, or color if she chose to keep it private.

Jason only cared about getting her healthy, and Eve's concoction seemed to be working already, thank God. Seeing her there in the airport, bone-thin and looking like a worn-out drug addict, had hit him hard. But oddly, within half an hour of being with her, he started seeing only Katie when he looked at her. When she met his eyes.

As she did now.

"Hey," she said, and he went to her, sat on the side of the bed.

"How ya feeling?"

"Scary good. When I woke up, before I opened my eyes, I thought I was still dreaming, because I felt so much stronger, ready to take my life back. That stuff Dr. Price pumped into me is magical."

Considering some of the psychic powers in the Meyers family, along with what he'd seen and heard about Eve's healing abilities, "magical," probably wasn't far from truth.

"She said you could try some soup if you feel up to it."

She sat up, and immediately clutched the blanket. He waited for what he assumed was the predicted lightheadedness to pass.

"Whewf. She wasn't lying about that part." Kate smoothed the blanket under her hand. "Or about the part that it would pass quickly. I'll give soup a try."

Jason braced for a quick rescue when she declined his help and wobbled to the bathroom. Dr. Price had given him strict instructions that Kate wasn't to be dependent on him. She was in a fragile emotional state, and needed to be able to help herself as much as possible so she could get her confidence back.

The woman brilliantly followed that instruction by acknowledging that it would not be easy for him, but in the end he would have a woman at his side he believed in again, instead of one he was afraid to leave alone.

So instead of standing outside the bathroom door ready to run in and rescue her if she fell, he picked up the phone and ordered room service.

Ravenous himself, he managed not to watch her while she slowly ate the soup, but it was hard.

"That was good," she said, putting the bowl on the tray their server had abandoned just inside the door and going to the window. "I'm sorry I scared the guy who brought our food."

Her instant fear when the stranger walked into the room had caught Jason off guard as well. She'd frozen in place, looking like she would keel over or shatter if anyone so much as touched her, and he was glad she brought it up now.

"You were okay at the airport, so I didn't expect…"

"I was empty then. Like a walking zombie, dead inside, and everything outside of me was a blur. I couldn't think, let alone feel."

Jason came up behind her, locked his arms around her waist, and rested his chin on the top of her head.

"And now, Katie?"

She smiled and lifted the palm of his hand to her heart. "It's beating. Can you feel how strong and steady it is?"

"Yes." A wave of relief engulfed him. "What are you thinking about?"

She smiled, "I was thinking about the days I spent up in the trees."

"In the trees?"

"I was hiding from Victor."

"Which time?"

"After he grabbed me in Vancouver at my base-ment suite, when I lost your phone. I woke up in the back seat of his car, and luckily he had to stop for a train crossing. I bolted out of the car and ran into the forest."

Every muscle in Jason's body tightened, but he somehow managed to keep his arms gentle around her.

"I climbed into a tree when daylight came so I could watch for him, and that became my survival tactic. Hiding in the trees when it was light out, and walking the train tracks at night. Took a week to get to West Vancouver. Sitting up in the branches, I used to close my eyes and imagine you holding me just like this, high above everything, and safe. I could even feel your chin resting on my head and your heart beating against my back."

Jason slipped his hands under her shirt and touched the scars. "You had to be in pain. Bleeding."

"The cuts weren't very deep. He had me by the wrist, and I was putting up one hell of a fight, trying to run backwards away from him while he was swinging the knife at me. My barn coat was good protection at first, but then the snaps popped open, and that's when he got in a couple of slices. Then he must have dropped the knife, because he started punching me. Knocked me out eventually."

Jason's heart pounded against her back. "The whole thing was recorded. First part on my cell, and the rest by emergency dispatch."

"There wasn't much to hear, really."

He hesitated. "Are you ready to go home now, Katie?"

She sighed. "I don't have a home anymore. The last time I talked to my lawyer, he told me it was sold."

"Your lawyer? You were in contact with your lawyer?"

"He's the only one I thought was safe. You know, the attorney–client confidentiality thing. He couldn't tell anyone where I was, and when I ran out of money a few times, I called him to wire me more."

"Have you known him long?

"Not really. He was Tanner's attorney, mostly. Contacted me after Tanner's death because of the will and my inheritance. His family are from the racetrack and everyone knows them. He's probably done work for half the backstretch at one time or another."

"Did you know he was very tight with Victor?"

"Hadn't really thought about it."

Jason said quietly, "Think about it now. And think about the times you called him, and how long, after each time, before Victor caught up with you."

Kate stiffened, then turned to stare at him. "Are you saying he was telling Victor where I was?"

"Precisely."

"But that's breaching his lawyer vow or whatever it's called."

"Which could have something to do with why he took the easy way out."

"Meaning?"

"He committed suicide three days after Victor's capture."

"Seriously?"

He nodded. "When Victor was arrested on attempted murder charges, he immediately tried to negotiate a deal by pointing at two of his accomplices. Your lawyer, Dan, was one of them. Dan was then arrested, and appeared relieved that it was over. He spilled his guts in a statement which included information about Tanner's murder and the attempts on your life. Dan's part was to write a phony will. Without it, you wouldn't have inherited the entire business, and Victor's tidy setup would have been gone. And once you were on the run, he kept Victor up-to-date on where you were. He was released on bail, but I guess he didn't want to stand trial."

"What about Mark? Did I put him in danger by leaving everything in his hands?"

"As soon as you disappeared we filled him in, and he worked with us."

"You trusted him so easily?"

"Because of the suspicions about Victor, and years spent trying to build a case, all of the barn staff were run through the system years ago. They are all clean, and none but you in Victor's crosshairs."

Nausea roiled in her gut. "Why did they want me dead, Jason?"

"At first Victor and his cohorts thought you had figured out their game, gone to the police, and were in hiding because you were going to be the witness who put them away."

"And where did they get such a far-fetched notion?"

"Apparently a small part of a shipment went missing, and it had to be either you or Leo who took it. And when you tied up all your loose ends before leaving Kentucky, including putting the townhouse on the market and giving your attorney a letter with the instructions 'to be opened upon my death,' they were convinced they were right.

"The mutual tickets he gave you and Jake were a test. When you didn't confront him, he was convinced you were already working with the authorities. Then you vanished and sealed the deal."

Kate was amazed. She had nearly died twice for totally bullshit reasons. "Talk about *my* wild imagination."

"Yes, let's."

Kate frowned.

"Besides the fact you thoroughly pissed me off, I was impressed by the convoluted methods you used to disappear and stay just a few steps ahead of me. I'd love to hear your thought process. When did you decide you needed to run?"

CHAPTER 18

———

KATE SWALLOWED AND WENT TO sit on the side of the bed. "It began as a plan to rescue Leo. You hadn't found him, and didn't seemed interested in going to High River, so I decided to go and find him myself."

Jason was shaking his head while he rolled a chair over so he could sit in front of her.

"I figured I could tour the breeding farms there, and chat up a few people for information quite innocently, without drawing attention."

She shrugged when Jason rolled his eyes.

"I needed to *do* something. I couldn't just sit around and hope. Leo dragged my ass back from the edge once, and I owed him."

"So you had this plan."

"Yes. And then he was dead. And there was nothing I could do. And after we spent that night together, and I knew how much I still cared about you, I started to think about what it would be like if you were next. And I panicked for a while."

"And then?"

"And then I decided to stick to the plan mostly, and just disappear. I could start a new and uncomplicated life somewhere else, and be content just knowing you were okay."

"What kind of a life were you planning, Katie?"

"A simple one. And it was working just fine. I had a good job at a riding stable. Lots of horses to care for, and a few dozen kids eager to learn."

"I thought the racetrack was your life."

"I used to think that too, but apparently I was wrong. In the past year and a half I haven't been anywhere near a track, or read a racing form, or been on a racehorse. None of it. Not even on the internet. I left it all behind, like my hair."

"I kinda liked your hair."

"So did I, but it was a bit of a symbol, part of the picture that was Kate Oliver, trainer."

"You didn't miss anything about your old life?"

"I missed The Princess, and I missed you phoning my pocket and making me angry by hanging up on me or saying things that left me wondering if there was a bug in my house."

Jason was grinning.

"Did you enjoy irritating me?"

"I was trying to stir you up. Hoping to make you mad enough to drop your guard. Wishing I really *was* in your mind."

"Oh, but you were." She looked him in the eye. "How did you know I was drinking chocolate milk that time?"

"Educated guess," he said. "There was pleasure in your voice when you spoke after every swallow, and I guessed that you still loved chocolate milk."

"And what about the ice cream?"

He grinned then. "I confess to inside information. The day you flung my cell phone around your kitchen it was still working, and I heard everything you said." He cocked his head to one side. "Do you always say shit so much when you're mad?"

She was caught between indignation and amusement.

"Made my day to hear you say you liked having me at your fingertips... Even though the ice cream comparison took a bit of the starch out of it. Knowing you had that phone in your pocket was comforting for a while."

"For me, too. I had no idea how comforting until I lost it, and suddenly I was so alone." She fought the lump in her throat. "I never stopped being afraid after that."

Jason sat beside her and gathered her close. "You will never be alone again, because I'm not letting you out of my sight."

"Are you saying you don't trust me?" she taunted, trying to lighten things up.

"Precisely." But there was teasing in his voice.

She pulled away just a bit.

"Don't even think about it," he said, and lowered his mouth to hers. Her hands slipped under his shirt, and he tipped her back across the bed, nibbled his way down her throat. He wreaked havoc with her senses for a while, but when the heat ratcheted up a notch, he stopped, wrapped his arms around her, and told her to go to sleep.

She lay still, wondering why he didn't want to make love with her.

Sometime later Kate woke up slowly and opened her eyes to find him staring at her. "What's wrong?"

"Absolutely nothing."

She touched his face. "I love you, Jason."

"And I love you, Katie Oliver." He placed a quick kiss on her lips. "Now turn over and go back to sleep."

Kate did as she was told, somewhat puzzled by his behavior, but not willing to think about it. She snuggled her back against him, and he held her tight against his heart while she waited for him to fall asleep.

She stayed as long as she could and then edged away. Slipped out of bed and made it as far as the table.

"Stop." His voice landed sharply between her shoulder blades, light flooded the room, and she spun around to face him.

He was halfway to her, and the pain in his expression was frightening. "What's wrong?"

"Where were you going?"

"I was tired of lying awake. Thought I'd sit up for a while."

He went back to the bed and rubbing a hand over his face, said, "Sorry. Just a little gun-shy."

That's when it finally hit her.

While she'd been living in fear, so had he. And while she at least got to make some of the decisions along the way, exert some kind of control now and again, he had none.

When she sat beside him and touched his face, he took her hand and pressed his lips in the palm. Put an ache in her heart.

She slipped her arms around him. "I am so sorry for what I did to you. For the torture you've lived through. I was only thinking of myself. Maybe if I'd known how you felt I wouldn't have run away, but somehow I can't say that with any certainty. I was completely wrapped up in myself and controlling my world. My perspective was totally warped."

"Kate."

With her fingertips against his lips, she said, "Jason, I've probably loved you forever. But unfortunately I've always thought I shouldn't. I've spent half my life proving I could live without you, when all I truly wanted was to be in your arms."

She'd been taught almost from birth to set goals and move heaven and earth to achieve them. Part of recovering from the death of her parents when she was barely out of high school was the realization that her heart had to be protected at all costs.

"Then why the hell—"

"I was locked onto a goal that I couldn't admit was unattainable. Giving it up would leave me nothing but you, and I had already learned that people were temporary. You would eventually leave me, and then I'd have nothing at all." She sighed. "Why was I so stupid?"

He took her face in his hands and kissed her with a tenderness that brought tears to her eyes. "I was equally stupid for not putting up a fight. But never again, lady. Moving heaven and earth won't be enough to get rid of me now."

She kissed him until her heart threatened to expand to bursting. Jason rolled over, pinned her under his weight, and gazed into her eyes. "Katie Oliver, there is something about having your warm body next to mine that makes me very, very content."

Her grin came unbidden. "Not the word I would have used."

The look on his face lightened. "Are you being

cheeky?"

"You always say to call a spade a spade."

He studied her for a minute before saying, "Okay, along with contentment, I feel the incredible desire to make love to you day and night for the next fifty years. Satisfied?"

"Not yet," she said, tipping him over.

"Don't go starting something that you can't finish," he said, sliding his hands over her butt.

"I will never be finished with you."

He reversed their positions, pinned her arms above her head, and lowered his mouth to her throat, teasing and tormenting her until stopping short of what she wanted…yet again.

———

Almost forty-eight hours later, Kate was at the window watching the palm trees sway in the wind, feeling much stronger, and the reality of what she'd been through over the past year or so was beginning to sink in.

Jason was very good at both pushing her to talk, backing off when she needed a break, and asking questions she found both irritating and enlightening.

When she asked him about the charges against Victor, he studied her for a minute before answering.

"They had enough to hold him on attempted murder because of the shooting in Kamloops, but they hope your deposition will give them more of the pieces."

"When do I do that?"

"As soon as you like. They're waiting for you in Vancouver, and I'm supposed to take you there on our way home."

"It won't really be over until then, will it?" She focused on him and frowned. "You look so worried."

"It's going to be hard on you. All the questions, going over everything again and again."

"Then let's go now. Get it over with."

Jason booked a flight for early the next day. Then he phoned Ted and told him their arrival time.

He ran what she called his measuring gaze over her. "Do you want to go home right after that?"

"Home?" Her stomach tightened. "I'm not sure where that is anymore."

He put his hands on her shoulders and said firmly, "I mean home with me. The only home you'll ever need, Katie, the one where I will keep you safe while you drive me crazy for the rest of my life."

Hope warred with the old enemies in her head. "Jenny said I could stay in her spare room."

"I've seen that room, and the bed is way too small for us."

She kept her eyes averted so he couldn't see the laughter. "But she's my friend, and I—"

"Jenny can't kiss you goodnight like I can." He lowered his lips to the side of her neck, teasing and tantalizing.

She turned to keep her mouth out of reach. "But she's a great cook."

"So am I."

Kate leaned back to stare at him. "You cook?"

"I do."

"And you have a bigger bed."

"And a fireplace in the bedroom."

"Okay, you win."

"That's it? A fireplace and you fold?"

"You wanted more argument?"

"Well, I wanted to at least get your clothes off to really convince you."

"Not necessary."

"It is for me."

"Speaking of clothes."

"You need help getting out of yours?"

"Seriously?" Kate laughed, because all she had on was his T-shirt and her pajama bottoms.

"Very serious," he said and slid his hands under the soft fabric.

"Jason. I have no clothes."

"Just the way I like you," he said into the ear he was nuzzling.

Kate pushed on his chest and locked her arms straight out between them. "I can't go to Vancouver dressed like this. Isn't it winter in Canada?" She did have the clothes she'd been wearing when she arrived, but even after they'd been laundered by the hotel—twice—the thought of putting them on again made her skin crawl.

"You would rather go shopping than stay here and fool around some more?"

"Yes." She needed clothes, and their fooling around was leaving her frustrated because Jason always called a halt before it got to where Kate needed to go. While his restraint had been admirable, considering the shape she was in when she arrived, she was much better now.

He loosened his grip, and she turned in his arms

to a walk away, but he didn't let her go. "I love you, Katie Oliver."

With her heart pounding in her ears, she leaned her head back against his shoulder and said quietly, "Do you have any idea how many times I've heard you say those words in my head? Some days it was all that kept me going."

She took a deep breath to steady herself. "When I was playing dead in that dark, snowy field, hoping Victor had gone away and wouldn't kill the girls when they came looking for me, I would imagine you saying, 'Hang on, Katie girl. Don't give up. Stay strong, because I love you." Her voice cracked, and a tear slid down her cheek.

Jason tipped her head back and looked into her eyes. "I said almost exactly that to the stars every night. I would stand outside wherever I was and beg you to hold on until I could find you. I swore to the heavens I would one day bring you home."

"So I had no options? No shot at going to live with Jenny?"

"No shot at all." He hesitated for just a moment. "Katie, I did something wild last summer. It was something I needed to do for my own sanity, and for us."

Definitely curious, she waited.

"I bought a farm."

Kate's eyes widened. "You bought a farm."

"The Princess needed a place to hang out until you got home. It's small. Thirty acres with a ten-stall barn.

"For The Princess."

"We have a thing. She fell for me when I went to visit her at Jim's barn. I cheated by always carrying something of yours in my coat pocket…along with peppermints, of course."

"Something of mine? Like what?"

"One of the riding gloves you left behind when you bolted from the hotel. Did you know she won a race while you were gone?"

Kate was amazed. "I didn't think Jim would even start her."

"He wasn't going to, but she was becoming unruly to gallop, and he figured a race was what she needed."

"And she won! Is she at your farm now?"

"Our farm. Yes."

A tiny trill of happiness rippled through her. "And Anchor?"

"She needed company, so he's there too."

"Where is it?"

"About ten minutes from Jim and Jenny's.."

"So they knew I wasn't coming to stay with them?"

"Let's just say they were rooting for me. However, they were also careful to warn me you were a tough nut to crack, and not to get my hopes too high."

Not so tough anymore, she thought. "We should phone and tell them."

Jason placed the call, then handed the phone to Kate.

"Hello?"

"Hi, Jenny,"

"Oh! Katie! Where are you? When are you coming home? How are you? Did Jason tell you…"

Laughing, Kate held the phone out to share Jenny's barrage of questions, and Jason took it from her.

"Jennn-i-ferrrrr..."

When she suddenly went silent, he said, "She's fine. Skinny enough to ride, but fine. We're headed for Vancouver tomorrow, should make it home a day or two later, and she doesn't need your spare room."

"Oh! Did you tell her you love her?"

"Yes."

"And did she say she loves you too?"

"I don't think so."

"Pass her the phone."

Jason handed it over.

"Katie Oliver, do you love him?"

"Yes"

"Then for crying out loud, hang up this phone and tell him so!"

Click.

Kate was still laughing when she put the phone down and turned to Jason. "I love you."

"What?"

"Jen told me to hang up and tell you I love you."

His smile widened. "She can be a pest at times, but certainly has her uses." He played with the hem of her T-shirt. "Still want to go shopping?"

"Not especially, but I really need something to wear."

Kate bought jeans, shoes, a sweater, and a jacket, and when Jason reminded her she hadn't bought underwear, she thought about the panties. The one pair she had left with a pocket sewn in. Every night in the shelter she had washed them in the bathroom sink, then put them back on wet. She could have left them to dry overnight, but was terrified of losing what had become her lifeline. But she needed to be brave now, and let go. She headed for the lingerie department.

On the way back, Jason suggested they have dinner in the hotel's restaurant. Kate hesitated for a minute and then shrugged. She was going to have to learn to be comfortable out in the open and surrounded by people again. Shopping had been easy with Jason at her side. Why not graduate to a restaurant?

While waiting for their meal, Jason left her to go to the washroom, and she was fine until she noticed a man on the other side of the room staring at her. Her heart thumped double-time, and sweat instantly soaked her back. She closed her eyes and tried to will herself to be calm, but her lungs were burning, and every muscle ached with the need to run. She tried counting backwards from a hundred and only got to eighty-seven. Scanned the room for exits. Shoved her chair back so she was ready to run.

A hand settled on her shoulder, and she jumped. Spun. Ready to fight if she couldn't flee.

"Katie, what's wrong?"

She blinked, and just like that, she was okay again. Jason was there. Her shaking hand covered his. "Holy crap." She shuddered.

"You're okay. No one is going to hurt you. Katie?"

"I'm okay. Just a bit spooked."

The server arrived with their food and she stared at it. "I don't think I can eat now. Maybe we could take it upstairs with us?"

Jason made the arrangements, and minutes later

she was safely behind their locked door.

"How you doing?"

"Okay."

"Not," he said.

"I guess that was my first panic attack."

"Out of the blue?"

"No. There was a man across the restaurant staring at me, and I was suddenly terrified and fighting the need to run."

"I shouldn't have left you there."

"I suppose you could have taken me to the men's room with you," she said dryly.

"Don't kid yourself, woman. Next time I will."

"Thanks." She wrapped her arms around him and snuggled in.

"Um."

She looked up.

"I like your new clothes and all, but…" He toyed with the bottom edge of her sweater. "Kinda warm in here for this, isn't it?"

"You might be right."

No further urging necessary, he slid it up and over her head, then laughed out loud at her white cotton bra with candy-apple red hearts all over it.

He unsnapped her jeans then slowly slid the zipper down, exposing panties to match the bra. "Cute."

She pushed him over to the bed, tipped him onto it, and enjoyed torturing him with her mouth while she took his clothes off very slowly. But when things were finally getting to where she wanted them, he stopped her. Tucked her in beside him and said, "Not yet, Katie."

On the flight to Vancouver, Jason stretched his legs under the seat in front of him and leaned back to watch Kate. She looked completely relaxed, just as she had right before someone bumped into her when they were going through security and he'd seen the fear in her eyes.

But she recovered well.

Walking from the plane to customs, she said, "This was the scary part for me before, hoping I wouldn't get busted for the borrowed passport. I barely look like the woman in the photo, yet time and again I used it successfully."

He laughed. "You weren't getting away with anything. When we caught you on video going through with Mary, we got the passport number, and you were put on a very special watch list. You were allowed to cross freely, but reports were generated each and every time—unlike when you ditched it and traveled on the police officer's ID."

They cleared customs and were nearing the terminal exit when Kate grabbed his arm and stopped him. Her expression was a mix of fear and anger.

"What's wrong?"

"Someone's watching me."

"Where?" he scanned the crowd.

She pointed to the doorway. "Right there a second ago."

Jason slung an arm around her shoulders. "I'll keep you safe."

"You shouldn't have to."

Working their way toward the wide expanse of

sliding glass doors, her grip on him tightened, and she was vibrating with fear. "There. By the pole with the T on it."

Just when Jason spotted the guy, Kate said, "Fuck it. I want my life back." And she took off, marching straight at the guy.

The crowd seemed to part for her, and in seconds she was right in front of the man while Jason was still trying to catch up. Then he couldn't believe his ears.

"Who are you, and why are you watching me!" she demanded.

The stunned look on the slightly droopy but tanned face was worth far more than a thousand words.

He opened his mouth, looked over Kate's shoulder at Jason, and said, "Ah—"

"Don't give me stupid! I want to know why you were staring!"

Jason got a grip on her shoulders and held her tight. "Kate, I would like you to meet Ted. A very good friend of mine."

She froze, then used both hands to cover her face and an embarrassed groan escaped.

"Nice to finally meet you, Kate." Ted was grinning.

Kate spread her fingers, then lowered her hands. "Guess I must be good witness material, being so mentally stable and all."

Jason and Ted both laughed.

"For the record I used to be more stable, but the last few months have been somewhat difficult."

Ted smiled over her head at Jason and said, "I think I like her."

"Forget it, she's spoken for."

"Then why bother to introduce us?"

The drive downtown only took a half hour, and the conversation was nothing but lighthearted banter. Kate felt comfortable and very relaxed by the time they arrived at the attorney's office.

Ted showed them into the boardroom where the prosecutor, Madeline Griffiths, and a court reporter were waiting, and after introductions, Ted excused himself, closing the door firmly behind him.

"I have a lot of questions for you, Ms. Oliver," said Ms. Griffiths. "We'll take our time, and whenever you need a break, please just say so. I don't expect this will be easy for you."

Kate gave her a wide smile. "Compared to what Victor put me through, this should be a breeze."

The questions began, and Kate was careful to answer each one as completely as she could. She didn't hesitate to ask for clarification when the question was unclear, or explain when her answer was uncertain. Jason never said a word, but occasionally touched her shoulder or arm when she seemed to need reassurance.

Hours later, having also been interviewed by representatives of a dozen government agencies, Kate was free to go.

Tonight, instead of staying at a hotel, they were going to stay at Ted's home, and on the drive there Kate savored the majesty of the mountains while the ocean renewed her spirit. Some of the weight lifted from her shoulders, and the tightness eased from between her eyes.

They stopped at a shopping center to pick up steaks for supper, and Kate took the opportunity to slip into a store and using some of the cash Jason had given her added to her wardrobe.

Arriving at Ted's house was like turning the page and starting a fresh, new chapter. The driveway led down the side of a mountain and deep into a forest until suddenly, there was a large clearing. Ted's house was nestled into a rocky cliff overlooking the ocean. Kate stepped out of the car and stared at what looked like three stacked wooden platforms surrounded by walls of glass and rustic patios.

The entryway on the middle floor opened directly into a huge open space dominated by a floor-to-ceiling fireplace with a comfortable seating area on one side and a spacious kitchen on the other.

The stairway to the right of the front door led up to Ted's office and bedroom. And the one to the left would take them down to the guest suite.

Kate went down and changed into her new, comfortable outfit—dark blue leggings and an oversized blue and white flannel shirt—and when she went back up, the intense conversation they'd been having ended abruptly.

"Classic Katie except for the hair," Jason said.

"What's wrong with her hair?" asked Ted "I think it makes her look spunky."

"You should have seen it before. Brown with streaks of sunshine all through it, and it hung right to her…belt."

Ted shook his head. "That would make her look like a kid. I think this is just right. Kinda cocky and opinionated."

"Oh, she's definitely opinionated."

"That's what makes a woman strong."

"Okay, then what is the cocky part good for?"

"It keeps you on your toes so you don't ever become complacent. I really do think she's a good match for you."

"Thanks, but I already knew that."

Kate had been amused by the banter—likely meant to distract her from whatever conversation she'd walked in on—but it was time to step in. "When you two are finished discussing me like I'm not here, I have a question."

Both faces fell, almost as if they expected her to ask for an answer they weren't prepared to give, which only made her more curious about what they'd been talking about.

"When's supper?" she asked.

"Just as soon as the table is set." Grinning, Ted passed her the cutlery she hadn't even realized he was holding.

The simple meal of steak and potatoes was followed by chocolate ice cream, and Kate savored hers while staring at Jason and, judging by the look in his eyes, he didn't miss the message.

Ted glanced back and forth between the two of them and said, "Before this goes any further and I lose you both for the night..."

Kate shifted her attention to her host, and he continued, "I think it's time you were filled in on the details of Victor's exploits and what part you played his game—aside from being a target."

CHAPTER 19

THE ROOM WAS DARK, BUT for the light of the fire. Jason sat on a small sofa, and gestured for Kate to join him, but she'd been leaning heavily on him for days and it was time she depended on her own backbone.

She chose an armchair and curled her legs under her while Ted poured them each a snifter of brandy.

"Victor was born into a family who made their fortune in the shipping industry," he said. "His upbringing was privileged, but when the family money began to..."

Kate held up her hand, "Ted, could we just cut to the chase and leave the other stuff for the jury?"

Jason grinned.

"Okay, then," said Ted. "How about I start with the most recent stuff and work back?"

Kate nodded. "Fine with me."

"When Rainbow and Anchor were flown back to Kentucky, the crate was confiscated after they were unloaded, and when it was taken apart, a huge quantity of marijuana was found densely packed within the stall walls where there would normally be two-inch-thick slabs of insulation material.

"Pot doesn't seem like a very big deal," said Kate. At least not big enough to get her killed.

"It was worth a million dollars on the open market, and is typical of backhaul. The prime product on this trip was the one going into Canada, not coming out."

Her eyebrows hiked up, but she said nothing, so Ted continued.

"Prior to that, the last horses he shipped in from South America were wearing millions of dollars' worth of stolen diamonds."

"Wearing?"

"Those fancy shipping halters were not actually designed for the safety of the horses, but for their bulkiness, which provided space for special compartments where jewels could be hidden."

Kate had a flicker of a memory. "Leo kept rubbing his hands on the sheepskin. He was searching them, wasn't he?"

"Yes,"

"Is that why—"

"I can't talk to you about Leo yet, Kate. I'm sorry. But I can tell you he managed to get a couple of stones out of one of the halters, and it was the break many agencies who'd been after Victor for years had been waiting for."

"So Victor is a smuggling magnate." Kate almost heard the click as the pieces came together in her mind. "He was laundering money through me by handing over that envelope of cash every month. Dirty money I plunked into my account to cover payroll and a good chunk of my feed bill."

"You couldn't have known any better. And if you had been suspicious, it would have cost you dearly."

"But it did anyway. Didn't it? Isn't that why he wanted me dead? He thought I knew?"

"True enough."

"Why did he kill Tanner?

"Tanner suspected Victor of insurance fraud and called him on it. One of the international horses was injured in an accident at the airport some years ago. According to Brett, it fell from a ramp during loading and was sent to a clinic and stitched up before continuing the journey to Kentucky."

Ted sipped his brandy.

"When the horse was unloaded from the van at Tanner's barn, the stitches had ripped open, the wound was a filthy, gaping mess, and the poor creature eventually had to be euthanized due to complications to his hooves caused by fever."

"Laminitis," said Kate. She'd seen it many times, years ago. These days, treatments were better, and it was more easily prevented.

"Tanner confronted Victor about his man Brett, who travelled with the horses and was supposed to care for them throughout their trip. Tanner said Brett was either negligent, or he contributed to the horse's injury on purpose, with a big insurance payout being the end goal."

Kate had a vague recollection of the story, but it was during the time she was reducing to ride, and not paying attention to much outside of her small world.

"All hell broke loose. A necropsy was done, and nothing suspicious was found. The only odd fact mentioned in the report was that the original injury appeared to be a clean incision as opposed to a traumatic injury, and the assumption was made that the vets had trimmed the area to make it neater and easier to stitch."

"So was it fraud, or wasn't it?" asked Kate.

"Yes and no. The horse was not supposed to die. However, the infection was caused by illegal actions."

"Meaning?"

"The horse didn't fall off a ramp. His hindquarter was opened and a package of jewels was sewn in under the skin for illegal transport to North America. When he arrived here, they tore open the stitches to get their package. The horse's system was already objecting to the foreign object, and the dirty, gaping wound was a prime target for a massive infection."

"The bastards."

"Exactly the term Tanner used when he called me. He wanted to blow the whistle on Victor, but he needed proof that would stand up in court and there was none. Years went by until for some reason Tanner finally lost patience. I warned him Victor couldn't possibly be working alone, and based on the amount of money involved, organized crime has to be involved. A week later I received a letter."

A chill skittered across Kate's skin.

"Before he left on his fishing trip, he wrote down every little detail he could think of that could be important in a case against Victor. When I couldn't reach him by phone after that, my contact told me he was dead."

Ice-cold words escaped through her clenched teeth. "The fucking bastards."

Ted took a deep breath. "From that moment on, we knew you could be in danger too, so you were watched carefully."

"By Leo."

"Among others."

"Jason?"

"Not until you called him. Leo thought Jason might be too close to remain impartial, but once you made the contact, we gave him some basic information."

"Only basic?"

"Like I said, I was uncertain if he could keep his feelings from getting in the way."

"Ouch," said Jason, and Ted smiled.

"Were I in your shoes, it would have been no different, my friend."

"Tell her about Pete," Jason said quietly.

Ted reached to the shelf behind him and picked up a black object, which he handed to Kate, who recognized what it was right away. "An earplug."

"Precisely, but take a good look."

She rolled it around in her hand and squeezed. Instead of the dense foam she expected, this one felt hollow. She ran a finger around the outside until she found a tiny slit and used her baby finger to explore further. The plug was, indeed, completely hollow.

"Victor used to insist his horses fly with earplugs because of the noise on cargo decks." She glanced at Ted. "Yet another place to smuggle jewels, I suppose."

"Exactly. And this one must have been left in the horse's ear by accident, and they had to go to Tanner's barn to retrieve it. That's when Pete caught them, and they killed both him and the horse."

Kate shook her head in disgust.

"I found Pete dead in the stall," said Jason. "A day later I found the earplug and took it to Ted. Two days after that his superiors sent him on a special mission, working with CSIS in Vancouver."

"Did you ever find out why?"

"Yes, but again, it's something I can't talk about."

They were quiet for a few minutes, each lost in their own thoughts.

"You have any questions?" asked Ted.

"Not at the moment, but I'm sure I will."

"I'll turn in, then. See you two in the morning."

Kate stared into the fire for a while, lost in the flickering of the flames, zoning out instead of thinking about everything she'd learned.

"You okay, Katie?"

"I wish I'd let Zeke punch him in the nose."

Jason smiled, "Zeke was at his bail hearing and enjoyed that just as much."

"Oh, I forgot he was a cop."

"An agent, actually."

"Whatever... So, tell me what happened after that. What happened to the horses and my grooms and Mark and—"

"Not until you come and sit with me."

"Let's go to bed instead."

"I thought you'd never ask," he said, and followed her down the stairs.

Once behind the closed doors, he kissed her thoroughly. "I have wanted to do that all day."

Kate smiled up at him. "Likewise."

When they crawled under the covers, Jason propped himself up against the pillows and pulled her over to lean her back against his chest. He wrapped his arms around her and rested his chin on her head while they watched the flickering lights of boats in the distance.

Kate had an entirely new perspective on her past. It was as though she'd been living in a bubble and now she was free. "I feel like my life has been part of some elaborate movie, and someone else has been moving my arms and legs. I'm not sure I know what to think."

She hesitated only briefly before easing open a door to her past, one Jason knew nothing about. And when she started talking it came out in a rush. "Kinda like when I found out I was adopted. It was as though my past, my whole history, had disappeared at the snap of someone else's fingers."

A tiny shaft of pain hit Jason in the chest. There was so much she'd kept from him, but now... He swallowed the hurt. What she needed was his support and encouragement. These deeper levels of communication would heal both of them. And with that bit of wisdom settling in his mind, he asked, "How old were you?"

"Fourteen."

"Bad timing."

"True, but I accepted it and moved on. It's what kids do."

"How did you feel years later?"

"Quite comfortable. I knew the people who raised me cared about me. My history was truly my own. Only the people I thought I'd come from, I hadn't."

"And did you forgive them for the lie, Kate?"

"Of course. They didn't intend to hurt me. They only wanted me to feel safe and not threatened by uncertainty."

"But you never talk about them, or go home. Why not?"

"My adopted parents died."

That was at least consistent with what she had told him before. "No other family?"

"My parents' children were twenty years older than me, and they were too busy fighting among themselves to be bothered with a kid they barely knew. I was just some charity case to them." She shrugged. "My parents gave me a home when I was a defenseless infant. What more could I ask for?"

"You left?"

"I'd always dreamed of being a jockey, like that girl in the old movie, *National Velvet*, so I packed my bag and headed for the racetrack."

"Do you ever wonder about your biological parents?"

"My mother was a drug-addicted prostitute and my father an anonymous John."

Jason had no idea what to say to that.

Kate was absently rubbing her palms together in a slow, circular motion. "When I was in a homeless shelter in LA just a few weeks ago, I was in the bathroom washing up one day...or night, I don't remember which...but I suddenly *saw* myself in the mirror. With barely anything left of who I used to be, I suddenly, unexpectedly, found compassion for the woman who gave birth to me.

"My own bony shoulders, hollow cheeks, and sunken eyes made me think, this could have been how bad she looked. And this could have been how terribly *desperate* she felt. And in a flash, a brief moment of clarity, it occurred to me that her giving birth to me, then giving me away, made her a good person."

She sighed, and Jason took her hands in his. Kissed her fingertips.

"What a wise woman you've become."

"Not really. Just more tired and thoughtful."

Jason rested his chin on the top of her head again. "I'm sure that over the next while you'll begin to realize how much you've learned."

She chuckled softly. "Mostly how to hide in plain sight and bleach my own hair."

"Which reminds me. How did you ever figure pink hair would make you inconspicuous?"

"If you were Victor, would you scan a crowd searching for me and bother to take a second look at a teenager with pink hair?"

"Point taken."

Kate turned over and nestled her face into the crook of his neck, "I'm tired of talk, Jason."

His arms tightened around her. "Go to sleep, my darling Katie, I promise to keep you safe."

———

It wasn't quite daylight yet when Kate woke up, but the sheets beside her were cold. After a long, hot shower she made her way upstairs, and the moment Jason spotted her he said, "Hey there, sleepyhead."

Once again, he and Ted had been talking about her, or about something they weren't going to share with her.

"Good morning, Miss Kate."

The simple greeting hit her like a punch in the

gut, because Leo sometimes called her Miss Kate.

"Morning, gentlemen," she said, and when Ted started to get up, she gestured for him to stay where he was. "I smell the coffee, and I'm sure I can find it all by myself. Anyone want a refill?" They both declined.

Kate chose a bright red ceramic mug from beside the coffee pot and filled it while savoring the heady aroma. Then she wandered out onto the expansive deck and leaned on the railing. Watched boats drifting through the morning mist while she gave Ted and Jason time to finish the conversation she interrupted.

Before long Jason was slipping his arms around her waist and planting a kiss below her ear.

Kate turned and found his face a study in contradiction. Excited, yet uncertain.

"What's wrong?"

He grinned then. "Absolutely nothing."

"Okay, then why are you so happy?"

Something flickered behind his grin for just an instant before he said, "Because life is good and I'm excited about taking you home soon. Come on and get some breakfast."

While they ate, Ted asked if she would mind remaining in Vancouver for a few more days.

She glanced at Jason, then back at Ted. "Why?"

He explained that she could wait here for a few days and finish everything up or come back in three to six weeks instead.

"So when I left the office yesterday, it wasn't really over." She made no effort to keep the irritation out of her voice.

"Kate, it won't really be over until he's convicted,

which could be years from now. All they need you for in a couple of days is signatures. In the meantime, Vancouver is an amazing city. Why not enjoy it? The guest suite is yours for as long as you want it."

She nodded. "Thank you."

"I'll give the office a call and let them know you're staying so they can get all the paperwork ready."

When he was gone, Jason reached for her hand. "What would you like to do today?"

Kate looked outside and said, "How about going to a park? I need to walk in the sunshine. On the grass, to get my strength back."

They spent the next couple of days wandering the parks and beaches of Vancouver's north shore and talking endlessly. Little by little and day by day, Kate told Jason more about her life on the run, and about the people who helped her survive.

And as she grew stronger, her mind became more and more clear, less consumed with the events of the last couple of years. On the third day she decided she needed to shop for gifts to take home to Jim and Jenny, and Ted suggested they shop in Gastown, which was just a short walk from the main street police station where he had to go for business that day.

While they drove into the area, Ted and Jason were engrossed in business talk, and Kate, riding alone in the back seat, gazed out the window and saw something that had her heart beating madly in her chest, then she was struggling to breathe.

Ted parked and hopped out, and Jason opened Kate's door for her, but she couldn't move.

He crouched on the sidewalk beside the open door. "Kate? What's wrong?"

All she could do was shake her head.

"Katie, please, let me help you."

It took a couple of tries, but finally she managed to say, "Please get me out of here."

He took both her hands and pulled her to her feet, tucked her in against his side.

"There's a park just a couple of blocks back. Do you want to go and walk there?"

"NO!"

Jason was obviously startled. "Where do you want to go? Gastown?"

She nodded and he led her up the street. Once they'd walked about four blocks, she stopped.

"Could we go back to Ted's place?"

"You bet." He flagged down a cab, and once they were safely on their way back to Deep Cove, he called Ted to tell him they wouldn't need a ride home.

"Jason, I need to talk about it," she said the minute they were in the house.

He led her to the couch in front of the fireplace, stoked the coals and added some kindling. She stared at the growing flames until he sat beside her and put his hand under her chin, turned her face to his and kissed her gently. "Okay, my love. Talk to me."

"I don't know where to start."

"What happened to send you into a tailspin? Was it something you saw? Heard? Thought about?"

"The soup line."

"What?"

"About a block before the police station, across

from the park, there was a lineup of street people waiting for a meal."

"I didn't even see them."

She looked up through swimming tears and said softly, "Exactly."

"Tell me."

"I couldn't do it. I couldn't make myself stand in line with them for the food, but it wasn't because I thought I was better than them, or because I wasn't hungry. Oh, God, sometimes I was *so* hungry."

Her voice cracked, but she took a deep breath and continued, "I couldn't look at them. I couldn't stand to see their pain and helplessness. It tore at my heart enough at the shelter every night when I was occupying a bed someone else needed. I couldn't do it for food too."

She gulped in a breath. "I couldn't stand to look at them because acknowledging their pain, their struggle, meant acknowledging my own. I went to sleep dirty and hungry. Grateful for a roof over my head and a measure of safety from the streets. I slept on a thin mattress, on the floor, in a room with nearly thirty women. Women who had no other choice but to be there."

She fought to continue past the lump in her throat, "But I had a choice, Jason, and that wasn't fair. I knew I could pick up a phone and get help, but I didn't. And maybe some of them could have done it too, but there were old ladies, Jason, old and broken and hopelessly alone, sleeping on those thin mattresses. Most of them don't ever speak. I couldn't reach out. I was afraid if I got to know anyone else's pain it would be the final straw, and my heart would never recover. I knew that someday I would go home. And I was just as certain that for most of the women there, they were as close to home as they would ever get."

Kate looked down at her hands, her voice barely a whisper, "In the face of their reality, I felt like a fraud."

Jason touched her cheek. "As always, I am amazed by your strength, my Katie."

"I didn't feel strong. I shut down. Couldn't allow myself to feel anything at all. I was afraid it would break me."

"So what happened today, Katie, when you saw the soup line? What exactly did you feel?"

"I felt the desperation that I know hides behind most of those faces. I felt the emptiness that torments them."

"What about the people who like the life? The ones who choose to be there, free of responsibility and expectations. The ones who don't want to participate in our society?"

"They're different, Jason. But my heart bleeds for the others, and I don't know if I will ever be able to deal with that. I think I'll always wonder if there was someone I could have helped if I'd just had the guts to risk my own heart."

She smiled vaguely. "But I was also afraid it would be like giving a starving person a tiny taste of chocolate. Would that be cruel or kind?"

She lay her head back against the soft leather and turned to look at Jason through half-closed eyes.

"Come here, Katie," He held his arms open, and when she came to him he drew her into his lap.

Jason rubbed the tension from the back of her neck, and when she started to drift off to sleep, he carried her downstairs to their room, where he propped himself up on the bed and cradled her against him.

CHAPTER 20

J ASON SLOWLY WORKED THROUGH THE
reality of where Kate had been for the past few
months, what she'd gone through. Even with the
state she was in when he found her at the airport,
it hadn't occurred to him that she'd been living on
the streets, homeless.

And now he understood. She had retreated
beyond the place of feelings and hopes and dreams,
behind a blank mask.

For a while he was angry with her. Angry that
she had kept running and putting herself in such
physical and emotional danger when all she had
to do was pick up a phone and he would have
rescued her.

And then he was mad at himself for not keeping
her from running off and then for failing to track
her down.

Victor was his next target. He would gladly wring
the man's neck for what he put Kate through.

And it went on. For the hours she slept, he
trudged through the gamut of emotions and eventually found some tentative peace for himself, and
recognized that their old habit of curing every-

thing with sex wouldn't work anymore.

It was full dark before Kate finally stirred.

Jason rested his lips against her forehead, and she murmured something as she lifted her face to his and gently touched his cheek with her fingertips. He pressed his mouth into her palm, caressing the soft skin with his lips.

Jason?"

"Katie?"

"Why was I afraid of this?"

"Of us?"

"Of how I feel when you touch me."

"I think it goes way back to the days when you needed complete control."

"I never cared about control when you were touching me."

"Exactly. And that lapse scared you when you thought about it, and you were afraid of yourself back then."

"And now I've been stripped of my power for so long, it seems like such a foolish thing to worry about."

Jason smiled. "You might never be so driven again, but your basic personality won't change."

"You think?"

"I know."

"What makes you so smart about me?"

"I have been a student of who you are for a very long time. As a matter of fact, I believe that by now I must have earned a PhD in Katie Oliver."

"Okay, smart aleck, what am I thinking?"

He rolled over and pinned her under him. Teased her with his lips and hands for a while, then raised up on his elbows and said, "You're thinking the exact same thing I am."

"Which is?" There was a definite huskiness in her voice.

"I want my skin to be touching yours." And he gently undid the buttons of her shirt and pushed it off of her shoulders. Even in the dark he could see the white bra with the red hearts, and he chuckled.

And then she was pulling his shirt over his head, using her lips, tongue, and teeth on his skin, and he let her have her way for a while before trapping her hands behind her back. "Not yet, my beautiful Katie."

"Jason, if this is to prove who's in control, you win. I give. Just please could we—"

He placed his fingers against her lips. "This isn't about control. It's about loving you."

They lay quietly together for a long time, each lost in their own thoughts, until Kate said quietly, "Jason?"

"Katie?"

"Feel like raiding the kitchen with me?"

He chuckled. "Only if you put a robe on first."

"If you insist."

"I do."

They'd just finished making a couple of sandwiches when Ted's voice startled them both.

"And I thought it was mice."

"Sorry we woke you up, Ted. Would you like a sandwich?"

"No thanks. Just wanted to see if everything was okay."

"It is."

"I can see that." He grinned at Jason, said good night, and went back upstairs to his room.

"What was that look about?" asked Katie.

Jason laughed out loud and then pressed his body against hers, pinning her against the counter. "You remember that look you wanted once, the one you gulped straight scotch to achieve?"

"Oh, really! But we didn't—"

"We didn't, but you look like we did," Jason said as his lips met hers and she no longer cared where she was. He pushed the robe off her shoulders and ran his lips down her throat to the middle of her chest, where he paid homage to one breast, then the other, while Kate slipped her hands inside his robe.

He lifted his mouth from her skin to look into her eyes.

"One more move, Katie, and I...we..."

She grinned for just an instant and pushed his robe to the floor. He reached behind him to turn out the kitchen light and then hooked a leg behind hers and lowered her to the soft fabric.

"Jason?"

"Now what?"

"Are you gonna throw on the brakes again?"

"Yep."

She lowered her mouth to his and kissed him teasingly, with a featherlike touch, until passion drove her to the edge, made her heart ache. "I think my soul belongs to you," she whispered.

"Our souls belong together."

She rested her head on his chest and sighed.

"You know, this floor is rather uncomfortable. Could we go back downstairs soon?"

She stood and held her hands out to him. "Come on, wimpy."

They took the sandwiches and a couple of cans of beer down to their room and sat by the window to eat. Then they crawled back under the covers and talked for hours.

Jason learned more about who she had been before he met her.

She told him of a childhood full of love and support from the people who rescued her as an infant, the ones she had called Mom and Dad. They'd pretty much raised her as an only child since their own kids were grown and gone before she appeared.

And she had been spoiled, for sure. There were skating lessons, riding lessons, birthday parties, and books, lots of books. The hours she spent reading were where her dreams came from, because she read everything she could get her hands on having anything to do with horses.

Jason asked about her parents and learned they were very busy doctors. They had raised a family of four kids while in their prime, then later they both maintained small private practices and worked together four days a month at a free clinic, which is where they met Kate's biological mother.

"How did you find out you were adopted?"

"I came home from school one day, and my mom was sitting in the living room crying. She had a letter in her hand, but quickly hid it and wiped away her tears when she saw me. Later I found it."

"You searched for it."

"True."

"What did it say, Katie?"

"It was a letter from Lilly, no last name, but it was addressed to me." She hesitated. "It was simply her explanation of why she had given me away and then stayed out of my life, even though she knew exactly where I was. She said she loved me, but the drugs had a hold on her, and she couldn't live without them. She knew it was better for me if she wasn't around, because she could give me nothing. She was homeless and addicted and didn't know how to love a child. She had managed to stay clean with the help of my mom and dad just long enough to deliver me safely, and then she went right back to the life."

"How did you feel, reading that?"

"I was fourteen. I felt everything and understood nothing. I was mad as hell that she was so weak, happy she had given me away, furious because I was deceived, sickened by the thought of being the child of a hooker, and confused about why the letter made my mom cry."

"So you confronted her, of course."

"And she told me the letters had been sent to her from the hospital where Lilly died. She had AIDS, and everyone died from it back then."

"Letters. Plural?"

"There was another one, thanking my mom and dad for helping her to do just one decent thing in her life. Deliver a healthy child and then give her a chance to grow up happy and loved."

"Pretty deep stuff for a fourteen-year-old girl to absorb."

"Absorbing wasn't my thing. I just chose to ignore the subject. I went on as though nothing had changed. As far as I was concerned, it was a good thing she'd died. That way no one would ever find out I was the bastard child of a weak and pathetic person, one who would rather sell her body to any passing slime just to get drugs than try to make a life for her own flesh and blood. I shoved her into a distant pigeonhole, nailed the door shut, and thanked my lucky stars my parents had been there to save me from her."

"Did it change you?"

"I was already a pretty strong kid, but after that letter I became unstoppable. I promised myself I would never live down to my heritage. I would be somebody. I would not die a dirty street tramp with a disease everyone knew came from a disgusting lifestyle. I would make my parents proud that they had rescued me. I would prove myself worthy of their love."

"Then what happened?"

"I became every parent's dream. I studied endlessly and achieved the best possible marks in school, I wrote scholarship exams and won everything I applied for, and I loaded up on extra classes, skipped forward, and graduated with honors a year early. I was going to be a veterinarian *and* a jockey."

"How did you end up at the track and not in university?"

"Three days after graduation, two policemen came to the door at about eight o'clock one night. They told me there had been an accident and my parents were both dead. I was seventeen...and suddenly very alone."

"What about their other children?"

"Kicked me aside like a stray dog while they fought over the money."

"What did you do?"

Kate smiled. "I did what would become my

go-to defense. I ran away from the pain and put all my energy into something else. A week after the funeral, I packed a bag, got in my car, and left everything I knew behind.

"I couldn't face going to university and vet school without my parents' support, and I had always dreamed of becoming a jockey, so I figured, why not take a shot? I drove to a racetrack where I went once with my dad, found the stable gate, and tried to walk in. Security stopped me, and I stood there waiting while they made a phone call. Then they gave me directions to Tanner's barn, saying he might be able to give me a job."

"And that was the day I met you." Jason smiled. "And finally I understand your drive."

"Too late."

"Why's that?"

"It's gone."

"I don't think so."

"Truly, Jason, the drive to be not-Lilly evaporated when I saw her in the mirror that day."

Jason waited.

"I understood her helplessness and pain. The drugs were not her enemy, Jason. They were her salvation. I understood what an incredible sacrifice she made in order to give birth to a drug-free baby, and I forgave her for not trying harder after I was born, for letting the life eat her up and eventually kill her."

Kate lay quietly against him, and he stroked her hair, waiting, but apparently she had no more to say.

"What a remarkable woman you are."

"A remarkably overwhelmed woman more often

than not."

He smiled at her refusal to acknowledge her own strength. He gently ran his lips across her forehead, and when she lifted her mouth to his, he ignored the invitation and said, "As much as you need to deal with what you've been through, you also need something lighter to think about sometimes, just to give your heart a break when you're feeling overwhelmed."

She smiled, "And what would you like me to think about? I mean besides making love with you, which is apparently something I can think about all the time but not actually experience—for some insanely twisted reason." She ran her lips across his chest, then back up toward his mouth.

Jason lifted her face away from him and pinned her with a stern look. "Don't think for one minute I'm enjoying any of the cold showers I've been taking lately."

"You're driving me nuts."

"Which is why you need something else to think about," he said. "Try this. If the world were perfect, and you had ten million dollars to spend, what would you spend it on?"

"I suppose buying sexual favors from you would be out of the question."

"Absolutely. Be serious for a minute."

"You just told me to lighten up!"

"Think about it. Ten million dollars to play with. Imagine the possibilities."

"Okay, I'll try, but I'm getting sleepy now."

Jason wrapped his arms around her tightly and said, "I do love you, Katie Oliver."

———

Morning brought reality with it. This was the day Kate had to go back to the prosecutor's office for the follow-up on her deposition, and she wasn't looking forward to it.

It was past time to quit looking over her shoulder, and she was more than ready to get on with her future.

On the ride up in the elevator, Jason rubbed the back of her neck. "Relax, Katie. This will be a breeze."

"I hate Victor," she said through gritted teeth.

Jason quickly pushed the stop button, and they were suddenly frozen between floors.

He took her by the shoulders and looked squarely into her defiant face. "If you take the time to hate him, you give him power and control. And hate takes up space in your heart."

He put his finger on her lips before she could respond. "Try to think of him as a parasite sucking the lifeblood from others so he can survive. If you deny him access, don't allow him into your mind, he will wither and die."

"I rather like that picture, but it might take me a while to get the hang of it."

"Just think about it, Katie, and don't give him your power."

"How did you get so wise all of a sudden?"

"I have a story not so different from yours, and had some amazing people to help me along the way. I didn't have to go it alone like you did."

He pushed the button to allow the elevator to

continue, and gave her a quick kiss just before the doors opened.

Her meeting with the prosecutor was completely anticlimactic, and over in less than thirty minutes.

Kate and Jason spent the rest of the day shopping and wandering around, simply enjoying the city and each other.

They took a water taxi to Granville Island, and Jason tried to buy live crab and lobster to take home for supper, but Kate said she couldn't do it. Couldn't stand the thought of dropping a living creature into boiling water.

Jason looked at her with something like relief and asked what they should get instead.

"I don't know. Steaks, maybe?"

"Ever seen how cattle are killed?"

"Jason!"

He shrugged. "Well..."

"Okay, how about chicken?"

Jason simply raised an eyebrow at her, and she stopped him before he could speak.

"Okay! I'm being unreasonable! Call me a lunatic, but..."

He laughed at her. "A little twisted maybe, but not a lunatic."

They finally settled on salmon. Not a whole one with eyes, just a nice, thick fillet, already cleaned and ready to cook.

Dinner was a happy meal. Jason and Ted teased her without mercy about her soft heart, and she took the ribbing gracefully.

They sat by the fire talking until it was very late and Kate began to yawn. "Okay, I give up. You two can keep talking all night, but I'm going to bed."

Ted shot Jason a look, which confirmed Kate's suspicion that they had something to talk about once she was out of the room. She said good night and went downstairs alone.

CHAPTER 21

—

THE NEXT DAY, WHEN TED saw them off at the airport, he hugged Kate and whispered, "Be kind to him. He loves you an awful lot."

Then he hugged Jason and whispered to him as well. Jason patted his friend's arm as they left and said, "I hope you're right."

Once they were in the air and on their way home, Kate realized how different she felt from when they arrived in Vancouver. She was no longer fragile, and the uncertainty was gone. It was as though learning about Victor, finally understanding what was going on for years, set her free of the fear.

She was slowly letting go of the past. Or mostly, at least. But there were flashes of memories, moments when anger surfaced, like when she remembered Victor standing beside her at Tanner's funeral, pretending he cared for the man. And she knew it would be impossible to ever forget Leo's last call.

Jason looked at her and swore softly.

She was startled. "What's wrong?"

"You. I could see the pain and sorrow on your face."

Kate touched his cheek "I'm sorry, Jason, but there will be times when I am sad or angry, and you can't change that. I'm learning that I have to let myself feel in order to be whole again. And it's happening already, just from the stuff Ted told me about Victor. I don't have that veil of uncertainty hanging over my head anymore. I know why he wanted me dead, I know why everything happened. I don't like what I've learned, but at least I can finally understand why things unfolded the way they did."

She frowned. "Sometimes it bothers me to think about how many people manipulated me—even Leo—and how gullible I was."

"Leo was your friend. Don't ruin your memories by being suspicious of him."

"It's okay. I know he loved me, and I believe he carefully pointed me right at you before he disappeared."

"How so?"

"Over those last few months, when we would sit together in the evening playing cards or whatever, I often found myself telling him about you. And now, thinking back, I'm pretty certain he purposely kept turning the conversations that way. As though he knew I was going to need you, and he kept gently prodding me to think about you. Does that make any sense?"

"It does. I imagine he was trying to help keep you safe."

She sighed and rested her head on his shoulder. Sometimes life sucked. And she really needed to stop going over and over what she couldn't change.

"Jason, tell me about the horses and Zeke and

what happened when they landed. We never did get back to it the other night."

"The long and detailed version, or the short one?"

"Short."

Jason grinned at her. "The FBI boarded the plane looking like cargo personnel, and once they had Brett in handcuffs, the horse crate was removed and taken to an empty hangar where portable stalls had been set up.

"Zeke was there to unload Rainbow and Anchor and settle them into the stalls, where they were examined by a vet, and their halters and bandages confiscated. Zeke stayed there with them for two days, until a judge released them. The crate had already been taken apart piece by piece."

"What happened to scumbag Brett?"

"He turned out to be a valuable source of information. In the name of saving his own ass, he told the authorities everything he knew, which was plenty. He gave them names, dates, and places." Jason half laughed. "As they say in those old shows, he sang like a canary."

Kate rolled her eyes.

"Victor had been under surveillance, but managed to get away just before the arrest team arrived."

"And that's when he started to hunt me down?" asked Kate.

"He'd been tracking you from the moment you disappeared."

"No kidding?"

"Don't forget about your lawyer, Dan. He told Victor you were selling the townhouse and not planning to return to Kentucky after the race in

Toronto. Victor saw a red flag and started his own campaign to test you, and you failed when you didn't call him on the mutual ticket he shoved in your pocket.

"Then, even though he and Dan figured there was something going on, Victor was stupid and arrogant enough to send just one more shipment of contraband home with the horses. And when it was intercepted he was determined to get rid of you. He believed you were the only one who could give the authorities enough information to hang him."

"When, in fact, I knew nothing. I was going to die for no reason at all."

"A horrible irony."

Kate shook her head. "And Dan tipped off Victor every time I called."

"I'm afraid so. We have phone records to prove it."

"I didn't even get to talk to him when I called from Kamloops."

"But the magic of caller ID gave him a location and a payphone number. He must have been pretty certain it was you."

How terribly sad it all was, and yet, looking at the positive, that phone call led to Victor's arrest.

"Katie?"

"You know, I may never be able to trust anyone again."

Jason scowled at her, "Do you trust me?"

"Of course."

"And Ted."

"Sure, even though he keeps secrets."

"How about Jim and Jenny and Zeke?"

"Them too."

"See? It's not as bad as you thought. From zero to five in just a few seconds."

Kate laughed. "Jeez, a motorcycle would give me zero to fifty at least."

Jason leaned over and kissed her sweetly until she put her hands alongside his face and kissed him back.

After a few minutes he held her away from him. "Have you ever heard of the mile-high club?"

"Yes. And no!"

"Then don't kiss me like that again until we're on the ground, woman, or we'll become full-fledged members."

Kate worked hard not to consider his words a challenge.

For the next hour they were comfortably silent, both lost in their own thoughts.

"That's a faraway look on your face," said Jason after a while. "What are you thinking about?"

"I know exactly what I would do with ten million dollars. I would buy a huge piece of land and build a soup kitchen where people could work. Gardens to grow their own food. Teach cooking classes and crafts for filling the empty hours of their days."

"Sounds wonderful," he said.

"Discarded people could develop pride in themselves through the work they did, and no one would ever be turned away. They would help each other and begin to trust again."

She grinned. "Some of the gardens would have tiny doors and secret places for fairies to rest, and of course, there would be lots of green grass for walking on and soaking up the healing energy of the sunshine."

Jason felt the passion in her voice. He watched her face become more and more animated by the minute. Katie finally had a new dream.

He smiled indulgently, "Since you don't have ten million, what about starting on a small scale? Buy a piece of land and build slowly grow over time instead."

Her eyes were wide with wonder and excitement. "It really is possible, isn't it?"

"Katie, for you, anything is possible."

For the last hour of the flight they talked about the details and logistics of such a project. Kate jotted notes on a napkin while Jason's heart warmed to see her so energized.

When Jason and Kate stepped into the terminal, they barely had a moment to blink before a tiny woman with flaming red hair catapulted toward them, throwing herself at Kate and holding on, rocking from side to side.

"My God, he was right. You're down to riding weight! What the heck have you been doing to yourself, Katie? I thought you learned the value of good health years ago. Why in heaven's name did you do that to your hair, Katie? It was so beautiful before. And what were you thinking, running away like that? Don't you know everyone was worried sick? You couldn't just call and say you were okay? Oh, Katie, I have missed you so much! Well, not as much as Jason did, of course, or The Princess and

Caly, but just the same..."

Jason and Kate were laughing, and Jim carefully pried his wife away and put a hand over her mouth. She glared until his hand slipped down to her chin and he planted a quick kiss on her mouth. "Let's get these good people home, shall we?"

Jenny rolled her eyes and stayed amazingly silent until they were in the car. Turning sideways in the front seat, she peppered Kate with more questions while they drove through the snowy landscape of an Ontario winter.

Jim turned off the road into a long driveway, and as they passed what looked like a cozy gatehouse, a man standing in the front window with a cat in his arms waved at them.

Kate swung to Jason, "Zeke?"

"Yep, and Caly stays with him when I'm away."

"This is your place?"

"Yep."

Having continued down the long driveway bordered on both sides by white-fenced pastures and old willow trees, Jim parked in a cleared space between a beautiful old white farmhouse and a matching hip-roof barn.

They got out and gathered Jason and Kate's meager luggage from the trunk, the four of them oddly silent, as though unsure what to do or say next.

"We'll be on our way," said Jim finally. "Kids are with a sitter, and Jenny planned your supper to be ready about now, so we'll leave you to it."

"Dinner's in the oven, so don't go forgetting about it and burn the place down or something stupid," Jenny added.

"Jennifer!" said Jim.

"They'll be in the sack before we're out the driveway." She turned to Kate. "Do me a favor and just walk through the kitchen on your way to the bedroom and turn off the oven, okay?" Her grin was wide and all-knowing, and Kate couldn't help but laugh.

Jim grabbed his wife by the arm. "Say goodnight, Jen."

"I'll call you tomorrow," she called out while Jim stuffed her into the car.

Jason and Kate stood laughing and waving as their friends drove away, then turned back to the house and Jason put his arm around her. "Welcome home, Kate."

She stared at him, again wondering about the odd feeling she'd had since she woke up this morning. Something wasn't quite right, but she couldn't put her finger on it.

He unlocked the door and pushed it open.

Two steps inside and the warmth of walls with a long history of family wrapped around her. Overstuffed couches, and a huge fieldstone fireplace dominated the living room he ushered her past, and the kitchen had an old wooden table and chairs set in the alcove of a bay window.

"So perfect," she said, imagining summer breakfasts there, gazing out at the horses in the fields.

After turning off the oven, Kate followed Jason to the bedroom, where he set their cases just inside the door, then lit the fire already set and ready.

There was a distinctly masculine feel to the room, with heavy, rustic furniture, but her breath caught when she recognized a patchwork blanket of bold colors.

"How did you get it?"

Jason's face was serious. "Sometimes I almost caught up with you."

Kate stroked the soft fabric. "It represented the bright, colorful life I was trying to build for myself."

"And I saw it as a piece of you that I could still touch and hold and keep safe."

Kate swallowed hard and turned away, going to the window to look out into the darkness.

She sighed as Jason's arms came around her, and she leaned back into him. "Do you have any idea how incredibly safe I feel when you hold me this way?"

His answer was to press his lips to her temple.

Kate closed her eyes and listened to the beating of her own heart, and Jason suddenly loosened his grip. She turned to look at him and was struck by his expression of uncertainty.

She touched his cheek. "My gut is screaming at me, Jason. I wish you would tell me what's wrong."

He kissed her instead, his mouth moving over hers with a sort of desperation that had her on tiptoe, giving back, trying to reassure him, determined to drive away whatever was bothering him.

She worked her hands up under his shirt, spread them wide over his back, up his shoulders, hanging on, wanting more, giving everything she had, but he groaned and pressed his mouth to the side of her neck.

"Not yet, Katie. Not yet."

She heaved a sigh. "It's time, Jason. I need you, and seems like you need me." She understood the denial up until now. She'd needed to heal, and they had needed to get to know a whole lot more about each other. When they were together the first time, sex was their answer to all problems. Mad? Have sex. Sad? Have sex. It got them over the bumps in the road, but not around the gaping holes.

Sex had been good. Great. A lifesaver. But it hadn't fixed what was broken between them.

And now? Now it was time to make love, and celebrate what was right. What was good and whole and made them who they were.

"I love you."

His smile was a bit twisted, and didn't make it to his eyes. "Good thing, because I'm afraid one of the surprises I have for you out in the barn will…"

She frowned. "Will what?"

He shook his head. "You're going to be pissed."

Great. Now she was feeling as unsettled as he looked. She hooked her hands behind his neck and drew him in for a sweet kiss. Smiled wide. "Probably a good idea to soften me up first then. Make love with me now, Jason." She pressed her body against his, and he put his hands on her ass, held her close.

"Too easy that way," he murmured. "Better if we wait."

She sighed. "Okay. Surprise first, then I'm going to have you right there, on the spot—living room, kitchen, driveway, wherever we are, and if you try to put a stop to it…"

Jason grinned and kissed her hard. "Deal." He towed her to a mud room at the back door, and they donned boots and jackets and headed for the barn, hand in hand.

It took a minute for her vision to adjust to the dim lighting, but nickers from the stalls at the far

KATHRYN JANE

end had her moving that way quickly.

Anchor was in the first stall, head out to greet her and instantly searching the coat pockets for treats.

Jason passed her a huge plastic jar filled with peppermints, and she grabbed a handful and the old horse was soon munching happily. She rubbed his forehead, then moved to the next stall and was shocked to realize it wasn't The Princess, but Rainbow.

Kate spun to look at Jason. "She was Victor's, how did you get her?"

"A long story for later, when we're indoors and warm. The important part is that she's yours."

"What?!"

"She was your Christmas present last year."

There was the slightest hint of something like sadness in his voice.

"I'm so sorry I wasn't here."

"I'm just glad you are now." He motioned to the next stall where the big mare was shaking her head. "One more."

Kate flung her arms around the mare's neck and, just like always, The Princess lowered her beautiful head and placed her jaw against Kate's back to hold her there. Face buried in mane, she inhaled deeply, savoring the sweet scent while tears trickled down her cheeks and she promised she would never leave her again.

When The Princess lifted her head, Kate kissed the soft spot right between her nostrils, receiving a soft nicker as a thank-you…and then there was an answer. A higher-pitched nicker from the back of the stall. Kate's heart did a skip and her eyes lit up when a gorgeous long-legged foal stepped into sight.

"OhmyGod, look at you. Look what you made, Mamma. He's beautiful." She swung to grin at Jason. "How could I possibly be mad at a surprise like this?" She planted a hard, fast kiss on his mouth before turning back to gawk at the baby again.

"Tell me who his daddy is."

Jason put his arms around Kate and pulled her back against him. "It's a secret," he whispered in her ear, and she laughed.

"I promise I won't be mad, no matter who you picked." She half turned to him in question. And froze.

There was a man standing so still in the shadows near the doorway he looked like a statue.

"Jason, there is someone in here," she said in a terrified whisper.

His grip on her tightened. "It's okay, he belongs here."

Every muscle in her body was on red alert until the figure moved and she sucked in a terrified gulp of air that came back out in a stunned whoosh.

She tried to move, but her legs had gone noodle weak.

The man came closer. And closer.

Tears started to pool.

And he reached for her.

Took her in his big, warm arms, like he had so many times before.

Leo held her tight while she cried like a baby. He wasn't dead.

"I'm sorry, Kate, so sorry for what you've been through," he said again and again.

And when she finally got a grip, pulled back

enough to see that face she'd loved for years, anger flickered somewhere deep inside.

Jason watched her. Saw the anger flash and thought, here we go.

"Wh—"

"It had to be this way," said Leo, stopping her before she could work up a head of steam. "It *had* to be this way. And it was completely out of my hands. I had to go into hiding or risk—"

"And you couldn't tell me? You left me beside myself with worry! And then wallowing in grief when they told me you were dead."

She swung toward Jason. "And you?"

"I found out at three o'clock this morning. Apparently my friend Ted didn't trust me to keep the secret from you." He grimaced. "And he was right. I couldn't have sat with you through that pain if I'd known Leo wasn't dead. I would have told you the truth."

Kate returned her attention to Leo. "Did you intend for me to go to Jason for help? Did you set me up?"

He smiled. "I was fairly certain you still loved him, and Ted said he thought it was mutual." He shrugged. "I figured even if you weren't smart enough to tell him how you felt, he would at least keep you safe from Victor."

Kate's mouth dropped open, and Jason laughed.

She shot him a look. "You were manipulated too, so why are you laughing?"

"Because they were right about something even we weren't sure of. And," he said to Leo, "thanks a million times over."

When Kate aimed a punch at his shoulder,

he grabbed her arm in midair, twisting it gently behind her back to hold her tight against him, and looked up to see Leo was headed for the door. "You are staying, aren't you?"

"Yup, I'll be at the gatehouse with Zeke and Caly for a few days."

The door closed behind him.

"That's all the surprises," Jason said.

"Thank you." Kate kissed him, then said, "Right here, right now."

She shoved his jacket out of the way and almost had his belt unbuckled when he grabbed her hands.

"Wait."

"Nope. Done waiting." There was as steely glint in her eye.

"But it's freaking cold out here," he tugged her toward the door. "And there's a soft, warm bed and a fireplace just steps away."

When he stopped to turn out the lights and properly latch the barn door, Katie took off at a run, leaving joyous laughter in her wake, and he was hot on her heels.

He kissed her while they shed their jackets and boots, and on that theme they carried on through the house, kissing and touching while items of clothing hit the floor one at a time, leaving a trail to the bedroom.

They were at the side of the bed when he managed to get out a breath and said, "Wait."

She stared. "Have I ever mentioned how annoying you can be?"

"Many times. But just stand still for one second, okay?"

Before she could argue, he grabbed the blanket,

her blanket, off the bed and stuffed it in a closet. Came back and tipped her over onto the bright white sheets.

"Fresh start tonight, Katie. Just you and me."

INTO THE SUNRISE

Kathryn Jane

D USTY'S EYES MET THOSE OF the mare, and she was transported to a place of great heat, riding bareback at a full gallop, bale strings wrapped around her wrists, pulling two horses along on each side of her.

A fiery branch was lodged between her inner thigh and the mare's body. Her leg was pinned by a filly pressing against her on the left, so she turned her toe outward to jab the offender in the side with the point of her boot, but in the middle of such panic there was no response.

She let the strings fall away from her wrists, and they galloped on blindly, relying on adrenaline and survival instincts until pain and lack of oxygen won. She collapsed over the mare's wither, looped her arms around her neck, laid her face in the thick mane, and held tightly to her own hands, praying she could stay on until they found their way out of the thick brown sludge hanging motionless where the air used to be.

But consciousness slipped away, and her grip loosened. There was no more strength, no more reserve to draw from. And when her limp, charred body slid off the horse's back, the last few burning embers of the branch fell away too.

"Dusty? What's wrong?"

She shook her head to clear away the images. Shuddered.

"Nothing, just hungry I guess."

The mare blew out a sharp breath, and Dusty felt it dance across her skin. This wasn't the first time she'd seen into the soul of an animal, but she'd never been a part of the images before, and it was disconcerting, to say the least.

She would always wonder what had happened to the woman riding the mare through the fire. Perhaps one day she'd find out. Or not.

DEAR READER

I really hope you enjoyed Kate and Jason's story. As former racehorse trainer, it was a joy for me to share some of the world I was a part of for many years. It was a delight to share a few scenes directly from the memories I still cherish. I will never forget the glistening dew on the grass the first day I sent Inish Glora onto the turf course at Woodbine, or the warm welcome I received there.

I'm pleased to also say I never encountered any of the "awful things or people" I conjured up for this story. All of that stuff was pure fiction thanks to being a voracious reader myself.

Some of what I experienced while running a ranch also slipped into this book and even became the focus of another book I just released. Callista Goes Country is about a woman who leaves her life in the city behind to help out on a goat farm. I too encountered the comedic devilment of goats, and I'm tickled to share some of the fun with you. It's a fun short read that includes a wonderful hunky man and of course, a happy ending.

Speaking of happy endings, if you are one of my CATS readers, Volume 5 is due to hit the shelves before Christmas.

If you want to stay in the loop, and get in on the pre-order news and links, pop over to my website at kathrynjane (dot) com and sign up for the news-letter. That way, you won't miss out on any of the scoop about new books, characters, contests, prizes, and of course a sale or two!

Cheers,

Kat.

PS. *For anyone who has ever taken the time to write a review for one of my books, thank you, thank you, thank you, a thousand times over!*

ACKNOWLEDGEMENTS

AS ALWAYS, I NEED TO thank my wonderful team, because I couldn't publish these books without their help. Whether catching typos, spending weeks on full blown edits, or taking me out to lunch when I need to get away from my characters for an hour or two, each and every one of my "people" play an important role in my life. (Yes, the four-legged ones too because who doesn't need a cat walking on the keyboard now and then, or a dog passing gas for comic relief.)

Many thanks to: Demon For Details for your fantastic editing; author L. j. Charles for your wonderful support, positive energy, and invaluable advice; Judicious Revisions LLC, and Barb for the sharp-eyed proof-reading; The Killion Group Inc. for another fabulous cover; Brenè Brown for Daring Greatly—an inspiration; Everyone who was part of my racetrack and ranch world; Nora Costigan and Anne Bailey, the eternally-brilliant smiles in the back of my mind; Al, my own charming prince, for baking bread and keeping me warm at night; Barb and Judy—how do I put it into words? You are the constants in my journey. You've egged me on and believed in me always. I love you all.

ABOUT THE AUTHOR

AWARD WINNING AUTHOR KATHRYN JANE lives on the west coast of Canada with her very own prince, a sweet dog, and an obnoxious cat. Among her favorite things are the smell of the ocean, crisp sunny days, cats with a sense of humor, faithful mutts, the warm breath of a horse, music, sunflowers, orange gerbera daisies, beach glass, rocks, and kind people.

A perfect day begins with a walk alongside the Pacific Ocean with her sisters.

For more information about Kathryn, her other books, and her painted rocks, check out her website and sign up for the newsletter. *www.kathrynjane.com*

MORE BOOKS BY KATHRYN JANE

ROMANTIC SUSPENSE:
INTREPID WOMEN SERIES

Book 1 – Do Not Tell Me No
Book 2 – Touch Me
Book 3 – Daring To Love
Book 4 – Voices
Book 5 – Lies
Book 6 – All She Wanted
Book 7 – Dance With Me
Book 8 – Missing
Book 9 – Diamonds To Die For

WOMEN'S FICTION:
Into The Sunrise

SHORT STORIES ABOUT COMMUNITY CATS:
CATS, A Collection of Heartwarming Furry-Tales

Volume #1 –2017
Volume #2 –2017
Volume #3 –2017
Volume #4 –2017
Volume #5 – (December 2018)